PRAISE FOR *THE BEAVER THEORY*

'A joyous, triumphant conclusion to Tuomainen's trilogy ... the comic thriller of the year' *Sunday Times*

'Quirky crime capers don't come more left field than the Rabbit Factor trilogy ... extremely funny, with a wicked line in social satire' *Daily Mail*

'The last book in a trilogy, *The Beaver Theory* is a fun and clever thriller in which a hero finds the right balance in all pursuits' *Foreword Reviews*

'Weird, funny, violent, funny and weird again ... bringing the absurdity to an almost state of normalcy and enveloping us in this world of wonderful, escapist delight' Raven Crime Reads

'Kooky, original and entertaining, *The Beaver Theory* is another must-read from Tuomainen and Orenda ... I'd recommend reading the whole series to avoid missing out on some of the best fiction you'll ever read' Emma's Biblio Treasures

'The pacing is superb, the story madcap but compelling, with the author's trademark humour *en pointe*, resulting in the delivery of a pitch-perfect finale' Jen Med's Book Reviews

'Antti Tuomainen has created a memorable and unique character, and David Hackston's fantastic translation has brought Henri's story to life in a way that absolutely reflects Antti's dry and delightful humour. I've loved every second of this trilogy and this is a terrific conclusion' Live & Deadly

'Written (and translated) with great wit, this delightfully funny black comedy of theme-park shenanigans and espionage, is a wonderful high note for the highly entertaining trilogy to end on' Rambling Mads

'Tuomainen's heroes are idiotic and lovable. They are each a bundle of ridiculous views, sincerely held ... Tuomainen reminds us that we can still inhabit a place where love, hope and sincerity may conquer all' Café Thinking

'Takes the bizarre and absurd and serves it up to the reader with tongue firmly in cheek and with a straight face that I have no idea how the author maintains ... This is the genius of his writing' A Little Book Problem

'A twisty, complex plot makes *The Beaver Theory* ... a fun and satisfying read' Blue Book Balloon

'An entertaining read with a distinctive and individual style that gets your attention and keeps you enthralled to the end ... Quirky and distinctive crime writing' Books Life & Everything

'I was intrigued all the way through ... I loved the roller-coaster ride on which Antti Tuomainen takes us ... I'm really sad to be leaving these characters behind, but I can't wait to see what the author has up his sleeve' Portable Magic

PRAISE FOR ANTTI TUOMAINEN

WINNER of the Petrona Award for Best Scandinavian
Crime Novel of the Year
THE RABBIT FACTOR is currently in production for TV with
Amazon Studios, starring Steve Carell
SHORTLISTED for the CrimeFest Last Laugh Award
SHORTLISTED for the CWA International Dagger

'Readers might think they know what to expect from Nordic noir: a tortured detective, a bleak setting, a brutal crime that shakes a small community. Finnish crime novelist Tuomainen turns all of this on its head ... The ear of a giant plastic rabbit becomes a key weapon. It only gets darker and funnier' *Guardian*

'The biting cold of northern Finland is only matched by the cutting, dark wit and compelling plot of this must-read crime novel' Denzil Meyrick

'Combines a startlingly clever opening, a neat line in dark humour and a unique Scandinavian sensibility. A fresh and witty read' Chris Ewan

'Brilliant. Absolutely brilliant. I enjoyed every single sentence' Thomas Enger

'A wonderful writer, whose characters, plots and atmosphere are masterfully drawn' Yrsa Sigurðardóttir

'An original and darkly funny thriller with a Coen brothersesque feel and tremendous style' Eva Dolan

'A triumph ... a joyous, feel-good antidote to troubled times' Kevin Wignall

'Finland's greatest export' M.J. Arlidge

'You don't expect to laugh when you're reading about terrible crimes, but that's what you'll do when you pick up one of Tuomainen's decidedly quirky thrillers' *New York Times*

'Right up there with the best' *Times Literary Supplement*

'Tuomainen continues to carve out his own niche in the chilly tundra of northern Europe' *Daily Express*

Also by Antti Tuomainen and available from Orenda Books:
The Mine
The Man Who Died
Palm Beach, Finland
Little Siberia

The Rabbit Factor
The Moose Paradox

ABOUT THE AUTHOR

Finnish Antti Tuomainen was an award-winning copywriter when he made his literary debut in 2007 as a suspense author. In 2011, Tuomainen's third novel, *The Healer*, was awarded the Clue Award for Best Finnish Crime Novel and was shortlisted for the Glass Key Award. In 2013, the Finnish press crowned Tuomainen the 'King of Helsinki Noir' when *Dark as My Heart* was published. With a piercing and evocative style, Tuomainen was one of the first to challenge the Scandinavian crime-genre formula, and his poignant, dark and hilarious *The Man Who Died* became an international bestseller, shortlisting for the Petrona and Last Laugh Awards. *Palm Beach, Finland* (2018) was an immense success, with *The Times* calling Tuomainen 'the funniest writer in Europe', and *Little Siberia* (2019) was shortlisted for the Capital Crime/Amazon Publishing Readers Awards, the Last Laugh Award and the CWA International Dagger, and won the Petrona Award for Best Scandinavian Crime Novel.

The Rabbit Factor, the first book in a trilogy that includes *The Moose Paradox* and *The Beaver Theory*, is now in production for TV with Amazon Studios, starring Steve Carell. *The Moose Paradox* was a Literary Review and *Guardian* Book of the Year and shortlisted for CrimeFest's Last Laugh Award.

Follow Antti on Twitter @antti_tuomainen, or on Facebook: facebook.com/AnttiTuomainen.

ABOUT THE TRANSLATOR

David Hackston is a British translator of Finnish and Swedish literature and drama. Notable recent publications include Kati Hiekkapelto's Anna Fekete series (published by Orenda Books), Katja Kettu's *The Midwife*, Pajtim Statovci's *My Cat Yugoslavia* and its follow-up, *Crossing*, and Maria Peura's *At the Edge of Light*. He has also translated Antti Tuomainen's *The Mine*, *The Man Who Died*, *Palm Beach, Finland*, *Little Siberia*, *The Rabbit Factor* and *The Moose Paradox* for Orenda Books. In 2007 he was awarded the Finnish State Prize for Translation. David is also a professional countertenor and a founding member of the English Vocal Consort of Helsinki. Follow David on Twitter @Countertenorist.

The Beaver Theory

ANTTI TUOMAINEN

Translated from the Finnish by David Hackston

ORENDA
BOOKS

Orenda Books
16 Carson Road
West Dulwich
London SE21 8HU
www.orendabooks.co.uk

First published in the United Kingdom by Orenda Books, 2023
This paperback edition first published 2024
Originally published in Finland as *Majavateoria* by Otava, 2022
Copyright © Antti Tuomainen, 2022
English language translation copyright © David Hackston, 2023

Hardback ISBN 978-1-914585-96-8
B-Format Paperback 978-1-914585-86-9
eISBN 978-1-914585-87-6

Orenda Books is grateful for the financial support of FILI, who provided a
translation grant for this project.

Typeset in Garamond by typesetter.org.uk
Printed and bound by Clays Ltd, Elcograf S.p.A

For sales and distribution, please contact *info@orendabooks.co.uk*

To my father, Eero
With many fiscal greetings too

NOW

By night, Somersault City smells very much the same as my own adventure park, YouMeFun: the plastic parts and metallic structures of the various attractions, the cleaning fluids and disinfectants, the residual aroma of the day's offerings at the café. The air conditioning is humming; outside the icy north-east wind is a billow of snow, testing the durability of the tall metal walls. Otherwise, all is silent.

But I can't claim to feel entirely at ease.

I am an actuary, not a burglar.

I'm only on my competitor's premises to ... gather information that I've been unable to obtain in any other way. But isn't that too a form of theft? Is this how burglars defend their actions to themselves? That they are merely scouting out other people's interiors and only taking the things they have otherwise been unable to get their hands on?

I take a deep breath. The time for such considerations is later. I remind myself that, in their short but all the more consequential career in the adventure-park business, the owners of Somersault City have threatened violence against me personally and made perfectly clear – this too, in person – their intention to drive my adventure park into bankruptcy, and the sooner the better.

Light seeps into the space here and there: from the windows by the ceiling a shimmer of the outside lights; the faint green glow of the emergency-exit signs; the Somersault City logo, lit up at the western end of the hall like a large, dim sun. As the seconds pass, my vision becomes clearer. The contours of the rides seem to sharpen, the space in front of me assumes depth and form, the different parts of the hall stand out from one another.

From my previous visit, I remember the topography of the hall with relative accuracy. And I'm only too aware of the lifetime ban I received on that occasion.

Meanwhile, I recognise the Dumbo Dodgems, the Kangaroo Course, the dizzyingly tall Eiffel Bungee and all the other rides, and again I wonder how on earth Somersault City is able to provide all this completely free of charge. In light of the known facts, their aim is either a precipitous descent into administration or they have financial backing from people for whom money is no object. Neither of these options seems especially plausible.

Naturally, I am something of an amateur when it comes to breaking and entering, but I note that at least I managed to select suitable footwear for the occasion. Not only are the cheap slippers I bought from a German supermarket chain colourful; they are soft too and have thick soles. My steps are silent. My first destination is the eastern end of the park, the administrative wing situated behind a climbing wall known as the Baboon Barrier. Of course, I don't expect to find a report on the CEO's desk neatly explaining how Somersault City plans to achieve the impossible: to run a profit while behaving in a way that is doomed to financial ruin. Nonetheless, I expect to be wiser by the end of my reconnaissance trip than I was when I arrived.

The baboons are quiet as I pass them. This is partly due to their plastic constituency, but the primary reason is that the electricity bringing them to life is switched off at night: there's no point in the baboons scaling the barriers without any little competitors to keep them company.

A short flight of stairs leads up to the administration

department. The doorway at the top of the stairs is open; there is no door or anything else to impede my view. I arrive in some kind of foyer. On the opposite wall there is a row of windows that allow me to see into what appears to be a conference room. I walk into the room and look around.

A long, greyish-white office table stands diagonally across the room; dark-blue plastic chairs have been left at a distance from the table. The only other item in the room is a flip chart. I walk towards it and flick back through its pages.

One page has clearly been dedicated to a straw poll of lunch options. Thai food received four votes, burgers narrowly lost with only three. I continue flicking through the pages until I reach the first blank page. I think for a moment, then turn back a page. All of a sudden, the page feels somehow crucial.

At the top, someone has written the year that has just started. Beneath that is a list of months. After January is the number 100. After February is the number 0. And after all the subsequent months, the numbers are negative:

March -100
April -200
May -300

And so on, exponentially, until we reach December (-1M).

Whatever these numbers are trying to express, their author has certainly opted for clarity and consistency of presentation.

I return to the foyer.

The right-hand wall is shorter and bears only a poster with a view of the national park – which feels rather curious given the park's employees, whom I have met and who do not strike me as the hiking type – but on the left-hand side there are two doors.

The first door isn't locked and opens the way most doors do: by simply turning the handle. The room beyond this door is more of a storeroom than an office, containing everything from a flat-screen television – still in its original cardboard packaging – to packets of oat biscuits destined for wholesale.

I look around for a moment and conclude that, given this space and the conference room, the people who tried to assault me and who have threatened the very existence of my adventure park are decidedly mundane in everything else they do. The next and last office space, however, appears to be the nerve centre of the entire park.

There are papers on the desk, but there are tools too. On top of one pile of papers is a set of pliers stained with chain oil, on another pile is a dirty workman's glove. I cannot immediately see its pair anywhere. What's more, I cannot see, at least not at first glance, the reports that were mentioned during my visit, reports whose figures I would be very interested to peruse. I walk round behind the desk and am about to begin a more detailed inspection when I flinch and realise two things at once.

My heart is beating so hard that I can't hear anything.

In addition, I've been using a small torch in the room, though the blinds are still slightly ajar. I switch off the torch there and then and try to breathe calmly, but the humming and drumming inside me only seems to be getting worse. As I realised earlier: industrial heists are not my forte. Eventually, my heart steadies itself a little, the booming dies down. As I try to establish the reason for this sudden anxiety, I move towards the door.

This is clearly the right direction, because I hear a thud coming from somewhere in the hall and realise I heard a similar sound earlier too. I wait. For the time being, there are no more thuds. I proceed silently through the foyer and remain waiting on one side of the doorway. I wait in silence for a long while. Finally, I peer round the doorway into the adventure park, allowing my eyes to pan from left to right.

The Eiffel Bungee, the boxing kangaroos standing almost as tall, the hefty Dumbo Dodgems and...

The Beaver.

The eighteen-metre Beaver and its countless activities, including a DIY foam dam, a tail with a bouncy castle, and a network of slides, is the number-one attraction at Somersault City. The enormous Beaver is lying on its stomach right in the middle of the park; from this angle the gargantuan rodent is partially hidden behind the bungee tower and the elephants. I can see the Beaver's mouth though. Its large, white front teeth gleam even in the dim. But that isn't what catches my attention.

Lying on the ground, beneath the beaver's teeth, there is ... something.

I can neither see nor hear movement anywhere. The Beaver's mouth is too far away to make out what it is about to eat. Of course, the steel-framed Beaver hasn't been left any literal supper, but this certainly looks real enough. Just as I'm about to take my eyes from the Beaver, I see movement at floor level. At first it seems as though something is trying to extricate itself from an otherwise dark and homogenous mass, then I realise what is really happening.

A hand slumps from a chest. On the floor beside the hand – and this, too, I see only now – is a Stetson.

My heart starts to thump again, there's a rushing sound in my ears, like standing beside a busy motorway. The calculation is simple – there are a very limited number of variables in the equation: someone is obviously injured and needs help, and it doesn't really matter whether I am here as an actuary or in some other capacity. (I'm still unsure whether this visit meets the specific criteria for burglary.) And because there is nobody else in sight, I must help this injured person. The result after the equals sign is clear.

I start moving.

I have to walk in a long curve to reach the Beaver because my route takes me past many of the park's other sizeable attractions. As before, my footsteps are silent. Finally, I walk around one of the Eiffel Bungee's legs and almost end up in the Beaver's jaws myself, but I stop before its teeth can reach me – and I might even take a step back too.

The cowboy costume is a familiar one: the boots, the jeans, the patterned Rodeo shirt and bolo tie with shiny eagles dangling at the ends. I know this man; I even know his name. He owns the park. I've met him, I told him what I thought about his business model, and I strongly advised a different approach. Above all: I told him – with witnesses present – that I have no intention of backing down, that I plan to respond to their aggression in my own way and that I will do whatever it takes to protect my own park.

But now he's not moving, nothing about him is moving. His eyes are open, his mouth is open. More to the point, his mouth is full. Protruding from between his jaws is a plastic ice-cream cone, approximately half a metre in length. The pointed, and presumably steel, end of the cone is wedged deep in his throat. I can't help thinking this looks a lot like an ice-cream advert gone badly wrong. I am about to take a step either forwards or backwards – I'm not sure I'm even able to decide which direction is best – when my heart implodes once and for all.

'Murderer!'

The cry comes from the main entrance. Just then, I hear someone running.

A lot can happen in a few fractions of a second. I look at the man lying on the ground, I look at the man running towards me, I make out the familiar blue face and realise quite how unfavourable the situation looks from my perspective. I turn and am preparing to start running when I hear another set of footsteps, this time coming from the opposite direction.

'Police! Stop!'

I finish turning, then – finally – I too start running. I hurry towards the back door, my original point of entry. I have just enough time to think of two things: my balaclava and the delivery ramp propped against the wall outside the door. The balaclava was a precaution against any security cameras. Now, at a modest estimate, it will be of immeasurable help.

As for the delivery ramp...

'Get him!' I hear behind me, and I'm almost certain I recognise the voice. 'That's our killer!'

I reach the door, push it open, press it shut behind me. In a continuation of the same movement, I grab the metal ramp from where I left it beside the wall, prop one end at the base of the railings around the loading bay and wedge the other end against the door. This I do at the last possible moment, as right that minute someone slams into the door from the other side. Fists pound on the door. I can still hear the shouting, only fainter, and now I can't make out any of the words. But there's no need. The situation is absolutely unambiguous and the joins between the dots are mercilessly and uncompromisingly direct: if they catch me or recognise me, then I'm no longer just a burglar.

I'm a murderer.

That chilly January day, the low, white sun shone straight into my face as I walked across the empty living room and stepped out onto the balcony. At once, the cold took me in its embrace. The pure snow glistered and sparkled; the trees wore their coats of snow in silence. Somewhere out of sight, a snow plough clattered into the distance. I took a deep breath, allowed my eyes to take in the familiar view. These houses, all designed with precise geometrical symmetry, enjoyed effective heating, functional layouts and a price that was unbeatable, given their size, and it had always been thus. And until now, I had enjoyed these things too.

It was my last day in Kannelmäki.

I noticed a faint tremor in my hands, and at first I tried to tell myself this must be the result of all the packing and carrying boxes here and there, the dozens of journeys up and down the stairwell, the endless positioning, the placing and fitting I'd been doing. But, as I quickly admitted to myself, this wasn't the whole truth.

Around nine months ago, I'd been forced to leave my job at the risk-management department of an insurance company. I was an actuary, a job and profession with which I still strongly identified, and I'd been forced into a situation in which I had to choose between a many-pronged humiliation and a demotion, or voluntarily leaving the company's employ. I handed in my notice. Shortly thereafter, I inherited an adventure park from my brother, who, at that precise moment, happened to be dead. At the same time, I inherited his debts too, debts that he had taken out with some decidedly hardboiled crooks. One thing led logically and inexorably to the next: a body in the fridge at the park's café, falling in love with art and the artist herself, defending the adventure park from unscrupulous investors and a cavalcade of criminals, and this in turn led to more bodies and, naturally, to my brother's resurrection from the dead and everything that ensued as a result. And finally to the fact that I was about to become a member of a family again, for the first time since the chaos that was my own childhood and adolescence.

Everything had happened very quickly. (I know lots of people say this after making a grave error – investing their life savings in an electric-car company at a grossly inflated share price, for instance, or taking a drunken decision to try slaloming along the motorway – and usually at the point when they wish such things as time machines existed.) Thankfully, I had already become used to the fact that, compared with the past, many things in my life were moving at the speed of a meteorite and that, more often than not, I had to take decisions once the train had already left the station.

Laura Helanto was my train, my meteorite.

We'd first met at the adventure park. Laura had worked as park manager from the time she had been released from prison, where she had ended up after becoming embroiled in her former boyfriend's many and varied financial improprieties. It quickly transpired that the park was just her way of supporting herself and her daughter, but that her real calling was as an artist. What's more, her art had a profound effect on me – a sensation that bore no comparison to anything I had ever experienced in the past and that was impossible for me to square with any known mathematical principles. It soon became apparent that Laura Helanto herself had an effect on me, one stronger still than her art. And now, evidence suggested that she had similar thoughts and feelings towards me too.

And yet...

I took another deep breath, the crisp winter air felt sharp in my throat, refreshing in my lungs. But even this didn't fully dispel the tremors, nor what was causing them. I concluded that, compared to how I might previously have acted, my behaviour was decidedly reckless. I certainly hadn't been following in the footsteps of Pascal and Euclid, as I had once resolved to do. How often had Schopenhauer and I wondered at people's foolhardy whims and general rashness; their actions and decisions, made without careful advance planning or even profitability and probability calculations, checked many times over? Yet what was I doing right now?

January reminded me of its presence. The sun was dazzling, but a chill ran through everything, first the clothes, then the skin, before settling somewhere deeper, right around the largest bones. I cast my eyes once more over everything to which I was about to bid farewell. Then I turned, went back indoors, walked through the empty, echoing apartment to the front door, carefully pressed it closed, descended via the stairs and climbed on board the removal van waiting by the front door.

The driver was a strapping young man with big hands, the kind of youngster who wore a T-shirt in the middle of winter and who took great care of his immaculate coif, even amid all the lifting and lugging; I'd twice seen him checking and adjusting his hair in the bathroom mirror after bounding up the stairs. I'd already given my destination when I booked the removal company, and now, while we were waiting for the traffic lights to change, for some reason the driver brought up the subject again.

'Nice neck of the woods, Herttoniemi,' he said, and glanced at me.

This woke me from my thoughts. Perhaps a little small talk, the kind I did my best to avoid, might cheer me up and lighten the mood.

'I like it too,' I said. 'Public-transport connectivity is excellent, the buildings are cost-effective and of high quality, their layout is clear and almost perfectly functional, and property prices in the area are expected to retain or even increase their value over the medium to long term.' I held a brief pause, looked the driver in the eye, and added: 'Assuming, that is, that there are no significant changes in the underlying macroeconomic situation.'

The driver was silent. Then, apparently with considerable effort, he managed to turn away from me and look straight ahead.

'We'll be there in a minute,' he said. 'How about I start with the boxes of books?'

We took the slip road from the dual carriageway up to a large roundabout, went almost all the way around it before taking the last exit and heading into what people called the old part of the suburb of Herttoniemi. We took an immediate left, passed a supermarket and a car park, then began climbing a hill curving round to the right. We travelled in silence after our brief attempt at small talk – either we had both got everything off our minds, or the subject of the pros and cons of life in Herttoniemi had been exhausted, and the driver didn't seem to need advice on how to find the right building.

We drove to the top of the hill, almost to the end of the road, took a short turn to the left, then continued up the steep driveway in front of the house. Geographically we were at the highest point in the suburb, which meant that we had *arrived*.

The driver switched off the engine.

I opened the door, stepped out onto the snow-covered driveway, and at that moment all my doubts about the rationale behind what I was doing quite simply vanished.

This wasn't just because I glanced up and saw the windows on the third floor glowing warm and cosy against the darkening evening sky. And neither was it because of how I had successfully consolidated the financing arrangement for Laura Helanto's recent pipe refit and her remaining mortgage repayments into a single loan, repayable over a longer period of time and with a fixed interest rate, thus making sure that, even with her monthly fee to the housing association, her outgoings would be reasonable long into the future.

No.

It was because of what happened next.

Laura Helanto appeared from the stairwell, propped the door open and began walking towards me. The closer she came, the more clearly I understood that I wasn't simply changing apartment. In fact, I wasn't even moving my belongings. (Though a moment later I was carrying them up the concrete stairwell to the third floor, careful not to bash things against the metal railings, which caused a low-pitched boom to echo up and down the corridor.) I was switching my life for a better one.

I was moving out of my old life and into a new one.

I looked at Laura Helanto and experienced the same joy that I always felt upon seeing her. I liked her appearance, her wild bushy hair, her bright, curious eyes framed by her dark spectacles, her broad, ever so slightly asymmetrical lips and distinctly angular jaw, and even more than that I liked her practical attitude. She often seemed to be a few steps ahead of me, as though she had read my thoughts or somehow knew in advance what I would do in a given situation, what I would think about a given matter. Right now, I couldn't say whether she had noticed this comprehensive shift in my thinking, but at least she knew what to say.

'Welcome home, Henri.'

We carried boxes for the next hour and a half. The driver did excellent work. I must admit, I was taken aback when I heard a short snippet of conversation between him and Laura Helanto. It seemed he *did* want to carry on talking about Herttoniemi after all; I heard him comment on the subject using almost the exact words he had said to me earlier. He and Laura then exchanged thoughts on the area, drawing on arguments that were largely emotional and therefore wholly incommensurable, and both seemed pleased with their conclusion. Straight after this conversation, the driver walked past me but refrained from broadening the scope of the discussion or continuing to debate the matter with me further. On the contrary: he quickly closed the door behind him and, judging by the speed of the footsteps echoing through the stairwell, almost fled the scene.

Carrying the print of Gauss's equations, I walked into the living room, where Laura was already unpacking my books and placing them on our shared shelf. Just then, Laura's daughter, Tuuli, and my cat, Schopenhauer, came out of her room to join us. In this respect too, I had been worried over nothing. Tuuli and Schopenhauer seemed to be getting on very well, and their age difference didn't appear to affect their interaction in the least: Schopenhauer was friendly and approving towards his new comrade, though this one talked more and moved more quickly than any other human being he had ever encountered.

That night, while I was lying in bed as Laura slept soundly by my side, her head resting on my shoulder, images flickered through my mind – not all of them pleasant: being pursued and chased on more than one occasion; sinking the body of a gangster who had tried to kill me into a murky pond; the constant suspicions directed at me by Detective Inspector Pentti Osmala of the Joint Division of the Helsinki Organised-Crime and Fraud Units; my brother's escapades, first dying then trying to take over the adventure park before one final disappearing act; and countless other events from the last few months, situations which I had survived only with the combined help of mathematics and a factor it was far more difficult to pin down. I believe the word 'love' is often used in such circumstances.

I listened to the winter winds whipping through the flues and to Laura's deep, peaceful breathing. My right arm was starting to grow numb, but I didn't feel the urge to move it. In fact, I didn't feel the urge to do anything, to go anywhere. I wanted to be right here. And at this, the unpleasant images began to fade, replaced now with more pleasant ones, from our first so-called date – a field of expertise and a use of time that until that evening I had considered very high risk and unprofitable over the long term – to the moment when we started unpacking my boxes this afternoon and began putting together our shared home. Eventually, these pleasant images began to fade too, and all I could feel was Laura Helanto's warmth.

My last thought before falling asleep was that I had come home. I had finally found my way to a safe place, both literally and figuratively. (As an actuary, I knew only too well, even as I began to slip into sleep, that there was only one thing in life we could predict with absolute certainty and that this factor was firmly linked to a well-planned life-insurance policy.)

The thought was every bit as warm, as real, as vital as Laura Helanto sleeping beside me.

I was safe.

And nothing could threaten me now.

2

'The parents' evening starts at six,' said Laura Helanto. 'If you get there fifteen minutes early, that'll be plenty of time. I would go myself, but I've got the interview across town, then I'm going to look at that workspace I told you about. If I get this job, it means I'll be sorted for the next six months.'

For the second time I told Laura that the matter was settled, we had formed a family unit and that meant from now on we shared things with a view to our mutual success. I told her she didn't have to worry about it in the least; the meeting wouldn't be the slightest problem. I very nearly reminded her that I had survived far trickier situations than this, but swiftly changed my mind and took the more sensible option. That was all behind me now, it was in the past. I had no intention of bringing park business into the home, not even tangentially.

Across the table, Laura was drinking her second cup of coffee, clinking the spoon against the sides of her large yellow mug as she stirred. Outside it was still dark. Tuuli had left for school a moment ago, and I was about to make my way to the adventure park. It was Monday, which meant we had the weekly staff meeting first thing, and I wanted to make sure I had all the necessary materials ready, which, in turn, meant I had to get to the adventure park in good time before the start of the meeting.

I stood up from the table and began gathering up the dishes.

Loading the dishwasher was a very satisfying, practical application of mathematical principles; it was about optimising space, exploiting the maximal flow of water, positioning dishes to make sure they were as evenly spaced as possible. One wrongly stacked bowl, pot or even a plain old plate might have a crucial impact on the overall cleaning process, its success or failure. I didn't explain the matter in quite this much detail when I told Laura that, from now on, I would take care of this household chore. Even without hearing my rationale, this seemed to suit her very well.

'How are you feeling otherwise?' I heard her ask.

I glanced at her as she sat beneath the dome light hanging above the table. Far behind her, the Arabianranta district had woken up too, the strip of light along the opposite shore ran the full length of the window. Laura was wearing grey tracksuit bottoms and a large light-blue hoodie. On her feet she had a pair of pink woollen socks. I was wearing dark pressed trousers, an ironed white shirt and a blue-and-grey striped tie.

'About what?' I asked as I arranged the drinking glasses in a tight but amply spacious row in the dishwasher.

Laura looked at me, smiled. 'In case you hadn't noticed,' she said. 'You've moved.'

'Quite,' I replied, placing the knives and forks so that they faced away from one another. 'I think this is a very mutually beneficial solution.'

'Nice to hear.'

Having spent a lot of time in Laura Helanto's company, I'd come to realise that in situations like this, one is expected to answer with similar questions. Until now, I'd never understood why this was necessary; I didn't know what to do with information about what distant acquaintances or perfect strangers had been up to recently, let alone how they were 'doing'. But I'd noticed that I was actually very interested in Laura Helanto's feelings and opinions, and so I asked:

'What about you? How are *you* feeling?'

She swallowed her coffee, and it sounded to me as though she did this a little more quickly than usual.

'I think this is quite ... mutually beneficial too,' she said, then chuckled; I didn't know why. She was still looking at me. I would much rather have concentrated on the lively twinkle in her eyes, but I was busy concentrating on making crucial decisions about the optimal positioning of several plastic containers, and I was certain I could hear the second hand on the wall clock edging me towards the front door.

'I know we've talked about this before but...' she began. 'After all that's happened ... I just hope that from now on everything will be ... safer ... safe.'

I believed I understood what she meant.

'The adventure park has overcome a number of difficulties,' I said. 'Everybody is working with renewed enthusiasm. Our customer numbers have remained constant, and our finances too. Soon we'll be in a position to think about more investments. Then there's the three of us. You, me and Tuuli. Our living expenses are relatively low, and our other outgoings too. Our finances are based on a sensible, long-term advance plan and predicated on sticking to that plan. As an actuary, I can't promise anything with one-hundred-percent accuracy – except the obvious, that is – but I will say that our financial margin is considerable and growing.'

Laura was silent for a moment. Then she smiled.

'Thank you, Henri,' she said and handed me her coffee mug, which I took from her hand and put in the place I had reserved for it in the dishwasher. Then I switched on the machine, and after a few brief displays of affection I was on my way to the adventure park.

My route was new now. First I took the metro to Itäkeskus, where I had to change and get a bus. And eventually, I did just that, but only after missing the bus I had been planning to catch, which would have got me to the park in good time. I wasn't in the habit of being late. Nonetheless, I decided to enjoy my new surroundings and the slowly brightening winter's morning as best I could. I reminded myself that I was unfamiliar with this route and that, these days, I seemed to be learning a great many new things.

When I finally got off the bus, I walked briskly, which wasn't only to do with being in a hurry, the -10°C temperature or the north-westerly wind. I had taken the weekend off, and I wasn't in the habit of doing that either. I usually worked at the park one day over the weekend, but now I'd been off since Friday afternoon. Key to this decision was moving house, but so was an observation I'd made about three weeks earlier. My employees had all grown into their respective roles, and nowadays they took greater responsibility for shared matters too. One afternoon three weeks ago, I realised that the day-to-day running of the park didn't require my constant oversight. Everything worked just as it should, things were taken care of, the employees did their work so well and so efficiently that I'd even considered giving them a pay rise and had reached the conclusion that this would happen as soon as our financial situation allowed it.

I crossed the road and continued across the snow-covered car park. As I arrived at the main doors, I turned and looked back. It was a curious thing to do, and at first I couldn't think why I'd spun around. I concluded it must have been from force of habit, a hangover from the time when I really did have to keep looking over my shoulder – for good reason. I looked at the car park a moment longer, judged it to be about as empty as on any median Monday, put my key in the door and stepped inside.

The aroma of fresh coffee and cinnamon buns hung in the air as I passed the Komodo Locomotive, the Strawberry Maze, the Doughnut and all the other familiar activities and contraptions. Our newest and largest acquisition, the Moose Chute, stood in pride of place in the middle of the park, its antlers reaching up to diving-platform heights and its dark flanks gleaming like a small ship. Whether I was looking at the machines, the floor, the walls, or anything at all, everything I saw was clean, in places almost sparkling. I mentally thanked Kristian, whose responsibilities now included organising and overseeing the park's cleaning operation. The hall even smelt clean, which also explained why the aromas coming from the Curly Cake Café were so overwhelming.

There were still a few minutes until the start of our morning meeting. I reached my office, switched on my computer, pulled up the documents and reports I needed and sent them to the printer. I glanced out of my second-floor window, adjusted my tie, grabbed the papers and walked into the conference room.

This was a new room, and it had come about at Kristian's initiative. Among his many suggestions for how to improve and modernise the park, this one had stood out in that it was genuinely feasible. He had even put up the walls himself, separating the room from the rest of the storeroom. Our marketing manager, Minttu K, had taken care of the interior design, which mostly consisted of shiny white surfaces and black leather. In addition, two black bollards had been positioned in the corners of the room. Minttu K called them sculptures. I'd seen similar rooms in a futuristic horror film I'd ended up watching years ago after a series of misunderstandings regarding the technicalities of buying a ticket.

Everybody was already sitting at the long white table: Kristian and Minttu K, and alongside them Esa, the park's head of security, playtime coordinator Samppa, and Johanna, who ran the kitchen at the Curly Cake Café. I walked to the head of the table, pulled out a chair and sat down. It was only then that I noticed that everybody in the room was looking at me. Their eyes then turned to the papers I'd placed on the table in front of me, then back to me again. The silence was new too. If this was a hint, I took it.

I lowered my eyes, examined the pile of papers in front of me. Then I remembered I had simply clicked open the report, printed it off, taken it with me and placed it on the white table – without so much as looking at it.

The uppermost paper was a report detailing ticket sales, customer numbers and the total takings. I had barely reached the end of the report when all the other observations I'd made that morning – the pristine snow covering most of the car park; the overall cleanliness that intensified the smells emanating from the café – little things I had noticed without knowing why, suddenly formed a clear picture.

Or rather, the picture they formed was distinctly unclear.

'What has happened?' I asked.

I looked at each of them in turn. Esa was staring straight ahead as though he was on guard duty, a black folder with a sticker bearing the insignia of the US Marines in front of him on the table. Samppa was adjusting his ponytail with sudden urgency, and once his hair was in a position of his liking, he turned his attention to his bracelets, the number and colour of which seemed to have increased since I'd last seen him. Johanna looked me right in the eyes, but I'd always found it impossible to read her: I suspected her lengthy spell in prison had helped her hone that stare into its current unflinching form. Sitting closest to me was Minttu K, but I could only see a small part of her face. Most of it remained hidden behind the giant coffee mug she was holding to her lips. As there were no windows in the room, I imagined the bouquet of window-cleaning fluid must be coming from the contents of her enormous mug.

'Footfall has suddenly ... collapsed,' I said and re-examined the figures on the page in front of me. 'Ticket sales only fifteen percent of what we would take on a normal weekend. Café sales only a tenth of what they usually are. Has something happened here?'

'Not here,' said Esa.

'Not here,' Kristian confirmed.

'Very well,' I said. 'Has something happened somewhere else?'

'Somersault City,' said Esa.

Somersault City was our new competitor, an enterprise about which I knew very little. My brother Juhani had defected and gone to work for them, but three weeks had been enough for him. Then he'd disappeared again. I only knew two things about Somersault City: the International Association of Adventure Parks had declined their membership but never formally explained why. In addition, I knew where Somersault City was located. The shining new building was almost diametrically at the opposite end of the city from YouMeFun.

'What have they done?' I asked.

'It all started on Friday with a massive radio campaign: free entrance and free hotdogs – normal, vegetarian, vegan,' said Minttu K. In the mornings, her voice resembled the growling of a laryngitic lion and her breath smelt of menthol cigarettes, even when she wasn't smoking them. 'Then at the weekend they brought in the celebs: on Saturday they had Aku Hirviniemi – four performances, all his funniest sketches. A six-figure fee and free hotdogs for the customers. Normal, vegetarian, vegan. And all this with free entry. On Sunday they had Anna Abreu – but that was adults only. She didn't sing. The dads bring kids to the park, then they get to take Anna on the rides: one ride per dad, per kid. Some of them were going around Espoo and beyond, looking for kids to take with them. One guy even packed his car with kids from the swing park and drove them all to Somersault City. Free entry. Free hotdogs. Normal, vegetarian, vegan.'

Minttu K took a thirsty gulp from her mug; this lengthy answer had clearly dried her mouth and throat.

'This all sounds like a temporary—'

'There aren't enough sausages left for us,' Johanna interrupted me. 'Somersault City has bought them all up. Their plan is to cook and sell over half the sausages sold in Finland this week.'

'But if it's only going to last a week—'

'Besides this unprovoked infraction, they have a long-term, more expansionist policy,' said Esa. 'Our intel confirms this. I've already conducted reconnaissance on the neighbouring plot. Would they be behaving like this if they didn't believe in their superior man power and endurance?'

'I'm not sure this is quite—' I said before yet another interruption.

'And they have already informed us,' said Minttu K, 'that the free entry is set to continue.'

'The park's about to open; I should go and open the doors,' said Kristian, and stood up; with his rippling muscles he looked as though he was heading in two directions at once. 'I'll make sure the first customers have tickets, then I'll be back. I've got some ideas.'

I glanced at my phone. Kristian was right about the time. I didn't know where the minutes had gone. I cast my eyes over the sales reports once more, the customer numbers, the various charts and figures. They posed numerous questions, that was certain, and not only for YouMeFun.

'Nobody can offer free entry and free hot dogs indefinitely...'

Minttu K shook her head. 'Not indefinitely, honey. Just long enough for us to close our doors. Once they're the only adventure park in town, they can charge whatever they like.'

Minttu K might have worded this thought rather differently from how I would have put it, but she was, of course, absolutely right. Silence descended upon the room for a second time that morning.

'Our defensive and offensive strategies in a nutshell,' said Esa, pointedly pushing his black folder towards me across the table. 'Land, sea and air. All readings taken this morning at oh-six hundred.'

I didn't know what was in the dossier in Esa's black folder, but neither did I feel a great desire to open it and find out.

'Thank you, Esa,' I said. 'Before we start—'

'Denying our true feelings,' said Samppa. 'That's mistake number one.'

'I don't see how—'

'That's exactly what I mean,' Samppa continued. 'Instead of suppressing our emotions, what we need now is a safe space where we can all share the feelings that this threatening situation is causing.'

'We should consider a militarisation sooner rather than later,' said Esa.

'There are no sausages,' said Johanna. 'I'm down to my last meatballs and fish fingers too, for the same reason.'

'Dialogue, dialogue, dialogue,' Samppa said, his emphasis growing with each repetition. 'What am I feeling, what are you feeling? And, once we've established that, what are *we* feeling?'

'I'm afraid it's too late for a pre-emptive strike,' said Esa. 'Stealth bombs and such.'

'Coffee might be next on the list,' said Johanna. 'And if the mums and dads can't get their coffee ... there'll be no way back.'

Samppa shook his head. 'We really need to let go of all this shame...'

I'd already raised my hand, and I was about to interrupt the increasingly agitated conversation, first to express my concern and second to stress that we should keep an eye on the situation and consider how likely it was that things would continue like this or whether our customer numbers would start to increase again in the next few days, but I didn't have the chance. Kristian returned to the conference room. He was out of breath. His tight white T-shirt looked suddenly very tight indeed. The same might be said of his expression.

'Nobody,' he gasped as he shook his head, as though he could hardly believe his own words. 'Not a soul.'

He paused for a moment, and it seemed that the last glimmer of hope flickered inside him, then snuffed itself out.

'I haven't got any ideas after all,' he said.

Later that afternoon, I noted that the adventure park was making history in a most unfortunate way: we hadn't had a single customer all day and the situation wasn't showing any signs of improvement. We also learnt (Minttu K had heard this from a sales rep working in outdoor advertising, who'd heard from her adventure-park-installation-operative cousin, who'd heard...) that next weekend Somersault City might be offering its clients free helicopter rides too. Even if this wasn't strictly true, it showed what people generally thought was possible and how they viewed the number and quality of our competitor's investments.

I went over the sums again, the same sums that I'd already calculated in a post-morning-meeting whirlwind of emotion ranging from frenzy to despair. The results were far from encouraging. We were still very reliant on our day-to-day takings, and our financial buffer was relatively small, though I'd been at pains to build one up over time. We didn't have the resources for large-scale publicity stunts. Giving away freebies would have been shooting ourselves in the foot; it would only speed up our demise. Based on the figures, it was hard to see how we could respond to our competitors, whose park was free, whose food was free, and who offered their clients helicopter rides and stand-up comedians.

I couldn't help thinking that, after everything I'd heard, I didn't actually know anything meaningful about Somersault City. At least, I knew nothing that might explain how they started operating as a business and how they'd come by a budget that seemed more appropriate for launching a space craft.

I stood up from my chair, looked outside.

Throughout the day the darkening, deserted car park had been covered in a thin layer of fresh snow, which only seemed to heighten the sense of emptiness. The longer I stared at it, the further YouMeFun seemed to drift into outer space.

During the course of the day, I'd had one-on-one conversations with every member of staff. Each of them had expressed their concern and given me their full support. This was a big change, especially given the situation when I had initially taken over the park. Not to mention what had happened when I'd been forced to tighten our financial belt. To put it mildly, I'd faced an amount of opposition. But once we had survived, and done so together, everything else had changed.

Now YouMeFun was *our* park, our shared interest.

All the staff had said this today, some more forcefully, some a little more reservedly. Esa was perhaps the bluntest with his suggestion of using landmines and a torpedo strike launched through a network of underground drains. Samppa wanted to allay the general hysteria and penetrate our underlying fears – his words – though he said he understood that in such a serious situation it was only natural to want to deny our true feelings. Johanna and Minttu K's views about the severity of the situation seemed to land somewhere between these two extremes.

And still, after dozens of calculations and all manner of different scenarios, I still couldn't work out how, even by pooling all our creative powers, we could ever come up with a solution to match our competitor. Let alone beat them.

Every thought, every last straw that my mind clutched, turned out to be another dead end, another snag. No matter how I thought about it, I remained on the outside, unable to see in.

Somersault City.

Snow fluttered lightly behind the window.

My phone rang and interrupted my musings.

3

The parents' evening was being held in the school dining room. I was still a little out of breath when I sat down and took off my coat: the pavements being now softened with a fresh covering of snow, the walk from the metro station to the primary school had been a little more arduous and therefore slower than I'd estimated. What's more, the route was new, as was the school itself, of which I naturally had no previous experience. Because of this, I didn't get there fifteen minutes before the start of the meeting – as Laura Helanto had recommended – but just as the meeting got under way, chaired by a black-haired woman who introduced herself as the deputy head. The intense blue of her blazer reminded me of Microsoft Word's branding. The deputy head welcomed everybody to the meeting and went through a list of upcoming events this term.

I quickly noticed that my thoughts were elsewhere, not here at the parents' evening as they ought to have been. For a while, it felt as though I hadn't actually arrived yet, as though I was still on my way from the adventure park to the primary school. I tried to push my work problems to one side and concentrate on the matter at hand, because I was here representing Tuuli and Laura Helanto, and in this new role I wanted to do my best.

As I listened, I cautiously looked around the room. The mothers and fathers were represented in almost equal number. Obviously, I didn't recognise anybody. For this reason, I was rather taken aback when a dark-haired man in a hoodie caught my eye, gave me a broad smile and waved his hand by way of a greeting. I was almost one-hundred-percent certain I'd never

seen the man in my life, but his behaviour seemed to suggest that
he knew who I was. I nodded back and gingerly raised my hand.
For some reason, the man thought my response worthy of a
thumbs-up. I looked away, glanced towards the other side of the
room – where I caught another pair of eyes. This time there was
no smile. This man was blond and small, though well built, and
despite his stature he seemed powerful and, one might say,
energetic. Before I could even think of responding, he looked
away and turned his attention to the front of the dining room.

I did the same. The deputy head looked like she was reaching
the end of her speech. Someone in the front row jumped to his
feet and turned to face those seated behind him. The man was
in his forties and had a sizable beard. He introduced himself as
Taneli, chairman of the parents' association, and then he began
talking about Paris. I realised this was the capital of France, but
I didn't understand quite how we had ended up on this
particular subject. Something must have happened during my
brief moments of eye contact. I concluded I must have missed
some short presentation or other.

It had to be said, the man with the sizable beard was a good
speaker. His words conjured up vivid images of the most iconic
sights in the French capital. For a moment, he sounded like a
travel brochure, before his tone turned rather more sombre and
he began to speak in a low-pitched voice about how important
it was for children to experience all of the above and how at a
young age such experiences have an effect comparable to that of
compound interest. Naturally, he was using these mathematical
terms in a loose, metaphorical way, yet I found it hard to disagree
with him on the substance, though I still didn't understand what
the wonders of Paris had to do with a school dining room in
Herttoniemi. Then the man asked something, and it took a
moment before I fully understood the question. It was at once

so obvious and yet so unexpected that I couldn't help myself raising my hand for the second time that evening.

'I can help calculate such things,' I said, honestly. 'I am an actuary.'

Because I was sitting right at the back of the room, I could see and hear a full dining room of people turn on their chairs and look at me.

'Brilliant!' said Taneli with the sizable beard at the front of the room. 'Now we've got the full committee together. Let's arrange a meeting for early next week.'

The rest of the meeting was reserved for the parents' questions. In addition to the deputy head, there was a younger teacher present whom I could easily have mistaken for one of the pupils. The teacher was nonetheless able to field a slew of questions and claims, even those that were beyond the realms of fact and science. And unlike some of the parents, she kept her calm throughout. Eventually, the deputy head, who had opened the meeting, brought proceedings to a close.

I stood up and was about to make my way to the front of the room to ask the man called Taneli for more information about the kind of assistance he needed with his mathematical problems when someone placed a hand on my shoulder.

'Henri, right?'

The dark-haired man in the hoodie was smiling again.

'Speaking,' I said.

'Sami,' said the man and thrust out his hand at once. I took it, and we shook hands. 'My daughter Ella is friends with Tuuli, they spend a lot of time together. Great to see you jumping on board like that.'

At first, I didn't understand what Sami was saying, then I realised that he must mean this event, the parents' evening, the fact that I was representing Laura Helanto. Which was important to me too.

'I'm only too happy to jump … on board,' I said.

'You're going to love it,' Sami nodded.

Sami had dark-brown eyes, and his cheeks were at once podgy and a little gaunt. This combination was only possible because the bones of his head were large, which made his cheekbones high, while simultaneously the general chubbiness of the rest of his body affected his face too – smoothing the edges, and in a way, softening the landscape. Sami was still smiling, and he was about to say something when he suddenly turned his head.

'Tuukka,' said Sami, 'come and meet Henri.'

I looked to the side. Tuukka appeared to be the small yet broad-shouldered, fair-haired Viking with whom I'd previously exchanged glances. He thrust out his hand even faster than Sami had done.

'A word of warning: don't believe everything Taneli tells you.'

'Why?' I asked.

There was a lot of commotion around us, and it soon looked as though most of the parents had already fled the scene.

'Tuukka's always joking about this, because Taneli's in the advertising business and Tuukka is in sales, so he's always saying he's the one who has to live up to Taneli's sales pitches,' said Sami, and Tuukka confirmed this with an almost imperceptible nod of the head. 'As for me, I've gone back to uni to study cultural anthropology.'

'I am—'

'An actuary,' said Sami. 'An insurance man. That's *actually* pretty reassuring.'

Sami laughed, again placed his hand on my shoulder, and I realised just how close to one another we were all standing. 'Sorry, I couldn't resist.'

'What…?'

Sami stopped laughing. 'We've got an informal dads' club,' he said. 'It all started because our kids play together and have loads of the same hobbies. We noticed we dads spent a fair bit of time together too. And the rest is *histoire*, as they say.'

I had no idea what Sami meant, and I was about to point out for a second time that I still had to talk to Taneli about matters of a mathematical nature, when I saw Taneli walking towards us. His reddish-brown beard looked even more sizable now that it was right in front of me. He had blue, slightly protruding eyes and more reddish-brown curls on his head, though considerably shorter than those on his chin. He wanted to shake my hand too.

'Welcome to the gang,' he said. 'We're going to give the kids the experience of a lifetime.'

'I've already told him about the dads' club,' said Sami.

'It's great to have another member on the team,' said Taneli, clearly trying to establish very close and intense eye contact with me. 'I suppose I should warn you, we're a bit different here in the heart of Herttoniemi. Some people call us hipsters, some hustlers, some people just call us weird, but at the end of the day we just enjoy rolling our sleeves up and getting things done. And for a good cause, like this one.'

I couldn't claim to have fully understood what Taneli was talking about, but neither did I want him to expand any further. I wanted to get back to our original subject.

'What kind of—?' I began but didn't get any further.

'Skiing, jogging, yoga, ice swimming, you name it,' said Tuukka. He sounded a little impatient, as though he was performing all of the above activities right here and now. 'During the winter, that is. In the summer it's football, street basketball, beach volleyball. For starters.'

'This is a really community-minded area,' said Sami. 'There's loads going on to bring people together.'

'I've got a few ideas about the initial finances,' said Taneli.

'Let's have a word about it before the first meeting of the Paris group next week. Speaking of Paris...' A phone had appeared in Taneli's hand. 'I'll add you to our WhatsApp group,' he continued. 'And maybe we can talk about that budget.'

The situation had escalated far more quickly than I had hoped or felt comfortable with, but at the same time I reminded myself that I had promised not only to represent Laura Helanto but to help Taneli too. I gave him my phone number and saw that Sami too was tapping at his phone.

'I'll add you to the dads' club group too,' he said. 'Don't be surprised if you get an invitation this evening or tomorrow at the latest. We all live within a radius of a few hundred metres, and there's always stuff going on with the kids' hobbies, and our hobbies too. Tuukka already told you we play loads of sports together. But we do plenty of other stuff too. Pizza nights, sports evenings, book clubs, and in the autumn there's the farmers' market too.'

'Skiing or skating?' asked Tuukka.

'What?' I heard myself ask again. It wasn't like me to give monosyllabic answers like this. The reason for my distraction must be trying to conduct several conversations at once and not being able to distinguish between them.

'Yoga?' asked Tuukka.

'Tuukka does a killer yoga routine,' Taneli nodded.

'I...' I stammered. 'I haven't really ... I agreed to help because I'm a mathematician...'

'Hey, now I know,' said Sami and turned to Tuukka and Taneli. 'We've got the kids' graffiti sesh this weekend. I know Tuuli's supposed to be coming; Ella's been talking about it too. That means the whole gang will be there. How about we take the outdoor ping-pong tournament that we missed back in the autumn and make it an indoor tournament instead?'

'Cool,' said Tuukka.

'Game on,' said Taneli.

'I'll post the tournament rules in the group, so Henri gets them too,' said Sami, and began using his phone with remarkable speed and dexterity. 'Let's start around half-nine, once the graffiti thing gets under way. Okay, cool, awesome. There you go. Now we've all got the time, the place, the rules and a list of participants with all the matches in order. Brilliant.'

I decided to dismiss Sami's decidedly confusing monologue for the moment – if need arose, which I thought highly unlikely, I could return to the subject later – and tried instead to ask Taneli what my mathematical expertise had to do with the French capital.

'This Paris thing,' I said. 'If I've understood correctly, this is some kind of class excursion?'

'A cultural trip for the kids,' Taneli nodded. 'We want to make this a once-in-a-lifetime experience for them.'

'And you're putting together a budget...'

'Right, and we've already started fundraising. Now we need someone who knows how to grow the pie,' he said. 'The bank balance, I mean. And come up with a budget that means we can all travel to Paris in a year's time.'

I thought for a second. 'How much have you raised so far?'

'We already had three small events last spring: two car-boot sales and a raffle,' said Taneli. 'So far, we've got about nineteen hundred euros in the coffers.'

I thought for another second.

'The teacher said there are a total of twenty-nine pupils in the class,' I said. 'A return flight to Paris costs at least two hundred and fifty euros, even for a relatively small passenger. The cheapest budget hotel costs around one hundred euros per night. And I imagine the intention isn't to fly all that way for only one night.

If we therefore assume that the shortest possible trip will involve two nights in a hotel, even then, the whole budget – not including food, transport at the destination, entrance fees and other unavoidable costs – will be exactly thirteen thousand and fifty euros. If we deduct the capital you have already secured, the budget deficit is a total of eleven thousand one hundred and fifty euros. If we try to make up that deficit using the aforementioned combination of raffles and car-boot sales, each turning an average profit of six hundred and thirty-three euros, at the current frequency we will have to hold no fewer than eighteen such raffles or car-boot sales over the course of the next year. For instance.'

The men looked at one another, then they looked at me. I stressed the rough nature of these basic calculations and was about to mention the fact that I thought holding raffles and car-boot sales every other week a rather ineffective way of raising funds and, in fact, one that could easily work against itself. And that all this must surely have brought them to the realisation that the project was on very shaky ground and that extra recruitments – by which, of course, I meant myself – were therefore unnecessary. But then, confounding all my expectations, Taneli began to smile, Sami began to smile, and even Tuukka gave a microscopic nod.

'Brilliant,' said Sami. 'I think we've found just the right guy to make the kids' dreams come true.'

'This really is going to be a once-in-a-lifetime experience,' said Taneli.

Tuukka said nothing. He looked at me without so much as the quiver of an eyelash.

4

'It all went brilliantly,' said Laura Helanto as soon as she walked through the door and was taking off her coat in the hallway. 'The space is perfect, they really liked my sketches, everything went better than I could have dreamed. They're going to let me know early next week whether I've got the job. How's your day been? Your first day as a member of our new family, as you said this morning?'

I'd been building up to this moment. I recalled my decision that morning not to bring work matters or other negative things into the home, into our new life. The cheerfulness and enthusiasm in Laura's voice were reason enough to think carefully what kind of news to tell her. I stood up from the living-room sofa, passed the closed door of Tuuli's room and found a chilly-cheeked but otherwise warm Laura Helanto by the coat stand. I had to admit that her embrace felt better than anything I'd experienced all day.

'Busy,' I said honestly, 'but I made it to the parents' evening.'

Laura was standing right next to me, I could feel a faint flow of air from her lips when she spoke.

'How was it?'

'I promised to do some calculations,' I said. 'For the possible trip to Paris.'

'Oh,' said Laura, confused. 'There was some talk about that a while ago, but I thought it was just speculation. They must have finally got some money together.'

I said nothing.

'But I'm a bit surprised,' she continued, 'to be honest.'

'Surprised at what?'

'That you'd jump on board like that, straight away.'

'I'm only too happy to jump ... on board,' I said for the second time that evening, as I drew in the scent of Laura's hair and skin, which I liked so much. At that moment I couldn't have imagined – after what might reasonably be called an eventful day – that the biggest shock of all was still ahead of me.

It happened at supper.

The rest of us were sitting at the table, while Schopenhauer had found a little alcove between the wall and the kitchen cabinets. He seemed content at being able to eat in peace and at least somewhat out of the sight of prying eyes. Tuuli, meanwhile, appeared very pleased indeed that I had made friends with her friends' fathers. It even seemed to matter to her that I was going to accompany her to the graffiti event on Saturday. I hadn't signed up for this myself, rather Tuuli, her friend Ella, and Sami, whom I'd met earlier that day, had taken care of this on my behalf. The matter even appeared to amuse Laura Helanto in a way that I couldn't have envisaged. In conclusion, I concluded that it was best to agree to their suggestions. Perhaps this is what family life is all about, I thought: needless hobbies, projects doomed to economic failure, and an array of awkward and uncomfortable situations that in the past I had assiduously avoided.

But it wasn't that simple.

Because what this particular and in all respects mundane event – a shared supper – made me feel and see was something I couldn't have predicted, or perhaps even imagined. When I saw Laura's glee and heard Tuuli's laughter, I felt a new, curious warmth rising up inside me, a mixture of happiness, pride and almost victorious joy. Here we were, all sitting together – now even Schopenhauer had sat down near us to clean himself – around the same table, and the soft light from the familiar dome lampshade seemed to cordon us off under our own sun, while outside the winter winds still whipped around the tall building. As mathematically incontinent as it sounded, this moment felt as though it was worth the day's tribulations many times over. And when I cleared the table later on, loaded the dishwasher, then took a cloth that was neither too damp nor too dry and wiped the dining table, the counter and the draining board, in that order, I realised perhaps more vividly than ever before that – assuming I had calculated the assorted factors and variables correctly – I had discovered something that to my knowledge practically everyone spent a lifetime looking for, longing for. I had found happiness.

After Laura had fallen asleep, I lay awake in bed.

Is this what so-called 'relationships' were? Were these the challenges?

I had been a live-in partner for a day and a half, and in that short time I had already found myself in a situation in which I'd had to conceal several matters. The spectrum of secrets ranged from the sudden loss of customers at the adventure park and YouMeFun's impending financial catastrophe to the budgetary crisis at the parents' evening, which I had ended up having to sort out for reasons I still didn't fully understand. Not to mention the fact that I suddenly belonged to a club with the other fathers, though I didn't recall ever applying for membership. Did these sorts of things happen to other people too? And if this was the average frequency of the manifestation of such problems, what could it possibly be like to be married for thirty years? For a moment, I tried to explain to myself that I hadn't actually concealed anything, that I had merely chosen a strategy that meant I would not bring anything unpleasant into our home, anything that might be comparable to what had happened in the past, and in this regard caution and discretion were part of my duties as a partner and a member of this family. And at almost the very same moment, I realised I was doing something that until now I had only seen in the cinema or read about in novels: I was stepping into the web of my own deceit.

I tried to steady my breathing, to relax. It was hard.

Even at the moment of drifting off to sleep, my mind was a flurry of aphorisms I had seen, whirling and swirling like a deranged carousel:

Relationships are about give and take.

Relationships need to be nurtured.

The best relationships are based on openness.

My dreams were restless, to say the least.

5

'Do you want me to go to the ticket office?' Kristian asked at the door.

I got up from my chair, looked outside.

The sun had risen, the day was as bright as it gets in January, like the faint glow of a reading lamp placed somewhere in the distance. The car park had been ploughed, turning the bright covering of snow into a general panorama of white and brown, with black spots here and there where the plough had scraped the asphalt with particular force. A quick glance was all that was required to give an answer.

'If the park is empty and nobody is buying any tickets,' I said, 'then what will you do at the desk?'

'Just in case there's a sudden rush...'

Again I looked at Kristian. With both his eyes and his words, he seemed as though he was fumbling for something.

'In case everybody suddenly remembers all the great times they've had here ... how amazing it is ... and because, well, this is still the best park and...'

Kristian looked like he had genuinely run out of words. I'd never seen him like this before. It was as though even his muscles were experiencing the same sense of withering. Then I realised something fundamental: he was afraid. This wasn't the Kristian I knew. He was even with me when we picked up our newest and biggest attraction, the Moose Chute, in a night-time operation in which we resorted to some decidedly non-mathematical tactics, and he had shown excellent skill and initiative in his new role at the park. Yet now he was panicking in a way that threatened even his considerable musculature. And so, I asked him:

'Have you heard anything new?'

Kristian didn't exactly squirm, but his body language wasn't far from it.

'Mr Fitness Finland,' he said, hushed.

It took a moment before I could truly take in the words I had just heard. I didn't know how to respond, so I decided to wait a moment.

'I'm entering this year,' he continued, his voice now even more hushed than before. 'And they're organising the competition.'

By now Kristian's face was puce. I believed I'd grasped what he was trying to tell me.

'Somersault City?'

Kristian nodded.

'When is the competition being held?' I asked.

A look of confusion spread across Kristian's fire-engine-red face. 'What, are you taking part too?'

'Kristian,' I said. 'I'm asking so I can glean more information about Somersault City.'

Kristian swallowed audibly, I could see the slump of his Adam's apple from across the room.

'Right, yes,' he nodded. 'April.'

It was almost three months until April. This meant that Somersault City was planning events long into the future. Which, in turn, meant that their recent antics were set to continue. Which, in turn, meant that Somersault City would be attracting our customers in the foreseeable future too – until we were forced to close our doors for good. But this information about Mr Fitness Finland still didn't answer one central question.

'Can I ask you something personal?' I began. 'Why is this so awkward for you?'

Kristian's face was like molten lava.

'Well, you see ... I'll have to go ... there ... to Somersault City.'

I stared at him. He looked as though he had just stolen the park's cash register or soiled the customer toilet. But he hadn't done anything of the sort: he had simply told me the truth, a truth that for one reason or another I had been trying to avoid.

'Kristian, you're absolutely right,' I said. 'We *will* have to go there. Thank you for reminding me.'

Kristian didn't quite smile, but his cheeks, now like a pair of distress flares, gradually began to cool down.

'Keep pumping,' he said. Hushed.

Somersault City was situated in the city of Espoo, just to the west of the Helsinki city limits. The complex was slightly larger than YouMeFun, in every direction. The Somersault City logo in neon lights on the building's roof was, at a conservative estimate, big enough, bright enough and powerful enough to direct all the air traffic in southern Finland.

I walked along the cycle path to the edge of the car park, crossed at the pedestrian crossing and began walking around the building. At the same time, I caught a representative glimpse of the packed car park. Cars drove around, accelerated, reversed and darted here and there in search of a free space. When people said that an event had the feel of a largescale sporting occasion, they probably meant something like this. I had to walk for a long time before reaching the entrance. The queue was considerable, and I joined it at the back.

Never before had I heard such enthusiasm.

Of course, most of the screams and whoops of the shorter people in the queue had something to do with the free hot dogs in front of them and – as I now recognised – the free waffles with free whipped cream and strawberry jam. The taller queue members, the majority of whom were the fathers, also seemed somehow more content with the situation than I had ever witnessed at my own park. My attention was drawn to a poster on the wall, itemising the week's programme of events. Every day there were performers, activities and special treats on offer. The bottom edge of the poster was dominated by large yellow lettering.

FREE ENTRY, it read.

And so, twenty minutes later, I walked into Somersault City completely free of charge – and mere seconds after this I felt that I understood more and, at the same time, less and less.

I recognised some of the apparatuses and activities at first glance. In the retailer's catalogue, I'd seen pictures of the Kangaroo Course, the Dumbo Dodgems and the Eiffel Bungee. And, of course, I had heard about and seen pictures of the contraption dominating the hall: the Beaver.

With a body almost twenty metres long (including the tail, the creature measured almost thirty metres), this giant rodent, jam-packed with activities and complete with a covering of high-grade fake fur, was such an imposing sight that for a moment I almost felt the need for more air. Meanwhile, the dozens of little customers running in and around the Beaver, on top of it, climbing its sides, charging through it and throwing themselves down the slides, didn't seem to suffer from a lack of anything, air or otherwise. In terms of sheer decibels, the noise from the customers was of a magnitude I'd never experienced at my own park, and at a cursory glance, I concluded that the levels of excitement around me were many times greater too.

I walked further into the park.

More equipment, more activities. More colours, more noise,

more dashing around. And in all this there was one common denominator: everything was brand new. Right from the smooth concrete floor beneath me to the fake comets flying overhead. I walked around the hall twice. In one corner of the hall, a celebrity business guru was lecturing the dads on how to be a permanent winner, and at the other end of the hall a shirtless male pop star was giving autographs to the mums.

For the second time, I came to a stop outside the door to the park's café. The prices on the backlit menu were senseless. Wiener schnitzel: one euro. Meatballs and mashed potatoes: one euro. Desserts were free. The queue wound its way round the hall.

I backed away from the door and experienced the same lack of air as when I'd first stepped inside. I had to move to one side, further away from the crush and the worst of the pandemonium. The throng of customers somewhat hampered my attempts at retreat, but eventually I managed to reach the relative calm of the Squirrel Trees to catch my breath. The Squirrel Trees might have been the most unpopular attraction in the park. It was a collection of trees of different size and thickness, and the object for the customers was to try and knock unusually large plastic squirrels from the branches with plastic peanuts that looked like tennis balls. Only one frustrated customer, standing just over a metre tall, was diligently trying to hit the squirrels. I didn't pay any attention to the plastic peanuts flying here and there, as I'd started to feel physically faint. Throughout the course of this visit, I'd been engaged in calculations that only served to make what I was witnessing with my own eyes all the more baffling. I decided to breathe calmly, to rest for a moment and only then decide on my next step. I drew air deep into my lungs and heard a voice behind me.

'Henri Koskinen?'

I had just filled my lungs, and now promptly coughed and spluttered the air back out again. Then I turned. In front of me I saw a man who was probably in his thirties; he had folded back the cuffs of his blazer and was wearing a pair of jeans that looked a little too short. I nodded, to confirm that I was, indeed, Henri Koskinen.

'We'd like a word,' said the man. 'Come, let's go and have a chat.'

The image of the man began to take shape. Grey eyes, blond hair combed tightly across his pate and a face that wasn't quite as youthful and sporty as his clothes and general style suggested. He looked like a man trying, at least in part, to hide who he really was. I followed behind him.

We walked back through the park. We progressed slowly, as if we were crossing a broad river. The customers around us were like a heaving, waist-height mass, and it would have been perilous to get caught up in its current. We both reached the other side of the park in one piece and without drowning, which was an achievement in itself. To my surprise, we walked around the Monkey Matrix, which I'd thought marked the end of the building. Behind this, however, was a space that seemed to be some kind of admin wing.

We took a short set of stairs and arrived in a space that one might call a foyer. The man gestured to the right, and it looked to me as though he was attempting a smile. But because smiling didn't come naturally to him, the result was something I might have expected from someone who has just filled their mouth with a handful of raw lingonberries.

We stepped into a conference room. Or, at least, I assumed this was a conference room. There was a long table and a set of chairs around it. A flipchart in the corner. The man who had escorted me closed the door behind me. We were alone in the room.

'Please, sit,' he said.

I looked at him, looked at the table and chairs.

'Sit wherever you like,' he said.

'Is this...?'

'A few minutes.'

I pulled a chair out from under the table and sat down. The man sat at the other side of the table, diagonally to my left. I adjusted my jacket, ran my fingers over my neck to check the position of my tie. I waited. The man was flicking through his phone. Approximately two minutes later, the door opened. At first I thought that the new arrival must be the identical twin of the man who had brought me here, then I realised that this impression was mostly to do with his clothes and body language. Smiling became him just as badly as it did his companion. He sat down on the other side of the table, diagonally to my right. Another man, who sat down in the middle, looked much more at ease in his youthful attire. He was perhaps in his forties, his dark hair, slicked back with gel, looked like the thickest of rugs, his stubble was peppered with spots of grey and silver. His eyes were blue, and they took stock of me for a few seconds before I heard him speak.

'Come to have a look around the park, right?'

'I wanted to see how your park operates,' I said, honestly.

'I told you,' I heard from my left. The man was still holding his phone, but now he wasn't even trying to smile.

'Joonas,' said the man in front of me. 'Put the phone away.'

Joonas suddenly looked as though he was either going to blow up or blow something else up. Nonetheless, with painful reluctance, he slid his phone into his jacket pocket.

The man in the middle returned his attention to me. 'Kotka,' he said.

Eagle? I thought, and waited for him to continue, but he was silent. I wondered, though it made no sense, whether he was expecting me to continue by suggesting some other kind of animal or winged creature. But, after a beat, he continued.

'Niko Kotka. And you are Henri Koskinen.'

I confirmed my identity for the second time in short succession.

'How do you like our park?' asked Niko 'the Eagle' Kotka.

'Impressive,' I said, again sincerely. 'I just don't quite understand everything.'

'Maybe you don't need to,' I heard from my right.

The third man spoke for the first time. I began to note just how much he differed from Joonas, who only a short while ago I'd thought was his spitting image. The folded-back cuffs and the all-too-short trouser legs naturally created a sense of déjà vu, but the differences were striking too. With flaxen fair hair in a bob and an almost translucent moustache, the third man looked positively shiny. But this shine couldn't hide the fundamental impression of dourness that the position of his head and body, and the piercing gaze from beneath his eyebrows, created. If I had to choose which of these three men was the most unpredictable, perhaps I wouldn't have chosen the phone-addict Joonas after all.

'What Olavi means,' Niko Kotka continued, 'is that it's completely okay if you want to take a look around the park, as long as you leave fairly soon afterwards.'

The manner in which Niko Kotka presented this proved essential to what happened within me in the following two and a half seconds. It was as though the intensity of the fluorescent lamps on the ceiling had increased many times over, as though for a moment I had seen not only everything that was happening in this park but everything that was *not* happening in *my* park, as though I was looking in two directions at once, to the past and the future. The levity in Niko Kotka's voice, the way he seemed to assume that he could speak to me however he pleased, and that his words would have the effect that he both desired and expected.

Electricity coursed through me – the adrenaline rush felt like a small nuclear reactor starting up.

I considered who I was, why I had come here and how much was at stake. I was here to defend my park, its employees, everything that I had built up with mathematics and my own hard work. At the same time, I remembered similar situations in the past: insinuation, intimidation, pressure, threats – both direct and indirect. I looked at these three men in turn. I believed in mathematics, I trusted it. It had saved my life, it had saved everything around me. With mathematics at my side, I would not back down. I would never back down again. I took a deep breath.

'I was just trying to see how your park works,' I said, and I could hear, almost from outside my own body, how calm my voice sounded.

'Why do you need to know how our park works?' said Niko Kotka. 'Shouldn't you be concentrating on how your own park *doesn't* work?'

Joonas let out a chuckle that I found it hard to consider benevolent.

'Your park isn't working, mate,' said Olavi, as if to reinforce Niko Kotka's comment.

'Seen many customers recently?' said Joonas, and slid his hand into his pocket.

'Joonas. Phone,' said Niko Kotka.

Joonas's hand stopped in its tracks and returned to its place on the table like an obedient dog.

'A big fat zero,' said Olavi.

'Olavi,' said Niko Kotka. 'Quiet.'

Judging by his expression, Olavi's comment appeared to have satisfied some kind of need: he looked smug and pleased with himself. Throughout this conversation, Niko Kotka's eyes had remained fixed on me.

'What if I were to say you're banned from Somersault City for life and we're going to throw you out by the scruff of your arse?' he said.

'How well acquainted are you with behavioural economics?' I asked. 'Without putting too fine a point on it, I would hazard that the business model implied in offering free entry to your park is harmful not only to me but it is harmful to you too and, what's more, it has a deleterious effect on the entire adventure-park sector, both in the short and long term. It gives our customers, the majority of whom are at a very impressionable age, the idea that adventure parks don't cost anything and that, in fact, they shouldn't cost anything. As such, offering free entry works against itself – against its own interests and objectives. Customers learn only to come to the park when it is free. And when it is free, we don't get anything in return. And when the customers don't come at all, we get even less. Everybody loses. Eventually, every adventure park will be out of business, not just mine. Which, of course, might be one of your aims. But even in this regard, I have bad news for you.'

'I told you he'd—' I heard Joonas say for a second time.

'I told you ... too,' Olavi chimed in, now sounding a little unsure of himself.

Niko Kotka glared first left then right. Then he returned, now clearly more agitated, to his previous tactic: staring right at me.

'You've got a reputation as a bit of smartarse,' he said. 'We know all about you—'

'Perhaps that was a careless choice of word, but I think you'll find that the term "smartarse" refers to someone who routinely resorts to a certain know-it-all *Schadenfreude*, if you will,' I interrupted. 'And, for the record, I try to avoid such behaviour as far as possible. In fact, what I am attempting to do here is to ensure in advance that we will have no need for the virtues of hindsight in the future. Is this policy of free entry really the way you want to run an adventure park under your ownership?'

'He doesn't own it,' said Joonas.

This answer followed my question almost instantaneously. It might have surprised me, but it appeared to have surprised Niko Kotka even more profoundly. Something happened to his expression. The fleeting moment of uncertainty and lack of control was easy to spot; he seemed startled by it himself.

'In that case, I'd like to speak with the manager,' I said.

'Shall I get V-P?' asked Olavi.

'Yes, please,' I said quickly.

Olavi stood up; he made sure to do this before Niko Kotka could say or do anything. In fact, he had opened the door and stepped out into the corridor before Niko Kotka could even turn to see his back speedily disappearing. Niko Kotka turned his attention to me again. There was no warmth in his blue eyes.

We waited a moment, then I heard footsteps. Olavi returned to the room and resumed his seat. Then I heard more footsteps, and a man entered the room with resolute steps and only came to a halt once he was standing behind the three men sitting at the table. The man was around my age, of average height and build, and nothing about him or his features attracted particular attention – except for his attire. He was wearing a pair of snakeskin-patterned leather cowboy boots, black jeans, a decorative shirt, the kind I'd seen on rodeo riders and country singers, and on his head, almost like a crown, he sported a broad-rimmed Stetson familiar from westerns. Upon closer inspection, I saw he had a slim bolo tie round his neck too. It was hard to look at him without thinking that, on top of everything else, I now found myself in the middle of a fancy-dress party.

'Ville-Pekka Häyrinen,' the man introduced himself. 'What's your business?'

Häyrinen was standing behind his men, meaning that they couldn't see him and Häyrinen couldn't see Niko Kotka's expression either. Right now, I thought this was an excellent set-up. I introduced myself and repeated what I had said a moment ago about the park's free-entry policy and the dangers that entailed. Häyrinen seemed to be listening to me, so I took the opportunity to present my arguments in greater detail. Then I stopped. Ville-Pekka Häyrinen touched the brim of his Stetson with his right hand in such a way that I had to remind myself that this was not some spaghetti western but a business negotiation being conducted under considerable duress.

'We've got a lot of expenses,' said Häyrinen, paused, then continued. 'But Niko here takes care of that, and he's convinced this is the way to drive you and your park out of business and wipe you right off the map, and after that we'll be the only adventure park in town.'

Niko Kotka's expression remained unchanged, but I was certain he was smiling. I returned my attention to Häyrinen and hoped I'd calculated the quartet's internal power dynamics correctly.

'And did Niko also tell you that it isn't going to work?' I asked. 'That nobody can threaten or blackmail me or my park, in any way? And that all the money you're currently spending will be gone forever? This is the diametrical opposite of a profitable investment. Regardless of the timeframe over which you're thinking of making a profit.'

For the first time, Häyrinen's face – which, admittedly, was quite hard to see beneath the broad brim of his hat – betrayed something approaching an expression, perhaps only a glimmer of uncertainty, a seed of doubt. I glanced at Niko Kotka. He wasn't smiling now, not even inwardly.

'Why should I listen to what our competitor has to say?' asked Häyrinen.

'Because I have experience of the adventure-park industry and a wealth of evidence and good results too,' I said. 'And because I am an actuary.'

'Beg pardon?'

'An actuary,' I said and, anticipating the next question, I continued: 'Actuarial mathematics is an application of mathematics and statistics in which we assess the probability and risk associated with specific events in order to calculate an insurance payment that is financially viable from the insurer's perspective. I realise it might be hard to see the connection between this and, say, the giant Beaver out there or the Kangaroo Course, but with some lateral thinking I believe we can get there. I assess risk; I assess probabilities.' I looked at all four men in turn, then added: 'I don't mean any offence, but I'd hazard I am more qualified in this field than all four of you.'

Häyrinen remained silent, his Stetson was still. Then the front of its brim rose a few millimetres.

'Even so,' he began. 'Why should I take advice from you?'

'Because by helping you and your park,' I said, 'I'll be helping my own park too.'

Häyrinen rubbed his chin, straightened the black tails of his bolo tie.

'Niko,' he said. 'You told me and Elsa that this Henri Koskinen was nothing but an unimaginative, introverted number-cruncher who doesn't even know what year it is, let alone what day. What I've just heard doesn't quite tally with that assessment.'

Häyrinen looked at the back of Kotka's head; Kotka kept his eyes fixed on me.

'That's how Koskinen's brother described him,' said Niko Kotka, 'and I think he was right. It shows quite a lack of imagination to turn up here and say things like that without understanding the consequences.'

Joonas chuckled, then regained his composure. Olavi was clearly having to restrain himself. Häyrinen remained silent, looked at the three heads in front of him one after the other, and then at me. Then he seemed to remember something and glanced at his watch.

'Elsa is waiting,' he said. 'We're going to look at another horse. You know Elsa, nothing is more important to her. She can never have too many horses...'

The three men sitting at the table all nodded in unison.

'That's fine, we'll take care of—' began Niko Kotka, until I interrupted him.

'I truly suggest you rethink the free-entry policy,' I said. 'And if I can help by explaining any of the mathematical concepts involved, I'd be only too happy.'

Häyrinen looked at me; he was clearly about to say something, then decided against it. Again he glanced at his watch, then turned on the heels of his cowboy boots and walked to the door. He was already about to swing out of view when he suddenly stopped in his tracks.

'Niko,' he said. 'Get me and Elsa all these ... numbers, okay?'

'I'll deliver them to both of you,' said Niko Kotka, but he didn't look at the door; he was looking at me. 'In person.'

Ville-Pekka Häyrinen's steps disappeared down the corridor, then everything fell silent. I stood up from my chair.

'Thank you,' I said, 'for this ... enlightening conversation.'

I walked out of the room. I was in the foyer when I heard Olavi's voice behind me.

'Hey, insurance man,' he shouted. 'Count this!'

I didn't turn to see what exactly Olavi was showing me.

6

Throughout the days that followed, the episode in the conference room at Somersault City began to swell in my mind like a giant wave, constantly gathering strength. The wave buoyed me while I was encouraging the park's employees, trying to cheer them up both together and individually, and it carried me when I searched for ways to survive our current challenging predicament and our even more challenging future. And though I still hadn't come up with a solution and couldn't bring myself to tell Johanna, Minttu K, Esa, Samppa and Kristian quite how we were going to win this knock-out competition that had emptied our adventure park, somewhere inside me there was a quiet certainty that, one way or another, we would survive. This certainty stemmed from a curious combination of my own personal history (particularly my recent history) and the simple truth that I had managed to turn the course of the conversation to my advantage – though there had been no fewer than four opponents sitting across the table.

Mathematics had nothing to fear.

And perhaps that was one of the main reasons why I wasn't shocked or even particularly surprised when I became aware that Olavi from Somersault City was following me. I'd simply thought it a natural and logical result of what had taken place. And the reason it didn't really worry me must have had something to do with this new-found certainty that things would eventually work out for the best. Naturally, I hadn't said any of this out loud, and I was sure that during the last few days I had scrupulously managed to keep to myself the waves surging within me, the appearance of Olavi in the corner of my eye, and the undeniable omnipotence of mathematics. And perhaps this is why, that Friday evening, Laura Helanto's innocent question surprised me as much as it did.

'Are things at the park going better than usual? You're in such a good mood.'

The question took me off guard. We were sitting on the living-room sofa; Tuuli was asleep.

Twenty minutes earlier, we had settled down to watch a television series that I hadn't been giving my full attention. To be honest, I didn't know what the story was about, and this time I couldn't blame the performance itself. I realised I was simply enjoying having Laura sitting next to me, being at home and the very fact that this *was* my home. If in the past the idea of telling Laura Helanto any kinds of falsehoods had been completely out of the question, now I could barely bring myself to look at her.

'I didn't realise it showed,' I said.

'You talked to Tuuli for an hour about what kind of phone to get, you did your calculations and cracked her up by working everything out in your head, and even you laughed, which I think must be the first time I've ever heard you laugh while you've been calculating. You played with Schopenhauer, brushed his coat for about half an hour, and you were smiling the whole time. You compared my new sketches to Pissarro's heyday because you know he's one of my favourites – though my sketches have nothing whatsoever in common with Pissarro!'

All this was true. I simply hadn't noticed it myself.

'I see...'

'Or maybe it's still the novelty,' said Laura before I could go any further, 'of moving in together?'

Laura's change of direction was a relief. Now I could be honest with her.

'I would discount the novelty factor,' I said, and it was the honest truth. 'It's hard to imagine the charm will ever wear off. In fact, quite the opposite is true. In this sense, I consider the charm a gradual accumulation, as I've said in the past. Conceptually, I think compound interest is the most apt metaphor for my feelings.'

I could all but feel Laura's eyes on the right side of my face.

'I have to say, right from the beginning this was one of the things that made me love you so much, that way you have of talking so ... romantically,' she said eventually, brought her face closer to mine, and kissed me on the ear. At the same time, I heard her whisper: 'But you'd tell me if there were any serious problems at the park or anywhere else, right?'

Her lips were almost right against me, sending shivers through my body with their every touch. For some reason I found myself thinking about space, galactic proportions, the age of the universe: the big bang, fourteen billion years ago, its ever-accelerating expansion.

'If there were any serious problems,' I said, 'I would tell you straight away.'

On Saturday morning, Tuuli seemed anxious to leave the house. I tried to assure her that the seventeen and a half minutes I'd reserved for the walk would be plenty and that I'd even factored in a margin of error to account for the weather and potential roadworks, and all this would make sure we arrived on time. Having said that, I sensed that perhaps her impatience wasn't entirely because she was worried about the time it would take us to get there.

Tuuli had been sitting on a stool in the hallway with her hat on for ten or eleven minutes already, and throughout that time she'd been talking about graffiti, how to paint it, famous graffiti artists, styles and other associated factors. Her knowledge of the subject was impressive, though her mode of presentation and the cadence of her speech were at times surprising to say the least.

I pulled on my outdoor clothes and we set off.

It was a bright morning, cloudless and windless, the snow had settled, our steps were firm, walking felt light and pleasant. In the past, I'd noticed that on January mornings like these the combined effect of the light, the mild weather and the faint chill in the air made the mind wander and think of spring, which, in factual terms, was still a long way off. As though I'd first given myself a glimmer of hope only then to trample on it by accepting that there was still a long sub-zero spell to come, snow, ice, slush, wind and, of course, darkness. For this reason too, it was good that Tuuli continued her monologue throughout our walk. The other reason why I thought her talkative enthusiasm was a good thing was because of what I noticed during the final third of our journey.

Olavi was following me again.

And, more specifically...

He was following us.

I'd known for a long while that not only was being an entrepreneur in the adventure-park industry fraught with danger, it was also completely unpredictable. But what I didn't know (and there was no way I could have known), was that the combination of adventure-park entrepreneurship and a newly found family life was more challenging still. I wasn't especially worried about Olavi – my main concern was that he might teach Tuuli the kind of vocabulary that could prove problematic later on – but the matter began to bother me so much that I could feel the irritation slowly occupying my thoughts. I'd already decided that I wanted to keep the adventure park's business separate from this part of my life and had resolved to do so in any way I could. Now Olavi, with his bulbous green eiderdown coat and translucent moustache, was bringing work matters across this clearly drawn boundary by force.

But while my irritation at Olavi and the people he represented continued to grow, I felt almost happy. There was something infectious about Tuuli's excitement and forward-looking attitude, and the very thought that she was able to do something for which she felt this kind of drive and passion lent the early morning a very pleasant sense of tingling expectation.

We walked along the long straight roads running through the industrial park, and because he could be more easily seen now, Olavi had to hang further and further behind us. In other words, he didn't know that I knew he'd been following us – and that he was still following us.

Seen from the street, the two-storey building was partially hidden behind the car dealership that fronted onto the street, so I could only see about a quarter of it. We found the entrance hidden behind the dealership and took the stairs to the upper floor, and I let Tuuli lead the way. The room we arrived in ran the entire length of the building. The left-hand wall was essentially all windows, right up until the wall at the end, while the right-hand wall was half covered in graffiti and half bare, grey concrete. The shorter attendees had gathered at the precise spot between the grey and the explosion of colour, where a couple of young women I assumed to be instructors were speaking to them.

'I've got to go,' said Tuuli, and ran away from me before I had time to answer. I was already walking towards the row of windows to look outside and establish where Olavi had positioned himself, when Taneli and his sizable beard were suddenly in front of me.

'Yo,' he said.

'Good morning,' I replied.

'Best get downstairs quick,' he said. 'The first round's already started.'

I glanced in Tuuli's direction, and she happened to glance back at the same time. I pointed to the floor to indicate I was going downstairs, she nodded and turned away again. I assumed my message had been received and understood. A moment later, Taneli was escorting me to the door and the concrete steps leading to the ground floor and into an atmosphere that was considerably more agitated than I'd been expecting.

The layout of the lower floor was an exact copy of the upper floor, and the whole space seemed unable to make up its mind about what it was for: it smelt of machinery, equipment and industrial chemicals, but nonetheless it was largely empty, with the exception of some piles of boxes and junk next to the doorway. The ping-pong table was at the other end of the room. I could tell right away that it was a good thing there was something to separate the two players. Even across the length of the table, Sami and Tuukka were in such disagreement that at first they didn't even notice when Taneli and I approached them. Sami, the stocky cultural anthropology master's student, was much more agitated than at our first meeting. It was only once Taneli and I stopped two and a half metres from the edge of the table that he finally noticed us.

'Tuukka is playing hardball,' he said.

'We're playing to win, right?' said Tuukka without looking at us. Something suggested he had noticed our arrival, though he hadn't reacted in the least. Given his stature, he looked like a sinewy lynx, tensed and ready to pounce.

'So much for a nice relaxing Saturday,' said Sami, 'when this guy's whacking the ball right in my face.'

'All my shots touched the table,' said Tuukka.

'That's not what I meant,' said Sami. 'Can't we just take it a bit easier? This is supposed to be fun, after all, and—'

'It's a competition,' said Tuukka. 'We have the group stage, then the quarter-finals, the semi-finals and then the final.'

'How about I just throw in the towel right now?' said Sami.

'You can't do that,' said Tuukka.

'Why not?' asked Sami.

'Here's the chart,' said Taneli. 'And I made a logo too.'

'What's wrong with you guys?' said Tuukka. 'Can't you play like you mean it?'

'Maybe not everybody takes it quite this seriously,' said Sami. 'Maybe not everybody is a former competitive sportsman...'

'Former?' Tuukka exclaimed.

Tuukka's posture was even more lynx-like now. I thought that, if the situation were allowed to escalate freely, he would soon have a rabbit between his teeth.

'Guys,' said Taneli. 'Can everybody just chill out? We've got a new member...'

'Member?' I'd asked before I even noticed.

The men turned to face me.

'Dads' club,' said all three at once.

I was about to open my mouth, about to say – once and for all – that I didn't realise I had become a member of anything and that there must be some misunderstanding, but I didn't. I glanced to the side, out of the window, and saw a sliver of that familiar bulbous green jacket lurking behind the corner of the car dealership. I carried out a quick calculation and reached a decision.

'Very well,' I said. 'I'm going to get some fresh air before my game.'

The trio seemed to approve of this. As I returned to the door, I heard that it was Sami's turn to serve. Before touching the handle, I stopped. A stack of boxes was piled up next to the doorway; judging by their contents, it seemed they were destined for the upper floor. Some of the boxes had already been opened. Because I didn't know what to expect, I thought it best to prepare for any eventuality. The decision was quick. I stepped outside with a can of spray paint in my jacket pocket.

The frozen air gripped me right away, clamping around me like an angry blanket. I waited for a moment, then set off. The day was at its brightest, and the sound of the snow crunching underfoot sounded almost amplified as I walked between the two buildings. I walked away from the green jacket, away from the road and the way we had arrived. I reached the corner of the brick building and turned. I made my way along the narrow corridor ploughed in the snow, turned again, and waited.

Everything was quiet and still.

This part of the industrial area ended at a small park, its nearest section nothing more than a strip of woodland about twenty metres long. Behind me was a thick, wintery forest, to my right a brown-red brick wall, to the left a bare rockface, and in front of me the windowless, corrugated-iron wall of the car dealership. Whichever direction I looked, I was hidden from sight.

I had a plan, by no means a perfect plan, but one that, given the conditions and probable outcomes, was, I believed, the best possible. The basic premise was simple: I wanted to take the initiative myself, gain the upper hand. And because I didn't want Tuuli, or that curious club to which I now seemed to belong, to know anything about Olavi or what he had in mind, when I took that initiative, I had to be somewhere other than standing at a ping-pong table.

A crow squawked behind me, followed by a gloomy whoop as it sluggishly rose into flight.

Then I heard the crunch of snow between the buildings.

It only took a few seconds before Olavi appeared from around the corner.

He took another two steps and stopped about three and a half metres away from me. We looked each other in the eye. I was probably right to assume that, of the two of us, I was the least bewildered.

'What the fuck…?' he exclaimed.

It was a perfectly reasonable question. Olavi looked irritable and frostbitten, and his blond moustache only heightened the ruddiness of his cheeks.

'You've been following me for a few days,' I said. 'Why?'

Olavi thought about how to answer this. 'I don't like you,' he said.

'Why do you think that is?' I asked.

Olavi squinted. As he did so, his upper lip tightened above his teeth, making his moustache even thinner.

'What?'

'Is it because I questioned your business model and expressed scepticism about its profitability in both the short and long term? That I suggested a simple, purely mathematical approach to the matter, the kind that would allow for a truthful assessment of the situation?'

Olavi looked like he was thinking hard.

'You can shove your numbers,' he said.

I waited a moment.

'What if I told you I find that kind of language quite offensive?' I countered. 'Because mathematics is important to me, and I've found I can rely on it. Always.'

Olavi shook his head. 'We don't need you or your fucking

maths at Somersault City,' he said, and took something from his pocket. With surprisingly agility – given he'd been standing in the freezing cold for some time – there was suddenly something around his fingers. He raised his hand. The steel knuckleduster gleamed in the sunshine.

'I don't want to see you hanging around Somersault City spying on us again,' he said, and took a step closer. 'I'm going to put you out of business that bit quicker. Then you can do your sums in peace and quiet.'

He took two more quick steps. My right hand slipped into my jacket pocket, I gripped the can of spray paint, took it out of my pocket, and in a single movement gave it a shake and put out my arm as though I were gesturing towards the obvious solution to a seemingly complex calculation, and once Olavi was right in front of me I firmly pressed my forefinger down.

The spray paint appeared to explode from the canister; I could feel the pressure in my hand.

The paint was a vivid, baby-blue colour. Olavi didn't stop at once; he had only partly managed to close his eyes. I kept my forefinger pressed down. Olavi opened his mouth, presumably in an attempt to say something. The fountain of paint covered his tongue and teeth. He stopped, let out a sputter and took a step back, so I released my finger, lowered my hand a little, and waited. I had guessed correctly. He could still see – his confused eyes were blinking frantically in the middle of his face, now covered in fresh, light-blue paint – but, assuming I'd read him right, he was startled too. So I raised the canister again. And he started to back away.

I took a step forwards, and Olavi took a step backwards. We repeated this. Then I took a quicker step. I achieved my goal: Olavi turned and ran off. I took a few running steps after him. We ran between the buildings. Olavi glanced over his shoulder,

I brandished the canister. At the corner of the car dealership, we turned and arrived at the road.

And Olavi ran.

He ran along the long, straight road and peered over his shoulder one final time. I raised my hand again and showed him the canister, and he continued running.

I looked around; nobody appeared to have witnessed the incident. I slipped the spray paint into my pocket, walked back to the brick building and into the empty warehouse space, and installed myself beside the ping-pong table.

And so, I played table tennis, which I had last played twenty-nine years ago.

Among their dozens of other catastrophic endeavours and failed business ventures, my parents had also been table-tennis entrepreneurs. My father, who would today surely be described as a dynamic businessman who liked to think outside the box, once returned from an unfortunate business trip involving a collection of fishing equipment and told us he had hired an air-inflated sports hall, and then set it up on a plot of land that he'd bought on the cheap. The unusually low price of this land was due to its location: the air-inflated hall, complete with its dozens of table-tennis tables, was situated at the end of an almost unnegotiable path in a national park somewhere in the north of the country by the Russian border. Ping Pong Paradise, as my mother and father christened the venue, echoed and boomed when my brother forced me to play endless rounds of table tennis there. I would much rather have concentrated on doing something useful, like algebraic calculation, because even back then I had obtained a deep understanding of mathematics, and mathematics was like an impregnable fortress protecting me from the surrounding chaos – which, in this particular instance, came in the form of table tennis.

(There was nothing especially new about this chaos. We had just moved to another town and discovered a new form of chaos; only a short while earlier, on the other side of the country, my parents had been running a milk-carton museum, whose customer numbers had doggedly remained much lower than they had hoped.)

After all this time, I still couldn't claim to enjoy table tennis.

In addition to playing table tennis, I gave positive and encouraging feedback on Tuuli's and her friends' graffiti plans and sketches, though I probably didn't understand all their processes and nuances. In their own way, both these actions felt unavoidable. I had already noticed that family life meant not only making a lot of compromises but also putting up with a considerable amount of discomfort, both physically and mentally. Thus, I didn't feel at such a loss about what actions and practices were required as I might have in the past. On top of this, I tried my best to, as they say, engage, to live in the moment, both in my table-tennis matches and in my assessments of teenage art.

Still, I only succeeded periodically; I couldn't shake off the thought of my encounter with Olavi.

Of course, I realised that it was only natural to remember the moment when you spray someone's face bright blue, but this wasn't the only reason that the series of events kept creeping back into my mind. Time after time, I heard his handful of words, and they in turn provided new connections, new understandings of what I already knew. On the way home, I made my decision.

'That was a great day,' said Tuuli as we stood waiting at the traffic lights. 'We learnt loads.'

I said I agreed, and again I concluded that if I'd had to decide what was best about this day, it would have been Tuuli's bubbling enthusiasm. And I couldn't deny that I too had learnt many new things.

'Are you coming next Saturday?'

'Pardon?'

'When we go spray painting next Saturday; are you coming too?'

'I don't ... know yet,' I said as the lights turned green. I checked the traffic in both directions one last time before we started crossing the road.

'Do you know how to spray paint?' Tuuli asked once we reached the pavement opposite.

The question was a logical continuation of the previous one, but still it took me by surprise. I hadn't thought of it from this angle.

'It would seem so,' I said, and heard the surprise in my own voice. 'I didn't know I knew how, but today I realised that, with enough motivation, I can do it.'

Tuuli looked at me, smiled, and didn't say anything. I smiled back. The next time she spoke, it was on a different topic, something to do with a show on TV later that evening.

We walked home as the winter's day faded behind us and the streetlamps flickered into life.

Later that evening, once Laura came back from her studio, I said I would have to pop into the adventure park. She said on the one hand she understands my sense of duty to the park, but thought it was a strange time of day. I said, honestly, that this was an acute problem and I was the only one who could resolve it. For a moment she was quiet, then said that was probably true.

And with that I set off to the adventure park.

Just not my own one.

I am a murderer.

In other respects, too, I'm not having the best morning. I've slept very badly. First I broke into my competitor's adventure park, only to find myself caught up in a terrible misunderstanding and having to flee both the police and a group of criminals. Then, after some considerable detours, I returned home, where I told a nonplussed Laura Helanto that I'd left my phone on the shelf in the hallway because I hadn't anticipated the operation would take quite as long as it did (which was true), and since then I've been lying awake in bed thinking about my new situation.

And speaking of phones: since early this morning my phone has been beeping frenziedly with a steady stream of messages – about the Paris trip and an upcoming pizza night from the dads, who don't hold back when it comes to WhatsApp messages; and from my panicking staff. The common denominator in all these messages is that everybody wants me to solve their problems right away.

I almost have to force myself to eat breakfast.

I'm hungry, that much is true, but even chewing and swallowing seem to require extra concentration. I also note that it's hard to think about the logistics of a trip to a local organic farmer to pick up ingredients for a pizza night when I'm constantly reminded that not only am I now a suspected murderer, but my business is being fast-tracked into bankruptcy.

It isn't the fault of the rye bread, the sliced turkey, the yoghurt or the tea that everything I put in my mouth feels tough and indestructible, as though I've bitten into my own shirt or the table in front of me, or something similarly inedible. But I manage to eat all the same, I load the dishwasher, and for the first time I'm relieved that Laura Helanto isn't sitting here having breakfast with me.

She woke up after me, I heard her in the bathroom, then in the hallway. She is heading off without breakfast, as she is expecting a delivery of materials at her studio.

Naturally, such a sense of relief isn't entirely unproblematic, and it doesn't come without guilt – the idea that I've moved in with someone only to studiously avoid her. Of course, it's not that simple, I know, and I ask myself whether this is how all couples behave when they're trying to keep secrets from each other: that because I can't tell my nearest and dearest about the murder suspicion, the pizza expedition and the badly organised trip to France, I hide in the kitchen and wait for her to leave and get on with her day – which I sincerely hope will not include the sort of things I seem to dabble in, namely industrial espionage, near escapes and lethal ice-cream cones.

I really have slept very badly, I think, as I close the dishwasher and walk into the bathroom...

... and bump into Laura in the hallway.

'Sorry, darling,' she says as she pulls on her coat, wraps her scarf around her neck and places a toothpaste-smelling kiss right in the middle of my face. 'I'm in a terrible hurry. I couldn't get to sleep properly until the early hours, and now I'm running late. How did you sleep?'

'Quite—'

'You got home really late,' she says, pulling on a thick woolly hat. 'I wondered whether I should be worried, but then I just thought, if you're at the park you'll be perfectly safe, and then you came home.'

'I came—'

'I've really got to go,' she says, giving herself one last check in the mirror.

Her bushy hair curls out from under the hat, the scarf is bundled around her shoulders like a soft mountain, her glasses with their large, dark frames highlight the blue-green of her eyes. She is beautiful, my Laura, I think, and I so wish I wasn't suspected of murder right now.

'I'll pop into the shop of my way home,' she says. 'Could you take the rubbish out? The compost bin is quite full.'

She is right, about this too. The kitchen compost bin is full. For a fraction of a second I wonder if that will be my last act as a free man. What if this is what I'll be remembered for? Henri took out the compost, then he was sentenced to life imprisonment. I want to give my head a shake, to put these thoughts behind me.

'It's probably best if—'

'Great, darling, thank you,' Laura calls out as the door is already closing. 'See you this evening.'

It's only once I'm on the bus from the station to the park that I finally recover my balance, once and for all.

As always before, help comes in the form of mathematics, order and logic. I place things in order of importance and urgency, consider what I can do about each of them, what each task will require both in terms of time and resources, and I draw up a realistic plan, based as much as possible on probabilities, and, where applicable, a separate budget. It says something about my confusion that morning and my momentary imbalance that when I finally hit upon what I've been racking my brains to find, the plan takes shape during the eight and a half minutes of my bus journey.

My first and most important task is also the most obvious one, and stems both from the night's events and my current situation. The owner of Somersault City has been murdered, and it is only a matter of time before the authorities are able to place me in the vicinity of the body. And by that time, nobody will look any further afield for a suspect, especially because Olavi will doubtless be only too happy to testify to the incident with the spray paint. (This was, of course, an act of self-defence on my part, but I don't think it is too far-fetched to imagine that people will have a keen interest in hearing the testimony of a man with a blue face.)

So, first and foremost: I have to find the real killer and point the police in that direction.

In fact, everything depends on the success of this first task: my family happiness, rescuing the park, practically every aspect of my new life. As the bus slows down at my stop, I decide there's no point placing the pizza ingredients or the funding for the school trip on my timeline. They will sort themselves out in due course, assuming I haven't been sent to prison; haven't ended up in the clutches of a gang of hardened criminals – a distinct possibility, I realise if my nocturnal visit to Somersault City were to be revealed to the killer or killers before the police find out; and haven't gone bankrupt.

There is a reddish tinge to the morning sunshine, as though it is considering setting instead of rising. I can feel the wind on my cheeks and the tip of my nose, the snow crunches and crackles beneath my feet. Walking through the deserted car park does little to raise my spirits, but there's nothing new about that.

The emptiness doesn't surprise me; it serves as a reminder. I walk into the park and greet Kristian, who is standing behind the ticket desk. He says nothing about the morning sales figures, which tells me there have been no sales to mention. I can see it in him too, his deflated posture, his lack of smile.

I look at him and wish I could find something encouraging to say, but my mind is so full of other things that I have my work cut out to think of anything at all. And so I find myself telling him a story I heard at a training session in my former workplace about an entrepreneur called Sanders who thought he had come up with something revolutionary – pieces of fried chicken – and started looking for someone to invest in his new idea. Over the next few years, around a hundred investors laughed at him and declined to invest in something so crazy, but Sanders was undeterred. Eventually he managed to put together a small amount of initial capital, and Kentucky Fried Chicken was born. I end the story, and though I'm not a great fan of using the powers of oratory to raise the spirits (the claims people make often lack any basis in truth, and such speeches are almost without exception employed at the point when one has already lost the argument), I am about to say something about never giving up, but Kristian beats me to it.

'That might work with chicken,' he says. 'But this is an adventure park.'

'That's not the—'

'I know you're trying to cheer me up,' he continues. 'But I know a thing or two about chicken. I eat a lot of it. For the protein.'

'I didn't—'

'And this Sanders,' Kristian adds. 'I wouldn't trust him.'

I am torn. On some primitive level, I am curious to hear why the late CEO of a highly successful American company doesn't enjoy Kristian's trust, while on the other hand I feel that the conversation has been somewhat derailed, to the extent that I feel the need to find something more productive to do. I open my mouth, and at that moment, I realise something.

Our conversation was so intense that it's only now I see that we have company. I turn, and my first thought is that I am looking at two of our customers. Perhaps a little older than our clients' median age, a little taller, broader shoulders. But only marginally. At the same time, the image somehow comes into focus and I understand that these are two young men who look considerably younger than their years. They might be around twenty-eight but could easily be mistaken for half that age. And their clothes – the sagging, baggy jeans, the puffy eiderdown jackets and hoodies beneath them – seem to knock another year of two off that half.

'Harry,' says the fairer of the two, staring at me unblinkingly. 'Koskinen.'

'The man himself,' nods the other, darker, spiky-haired one.

Both men slip their right hands inside their hoodies. I hear the clink of chains; something appears on their chests. I would recognise these police badges anywhere, any time; I've seen one hanging around Osmala's neck many times. I can't see their names, but the badges are real.

'Let's have a chat,' says the blond one.

The darker one says nothing. His tongue touches the top of his palate, and I hear two clicks from his open mouth.

&

The men seem very at ease in my office. The fairer one slides into his chair as though he has left his skeleton in the foyer, places one of his legs on the arm of the chair and ends up slouching diagonally across it in a position I'd thought only the most phlegmatic of teenagers could ever achieve. The darker one hops up onto the table and swings his legs in the air as though he is waiting for his parents to pick him up and take him home. Their eyes don't fool me in quite the same way. They are watching me constantly, reading me, waiting, ready. Obviously, I don't know what they are waiting *for*, but I have my suspicions. I am grateful for the almost full minute it took us to walk from the foyer to my office and which I used to calculate these new variables.

'May I ask what this is all about?' I ask once I've sat down in the chair behind my desk.

'Sure,' says the fairer one, and points a thumb first at himself, then at his companion. 'I'm Lastumäki, and that's Salmi. We're with the Helsinki police, where we work with different units, take on different assignments – sometimes we're out in the field, gathering information, getting to know people. We thought today would be a good day to get to know you.'

Lastumäki has both answered my question and dodged it, and I sense he knows this only too well. I don't think I'm wrong to assume this isn't going to be an easy conversation.

'I am the actuary Henri Koskinen and—'

'I mean really get to know you,' the man who introduced himself as Lastumäki interrupts. 'We've just driven all the way from Espoo, and there's an adventure park over there just like this. Do you know it?'

I admit I am aware of the existence of Somersault City. Lastumäki looks at me but doesn't speak.

'How would you compare the two parks?' asks Salmi.

'In what sense?'

'You choose,' says Salmi, his legs still swinging beneath the table.

'Somersault City is much newer,' I say. 'Their equipment is

newer and more expensive, their marketing more visible, their customer numbers are currently larger.'

'So you know the place well, then?'

'I've been there,' I nod. 'I've been inside too.'

Salmi and Lastumäki glance at each other.

'So it's newer and more expensive—' Lastumäki begins, but I interrupt him.

'Their equipment is newer,' I say, 'but entrance to the park is free. So, you could say that their park is cheaper. It all depends how you look at it. I conducted a quick, superficial comparison, in a purely professional capacity.'

For a moment, Lastumäki is quiet. Now he is no longer sliding out of his chair.

'Okay,' he says. 'Let's talk about the owners of that park. When you visited Somersault City, did you encounter any of your professional colleagues?'

Two images flash through my mind: Olavi, his face covered in fresh blue paint, and, even more vividly, a man in a cowboy costume lying in front of a great beaver with a steel ice-cream cone jutting from his mouth.

'I've met them,' I say.

'When you say *them*…?'

'I mean the four men that I met on that occasion.'

Salmi clicks his tongue again.

'And what happened … when you met them?' he asks.

'We talked.'

Both men remain silent.

'You talked,' Lastumäki says eventually. 'What about?'

'I tried to get them to understand the short-sighted nature of their business model,' I say.

Salmi and Lastumäki exchange glances again.

'What does that mean?'

'If a business is engaged in heavily unprofitable practices—'

'Not that,' says Lastumäki. 'When you said you tried to get them to understand. What does that mean? How did you do that exactly? Threats?'

'Of course not,' I say honestly. 'I offered them my help.'

I can see that my answer has taken the men by surprise, and both Salmi and Lastumäki seem to be considering their next questions and perhaps the general direction of this conversation very carefully.

'There's been a violent death at Somersault City,' Lastumäki says eventually.

'I'm sorry to hear that,' I say, sincerely.

'The park's owner, no less,' says Salmi. 'Maybe you remember him.'

'I remember him very well.'

'He liked Clint Eastwood,' says Salmi. '*The Good, the Bad and the Ugly*. Jesse James. The fastest draw in the west.'

'Right,' I say, though I can't quite see how these things are related.

'There's a backlog at forensics right now,' says Lastumäki, 'so we'll have to wait a while for the results. But we're looking into the adventure-park sector, because my instinct tells me the perpetrator will be someone pretty close to all this. Of course, for technical reasons I can't tell you why I think that, but I do.'

I say nothing. Salmi and Lastumäki have kept their eyes fixed on me throughout, and it's beginning to feel disturbing, exhausting. Which is presumably the point.

'Seeing as you know the business,' Salmi begins, 'do you have any idea why something like this might happen?'

This is a question I've been asking myself since the early hours of this morning. Naturally, I don't have any answers, not even for myself.

'No,' I say, 'I have no idea whatsoever.'

My answer is met with more silence. In fact, it's only now that I realise quite how quiet it is around me. Lastumäki seems to have read my thoughts. Again he points with his thumb, this time behind him.

'It's pretty quiet back there,' he says. 'Is the park closed?'

'No, we're open,' I say.

'But there was nobody there when we walked in.'

I suspect Salmi and Lastumäki already know what the situation is – and the reasons why.

'We've been losing customers to Somersault City,' I say.

'Oh, really?' asked Salmi.

'Quite significantly,' I nod.

'Wouldn't something like that arouse any suspicions?'

I know what Salmi means. And I cannot deny the situation has aroused my suspicions. In fact, it has aroused them to such an extent that I visited our competitors in the middle of the night. But this visit right now is about something else altogether.

'I have nothing whatsoever to do with the death at Somersault City,' I say. Honestly.

Salmi and Lastumäki wait for a moment, neither of them speaks. Then, as if agreeing telepathically, they both move at once. Lastumäki hauls himself up from his chair, as if putting himself back together piece by piece. Salmi hops down from the table and stands firmly on the spot, which seems out of place after all that leg swinging. For some reason, they look even younger now, and in trying to stand up to their full height, they actually shrink. Once again, they look like little boys at the park.

'Now that we're acquainted,' says Lastumäki, 'I'm sure it won't be a problem if we come back another time.'

'Seeing as there's plenty of space here,' says Salmi.

And again, as if by common, unspoken agreement, the two

men turn and walk out of my office. I hear their footsteps, until I don't hear them anymore. I stand up from my chair and look out of the window as the men walk to their car. The small, old, white three-door BMW starts up, sets off. Then it speeds across the snow-covered car park, brakes suddenly, and spins around a few times. As though sitting behind the wheel is a young male driver who has just got his licence.

The compost bag is waiting on the mat right behind the front door. The bag is full and stretched, and it stinks. Laura Helanto has moved it from the kitchen because I've forgotten all about it. It's not like me to forget things, but I decide against trying to give her an explanation. I go back out into the frozen evening and drop the bag into the communal bin. For the rest of the evening, and even as I'm about to go to sleep, it feels as though the compost is still right there in the middle of the room, between me and the others present – Laura, Tuuli, even Schopenhauer – as though we are all keenly aware of it but pretending it isn't there.

2

Esa likes my suggestion right away. In fact, he likes it so much that I'm a bit nervous when, two days later, we walk through the morning calm towards the storeroom at the western end of the park.

I make sure to walk by his side, and preferably a little ahead of him. At times I've wondered whether, as his boss, I ought to recommend he gets treatment for his gastric issues, but each time I think this I reach the same conclusion: the matter doesn't seem to bother him, and it doesn't affect his concentration or efficiency at work, so I let it go. Right now, however, as my nostrils are stinging once again, my throat begins to tense and flashes appear in my field of vision, like augurs of the end of days, conjuring up images of a freight ship full of rancid pork pies, I wonder whether I have neglected my responsibilities. If one of my employees is having an internal nuclear meltdown, am I not duty-bound to help him?

'We should develop the park's intel capabilities,' says Esa, putting an end, for now, to further consideration of human fission. 'As for our general defence strategy, I've done everything the budget will allow. With extra funds, I could start up an intelligence-gathering service and work as an officer myself. A fringe benefit of an independent operation like this is that it would allow us to smoke out any moles and double agents.'

In practice, given the plan we are about to hatch, Esa's proposal suggests he would have to spy on himself; he would defend the park from his own possible attacks and try to catch himself – in the act. I don't want to dwell on this thought. As I see it, we have far more pressing matters to attend to.

Esa opens the door to the storeroom and we walk inside. The storeroom is a large space, as tall as the main hall – for obvious, practical reasons. This is where we store everything from spare parts to items that customers have left behind. Part of the space is reserved for repairs, apparatus construction, and the storage of hundreds of tools. Esa walks us to a pirate ship that has been taken out of use, opens an artillery hatch in its hull and takes out a long, camouflage-coloured bag. He lets the bag slump to the floor and opens its long zip. As he crouches down, he lets out a long wheeze, akin to the opening of the zip, and I realise now is the time to hold my breath. Esa might be a danger to my health, but he has demonstrated on more than one occasion that for him the park is more than a job: it is a calling, his heart and soul.

The contents of the bag meet the specifications of my plan.

Once we are disguised, we stand in front of the discontinued Banana Mirror and check one last time that we are ready. We look as though we repair adventure-park equipment for a living. What's more, in my overalls, blond wig and fake blond moustache, and thanks to the partial face mask that makes my cheekbones appear raised and a little cruel, I look as though I have been called out to repair this equipment in the middle of filming a music video for a heavy metal band of yesteryear. For Esa, the change is even more radical. This is curious, because virtually all he has done is comb his hair back and put on a large pair of glasses. He looks like a serial killer from a 1970s horror film. I decide not to tell him this. Instead, I say that we look ready to go and suggest we set off.

'What's our safe word?' asks Esa.

I'm not sure he means what I understand that term to mean, and I am about to ask him to clarify when he continues:

'In case we're forced to retreat,' he says. 'We don't want to blow our cover. The word should be simple and rare. I suggest "panda".

'That is a rare word,' I admit, trying to think of sentences that two repair men might say to each other and in which the word 'panda' would fit naturally. *This one seems to be working fine, but what about the panda?* I conclude that the probability of having to resort to the 'panda' is extremely small.

I give Esa a nod and feel the weight of my new moustache on my lip. Esa looks at me from behind his serial-killer spectacles.

We set off.

Somersault City is in the same place as before, and it is exactly as big as it always was, but now it seems to dominate the surrounding landscape with greater determination, like a despot. Which, right now, it is, in the war of the adventure parks at least.

The car park is so full that people have left their vehicles in places and positions that suggest an almost manic desire to get into the park. Some of the cars have been left on the side of the snow verges, almost vertical, some have been boxed in in a way that will require hours to unpack, and some cars have even been driven onto a frozen pond, even though distinct cracks across the ice suggest that it might give way at any moment. And all around, even outside the park, the air is filled with frantic screaming and squealing, to which the adult customers are contributing their fair share.

Esa and I neither scream nor squeal, we don't even speak as we walk through the front door and show our badges to the park's security guard. The man is around twenty-five years old and looks a little like Olavi before our blue-tinged encounter. He examines our badges long and hard, then gives a contented nod. Esa has done excellent work here too: we are now Jaakko Bourne and Eemeli Hunt from the mechanical maintenance company Component Installation Automatic. I realise that our name bears the acronym CIA, but as to where our undercover names have come from, I'm at a loss. I decide not to think about this any further, as we walk into the park and head directly towards the scene of the crime.

Where else would I start my murder investigation?

The Beaver seems to grow as we approach it. I note the area in front of the creature. It should be said that this time I am looking at the Beaver and the area around it with fresh eyes. I have been thinking about what happened; it's no exaggeration to say I've gone over it hundreds of times. I've tried to remember everything about what transpired that night and tried not to overlook even the slightest detail.

Naturally, there is nothing in front of the Beaver to suggest the events that recently took place here. Customers are running around, shouting and occasionally bumping into one another on the exact spot where I saw my competitor lying dead. But this is irrelevant for my investigation. Because although the location itself is important, vastly more important is how one gets there.

The Beaver is located right in the middle of the park, and from the Beaver it is a long way to anywhere else.

Of course, I remember this from my own escape, but as I see it, the fact bears other significance too, especially since I already know where I heard the thud coming from, though curiously no footsteps; I know what direction I used to approach the Beaver and from which direction, mere seconds later, I finally *did* hear footsteps approaching, and what direction I eventually ran and fled.

My theory – the strongest of them – is linked to the Beaver itself and the opportunities it presents.

The noise in the park is considerable, as is the commotion. To some extent, this is a risk factor – there is a chance that we won't notice anyone watching us or approaching us – but, on the other hand, the general hubbub provides excellent cover. We lower our heavy tools by the flank of the Beaver on the side facing the Kangaroo Course. The course's back wall also helps hide us from view.

We take out our tools.

Once I have found what I'm looking for, I leave Esa taking measurements at the Beaver's mouth and begin my inspection. By this point, Esa has already begun his task without my having to prompt him. Furthermore, he hasn't once asked why we are here or why the Beaver is the focus of our attention. It seems he is content in the knowledge that our park is under attack, and this is enough to spur him into action. And whatever one might think of Esa and his organic-toxicological challenges, one thing is certain: few customers will dare get too close to him. From time to time, one of the customers makes the mistake of entering the exclusion zone around him, but quickly backs off once the situation becomes clear – or rather, once it becomes murky: I see one of the park's customers stagger in an attempt to get away. Esa is left to take his measurements in peace.

I get to work too.

The first part of my theory concentrates on the seconds immediately after the thud I heard. I did not hear anyone walking calmly away from the dead man – or running, for that matter. And neither did I hear anyone leaving the park, at least not via any of the exits I knew about. I recall the perfect tranquillity of the hall after that thud, a tranquillity that was shattered only by the arrival of the police some moments later. Thus, whoever killed Ville-Pekka Häyrinen must have moved away from the body in such a way that didn't cause the slightest sound. To this end, there are only a limited number of realistic options. I don't think the killer could have used ropes to hoist himself up to the roof, because I would have heard and seen this all too easily. Therefore, the manner and route of the killer's escape must be closer at hand.

I have found a schematic drawing of the Beaver online – the database of the International Association of Adventure Parks is a real treasure trove of information – and examined it the way I used to examine mathematical problems. I try not to dwell on the fact that it is hard to remember a time when my problems were of a purely numerical nature and weren't to do with finding a balance between family life and solving mysterious homicides.

At its tallest, the Beaver stands at almost seven and a half metres. What I am looking for, however, must be found around two and half metres from the ground, because nobody could climb or jump higher than that in a matter of only a few seconds, and certainly not after using their energy to wield an enormous steel ice-cream cone. Every now and then I stop, examine the seams of the fake fur, run my hands along the surface of this giant rodent, looking for a secret door, a hatch or other corridor. But the only things I find are all indicated on the schematics: joints, the tunnel running through the animal (its walls sealed), more joints, appendages, slides, sturdy structures. My inspection takes almost exactly an hour and a half.

I return to the mouth of the Beaver and find Esa, who looks like he is still taking measurements. I tell him I haven't found what I'm looking for, and I am about to suggest we leave the premises when Esa suddenly jumps to his feet, quickly looks around, walks right up to me and, his eyes darting to both sides, speaks in nothing but a low-pitched whisper.

'Ultimately, it was so obvious that I even wondered whether this was some kind of decoy. But no, this is not an ambush.'

I say nothing. I genuinely have no idea what he is talking about.

'The Beaver's left tooth,' he says. 'It's two centimetres lower than it should be.'

I glance to the side. The Beaver's teeth are two metres long, they look strong, and, at least from this angle, they are even. I ask Esa to continue his measurements or whatever other tasks his role as an employee of Component Installation Automatic entails, while I look into the matter.

Then I step into the Beaver's mouth.

Its mouth isn't especially large; there is virtually no space behind the teeth. It's as though the mouth stops halfway, and there is a wall preventing people going any further. Then I turn and examine the spot where the teeth are attached to the gums, the place where the two materials are glued together, and I see that Esa is right. Between the tooth and the gum there is a gap of about two centimetres. I raise my hand and feel the gap. As I do so, I try to recall the Beaver's schematics, and it's then that I realise something.

I am about to turn away when my fingers come across a piece of paper. At least it feels like paper. I manage to tease it out of the gap and examine what I have found: a protein-bar wrapper. One thing is certain: the park's underage customers can't have left it there because the gap between the tooth and the gum is about one hundred and eighty centimetres from the ground. I can't put my finger on it, but for some reason this wrapper feels important. I slip it into the breast pocket of my overalls and turn, as I had been planning to do a moment earlier.

If the tooth is positioned two centimetres lower than it should be, that means that the metallic beams running underneath the plastic surface must be two centimetres further forward than they should be. Which, in turn, means that their other end won't quite reach the top of the mouth where they should, and therefore...

A small part of the wall must be loose.

I glance over my shoulder. Luckily, I am hidden by the Beaver's teeth, and judging by the fleeting glimpses I catch of Esa, I can see he is taking his role as a maintenance man very seriously and maintaining full control of his own territory. I imagine he is using all the qualities at his disposal to keep the customers and other curious onlookers at bay. So I have a little time.

The moving metallic panel is long and narrow, running the full height of the wall. It is only around thirty centimetres wide. Its movement is so slight that only those familiar with the design of this apparatus would realise quite how decisive this movement is – or what it will take to remove the panel altogether. I press the panel slightly inwards, then carefully slide it to one side. The Beaver is constructed like a jigsaw held together with a series of firm structural joints. But due to an almost imperceptible design flaw, at this specific point the parts of the jigsaw don't fit perfectly together. Now, in the middle of the wall, right at the back of the mouth, is a gap around thirty centimetres wide. I take out my torch, switch it on...

And slip inside the Beaver.

The Beaver is almost as impressive on the inside as it is on the outside. Particularly if one has a passing acquaintance with adventure-park equipment and their construction. Even on the inside, the streamlined French design is in abundant evidence. But I am not here to admire things; I'm here to investigate them.

I try to work quickly. I walk the full length of the Beaver, from its mouth to its tail. Once in the tail section, I find what I have unwittingly been looking for. When I come to a stop, stand still and focus my senses, I feel a wisp of air coming from outside the hall. Thus, the Beaver's tail is connected to the world beyond Somersault City. I lie on the concrete floor and point the beam of torchlight to where I imagine the current of air must be coming from. I see a very low and cramped corridor that veers off to the right after a few metres. The turn is sharp, and I have to admit I wouldn't fit down there. I am too tall and not supple enough. But someone who...

I hear a whistle: Esa's signal.

I stand up and head back towards the mouth of the Beaver. I switch off my torch in good time before the entrance to the mouth and tread carefully. Through the narrow gap in the wall I can see Esa working with one of the Beaver's front teeth.

'Orange alert,' he says without turning around, obviously aware that I have arrived. 'Another maintenance unit arriving from the north-east. It could be a counter-reconnaissance team, disguised – like us. We might have some questions to answer. I've got plenty of experience with interrogation techniques, but I'm worried about you.'

I admire Esa's concern, though I'm not entirely sure of the details. I slip through the narrow gap and back into the mouth of the Beaver, then begin sliding the wall panel back into place.

'Still north-east,' says Esa. 'Two males. Visual confirmed.'

I've almost got the panel in the desired position and try to lift it into place. I locate the right runner at the bottom, and eventually the right one at the top too. Finally, the loose panel is in the same position as when I stepped into the mouth for the first time. It also occurs to me that now I know quite how quickly someone else might have completed the same operation.

As unpleasant as it momentarily is, I follow Esa into the foyer and out through the main doors. But despite the fact that the cloud of noxious biogas that Esa has produced in front of me makes my false moustache feel like it's about to burst into flames and that my wig is ablaze on my head, I feel a deep gratitude towards him.

Once again, he has helped me in a way that might just prove decisive.

3

'I can't decide,' says Laura Helanto.

I look at her across the dining table, and as curious as it sounds, it's as though I am seeing her for the first time that evening. Outside it is dark, the soft light from the dome lamp above us is reflected in the windows. The potent, fatty aroma of herring cakes still hangs in the room, though we have already eaten everything we fried, right down to the last fishtail. The only leftovers are a small amount of mashed potato. Laura has wound her hair into a bun and tied it perhaps a little more loosely than usual. At a quick glance, the final result looks like a youthful Mohican. But her hair isn't the only reason I have to sharpen my attention. As far as I can remember, this is the first time during our relationship that I don't have the faintest idea of what she has just said. Of course, I registered that she was speaking, but as to the content of her words, I haven't the foggiest.

'What do you think?' she asks and leans her elbows on the table.

I can see she is excited about the subject and thinks it is important. Even her tone of voice seems to indicate this. Which makes the situation all the more awkward: I realise I am supposed to show interest, even to show that I care. And, of course, I *do* care. I just don't ... know what we're talking about.

'Of course, there's always the third option,' she adds. 'The one I mentioned first.'

'Right,' I say, and I have the distinct feeling that I have just stepped onto a path from which there is no return: I cannot back away, but I cannot ask exactly what we're talking about.

'I mean, it's definitely the most challenging of the three, the most complex,' Laura continues, 'but if I can pull it off, it would be something completely new.'

'You have a unique ability to overcome challenges,' I say, and that much is true. 'I've been struck by this ability right from the start.'

'So, the third then?'

Laura looks me as directly in the eyes as it is possible to do.

'Of course, I can't really say—'

'I don't expect you to make decisions for me, I don't want that, I don't even want advice or recommendations. I want to know what you're thinking.'

What *am* I thinking? I'm thinking about the enormous Beaver. I'm thinking about the murder for which I am a prime suspect. And yet, one way or another, here at the kitchen table, I have to proceed.

'Right now,' I say, again sticking to the known facts, 'this third option is speaking to me most of all.'

'Henri,' says Laura, then gives a long sigh. 'There is no third option.'

I sit there in silence. The mashed potato looks a little yellower than a moment ago.

'I don't think you've been paying attention,' she says.

'I'm sorry,' I say. 'How about you start from the beginning…'

'The beginning?'

Something about Laura's posture tells me this is the wrong way to proceed. Before I can rectify my mistake, and before I can present a more precise assessment of how far back she should go to make sure I really understand everything, she leans even further forwards across the table, now almost directly beneath the dome lamp.

'I was talking about my new project. It looks pretty certain that my offer will be accepted. The final decision will come sometime next week, but I've already received some follow-up questions, the kind of questions that suggest I've got the job.'

'That's excellent news,' I say.

'I think so too,' says Laura. 'But I don't like having to say the same things again and again.'

I say nothing.

'Is there something on your mind?' she asks eventually. 'Seeing as you're so distracted?'

The question takes me by surprise. Of course, I realised she might ask me this, but nonetheless this quick turn in the conversation feels surprisingly difficult. Particularly because I don't want to lie to Laura Helanto under any circumstances.

'I've been thinking about the park,' I say.

'What about the park?'

'Financial matters.'

'Financial matters?'

'And various questions about the equipment,' I nod, and nod firmly, because in a very broad sense, I am thinking about all of the above.

Laura is quiet for a moment.

'I'm sorry to hear that,' she says eventually. 'I thought everything was going smoothly.'

'In many ways, it is,' I admit.

'That's good to hear.'

We sit in silence for a moment. Laura seems to be thinking about something.

'I realise I haven't thought about the park for a while,' she says. 'In a way, it feels quite distant now, though I worked there for years. And I haven't spoken to any of the staff, not even Johanna. But that's normal – sometimes we go for ages without talking to each other.'

I hope my relief isn't obvious. It would only take one comment from Johanna – 'not a single customer all week' – and the whole thing would start to unravel.

'I know how important the park is to you, Henri. I know how meticulous you are about everything. And that might cause you some degree of stress. Have you ever thought about that?'

'No,' I say.

'That's exactly what I mean,' says Laura. 'I know it might sound a little paradoxical, but do you know what might help relieve your stress?'

Finding the killer, I think. Understanding how Somersault City fund their operations. I don't say any of this out loud, and instead admit I don't know how best to alleviate my stress.

'By paying attention to other people,' says Laura, now more emphatically, and I realise she must still be hurt that I didn't know what we were originally talking about. 'By giving other people time and thinking about something other than your park. You have a family to think of now.'

Of course, she is right. And I agree with her. I tell her so. She smiles, cautiously. She reaches her hand across the table top. Instinctively, I grip it.

'The worst is behind us, Henri. You should relax.'

Whatever relaxing means, this surely can't be it, I think, as I lie awake in the early hours of the morning. My neck is sore, my head aches, and it's all I can do not to twist and turn and wriggle my legs around: keeping them still requires particular concentration. Which isn't to say that my thoughts aren't still racing in all directions, even speeding up. Laura shifts position slightly, then continues her deep breathing and, I assume, her deep sleep too, and I return to what I was thinking about a moment ago.

If I combine the probabilities I have already calculated with the known concrete facts – again, I realise that one could not possibly exist without the other – I am able to construct a theory that will withstand some level of scrutiny.

On a tangent, I consider that this particular working strategy would be hard to explain at the actuaries' seminar where I once gave a brief, simple presentation on the best and most reliable methods for calculating probability models to predict future dividend-based third-party insurance payments. Though it might bear relevance for the final result, I cannot repeat the benefits for this calculation by disguising myself, pretending to be someone I am not – say, an employee of an imaginary maintenance company – let alone judge how pressure from the police, threats from criminal entities, and the adventure park's financial woes might serve as guiding factors in the overall calculation.

I take a deep breath. I stare up, let my eyes pan across the ceiling. My eyes can't seem to latch on to anything, and this proves beneficial to my train of thought.

My theory is the following:

Whoever killed Ville-Pekka Häyrinen – Somersault City's erstwhile CEO and wannabe John Wayne – with a giant steel ice-cream cone, must have been very close to him. Both literally and figuratively.

In fact, the perpetrator must have got close to Häyrinen on two separate occasions. First, he must have entered and exited the park via the Beaver. In practical terms, this is all but certain: had this not been the case, I would have heard and likely also seen something. What's more, I have ascertained that the route is quick and unimpeded, assuming certain factors about whoever was taking the route: he needed to be strong enough, agile enough, with a good enough understanding of how the Beaver is constructed and where to find that particular design flaw.

The perpetrator was probably waiting behind the Beaver's teeth for a while, long enough to eat a protein bar to pass the time. This isn't nearly as far-fetched as it might at first appear. It is hard to imagine a normal situation in which an adult would choose the Beaver's mouth as an ideal place for a quick snack and then go to extra lengths to hide the evidence. Moreover, the wrapper was fresh: it still smelt of dark cocoa and starch, it had the same smell as a fresh bar, and the smudges of chocolate inside the wrapper, where the fingers holding the bar had melted the coating, were still moist; there hadn't been enough time for them to dry properly.

And when the perpetrator saw Häyrinen approaching, he stepped into view. Even then, Häyrinen did not move aside, let alone run for cover. This indicates that Häyrinen must have known his assailant, at least in passing. This is corroborated by the fact that Häyrinen did not shout or even raise his voice. If this had happened, I would have heard it. It seems he just stopped – and found himself on the business end of an enormous ice-cream cone.

Who would benefit from Häyrinen's death? As I see it, consideration of this matter is linked both to the previous question and the next one, which is crucial: based on my two visits, what do I know about Somersault City and the people who run it? I quickly bring myself back to that moment in the administrative wing at Somersault City. From my first visit I remember the man sitting across the table, the one who was very clearly disgruntled when Häyrinen was invited into the room. And who then, more importantly, was visibly outraged that Häyrinen looked likely to receive those reports on Somersault City's financial situation.

Niko Kotka.

And every bit as important as his reaction during my first visit is how he fits into the rest of my theory.

Of course, it's hard to assess a person's height, other physical attributes and general agility based solely on how he walks into a room, then sits down, but in the case of Niko Kotka this isn't entirely based on speculation. He is exactly the right size, the right build. For a man his size he has large, strong hands and fingers, the kind that would have no trouble wielding a heavy object quickly and effectively.

I go through everything I know, filter the probabilities, and the more calculations I complete, the more vividly I can see Niko Kotka carrying out a plan that would see him depose the leader and make him king of the realm.

The sole sovereign of Somersault City.

4

For January, the morning outside the window is surprisingly bright and sunny. I sit in my office and listen but cannot hear a thing. The silence seems to underscore the urgency of matters, and the cloudless sky reflects the clarity I have achieved in my mind.

The park's Renault, a cheap maintenance and transportation vehicle that I got second-hand and that should be an unattractive proposition for even the most desperate car thieves, is packed and ready for departure. The vehicle is waiting for me at the back of the building, in the staff car park. I have been planning to spend a lot of time in and around the car, so the footwells are stocked with bits and pieces I've bought to get me through the morning.

I turn back to my computer and am about to switch it off when my hand stops. I'm not expecting anybody, but I recognise these footsteps instantly. For a variety of reasons, I was sure I wouldn't be hearing the approaching patter of those tiny patent-leather shoes again. But they are approaching me all the same and, as before, they come to a stop just outside my door.

Detective Inspector Pentti Osmala of the Joint Division of the Helsinki Organised-Crime and Fraud Units looks the same as he did on all the other occasions he has turned up at the park to talk to me. He is a largish and heavy-set Finnish man in late middle age, and there's something distinctly reminiscent of the Easter Island statues about the shape and size of his head. He is very attached to his grey blazer, which he seems to wear all year round, and his light-blue shirt and slightly puffy trousers, and he is still wearing the same light-brown, Italian-looking, surprisingly delicate leather shoes – the worst imaginable footwear for the current snowy weather. There must be something very hard and firm on their heels, and on a man the size of Osmala the clack they make is a curious fusion of angry maracas and an insistent pile-driver.

'Not disturbing, am I?' he asks from the doorway.

I cannot remember how many times he has asked this. This is how he always initiates our exchanges.

'Of course not,' I reply, as I am now in the habit of doing. Our communication mostly follows this same pattern: I suspect we both know that Osmala undoubtedly *is* here to disturb me and that the disturbance *does* disturb me. He maraca-pile-drives himself into the room and stands in the middle. The reason I wasn't expecting him is, I believe, good and justified. I assumed the authorities' interest in this affair had already been demonstrated by the appearance of the two younger officers, Salmi and Lastumäki. And moreover, they seemed to be scrutinising both me and the events at Somersault City – and my possible connection to them – with a similar investigatory approach. But now Osmala is here too, and probably not without his reasons.

'I don't recall that kind of silence on my previous visits,' he says, pointing towards the door and the hall.

'It's a rather recent development,' I admit.

Perhaps Osmala thinks about this for a moment – or perhaps doesn't. After all this time, I still can't read anything into his gestures or expressions.

'I assume the artist is doing well,' he says eventually. 'I still find myself thinking about her murals, their ingenuity, the relaxed, masterful way they combined different styles and eras.'

'Laura Helanto is planning a new work,' I say. 'We're hoping she's about to receive a large commission. Things look promising.'

Osmala nods, his raised eyebrows showing that he is suitably impressed. At least, that's how I interpret it. And I think I can read something into the fact that so far he has only asked about Laura Helanto and her work. Of course, I know Osmala is interested in art, particularly contemporary art, and that the three-dimensional murals that Laura designed, built and dismantled at the park made a big impression on him. Perhaps Osmala doesn't need to ask how I am doing because he already knows.

'Something rather unfortunate has happened,' he begins. 'Over at Somersault City. I imagine you're familiar with the nature of this incident. The owner and CEO; Häyrinen his name was. And his death.'

I confirm that I am aware of the incident.

'And I gather you've already met Detectives Salmi and Lastumäki?'

'I have indeed.'

Osmala nods. 'And everything went well?'

This question takes me by surprise.

'I think so,' I say. 'Yes.'

'That's good to hear,' says Osmala. 'I sometimes have trouble accessing – how should I put it? – their youthful wavelength.'

I say nothing. I'm starting to feel as though we're not just talking about the homicide at Somersault City anymore. Having said that, I'm not sure quite what we *are* talking about.

'I can't say I understand everything myself—' I begin, but Osmala interrupts me.

'Maybe it's the age difference, maybe it's because I'm too old a dog to learn new tricks,' he says, then seems for a moment to consider how to continue. 'Or maybe it's because I don't really understand why they came here in the first place.'

Osmala looks at me, a certain gravitas in his expression.

'Because you didn't kill Häyrinen,' he says.

I don't know what happens between us, don't know how to interpret the silent messages flying across the desk like bolts of lightning in the cartoons I used to read as a child. But the result is that in merely a few fractions of a second, we have, as it were, given up something and stepped into something new. Therefore, I reply, with complete honesty:

'No, I did not.'

Osmala waits a beat.

'And yet Salmi and Lastumäki have got you down as the perpetrator,' he says. 'Now, I don't know about you, but I think that's fascinating.'

I run through Osmala's words in my mind one more time. I want to make sure I've heard them properly before responding.

'It is,' I say. 'Decidedly fascinating.'

'And, taking all the evidence into account, it means that you'll have to prove your innocence,' he says, 'before, one way or another, they prove that you're guilty.'

Whatever people mean when they talk about 'tectonic shifts' in people's lives or their immediate circles might be an apt description of the events and mood in my office.

'These are,' I begin, 'manifestly, the prevailing circumstances.'

Osmala nods, slowly. 'So, you might be very interested to learn that Salmi and Lastumäki aren't focusing their investigation on the people running Somersault City. On the contrary, they seem to have put a ring around those people, cordoned them off from any and all suspicion.'

'That sounds odd,' I say. 'In many ways.'

'I thought so too,' says Osmala.

He doesn't need to say more. Finally, I understand what he's driving at. At least, I'm relatively sure I understand.

'Salmi and Lastumäki,' I say. 'You're interested in them too—'

'If I've understood correctly,' says Osmala, interrupting me in a very carefully considered manner. 'Ms Helanto makes a great many sketches before she gets down to the work at hand.'

'That's correct,' I say. 'Dozens of sketches. Of course, it depends on—'

'I think that's an excellent way of approaching things,' says Osmala. 'To look at what works, what stands out, what comes to life, what is strongest about each work, and what eventually turns out to be the best option.'

Naturally, I can't be sure quite where Osmala is going with this comparison, but I think I've understood enough.

'If they come back again,' I say, 'I will try to form an overall picture of the situation and pass it on.'

Osmala nods. 'This sort of reciprocity could really help us distinguish the wood from the trees, as it were.'

After this, Osmala asks me to pass on his warmest regards to the artist – by which he means Laura Helanto – and his wish to be invited to the opening of her exhibition. He stresses that this isn't a prerequisite for anything, which naturally means, particularly in my current situation, that it most certainly is a prerequisite. Osmala turns, his Italian shoes, which still look far too small for him, squeak against the floor, and he walks out of the door. This time he doesn't even stop in the doorway, the way he usually does, but continues down the corridor until I can no longer hear him, or anything else.

5

Osmala's words are still echoing through my mind a full five hours and eighteen minutes later. To put it mildly, the situation in which I currently find myself is new and unexpected. In addition to investigating a murder and organising a school trip to western Europe, I have to provide the police with information about the activities of other police officers, and all this I must do without disrupting my new family life – while sitting in YouMeFun's Renault in the car park outside Somersault City while my phone is quickly filling up with messages from the group of frenzied fathers.

A moment earlier, I made what has proven to be a fateful error by replying to *Le Groupe Paris*, the name of our WhatsApp group – and saying openly that, in light of the facts regarding the timing of the trip and how to finance it, I see a number of significant challenges, perhaps insurmountable ones. Some of the fathers think we should call an emergency meeting, some even suggesting it should be later this evening, and they are all asking me for an updated budget. Of course, the times the fathers suggest are wholly inconvenient for me, and not just today. Of course, I cannot tell them why. I cannot tell them that, in addition to running an adventure park, my evenings (and quite possibly my nights too) are spent trailing and spying on my competitors.

An undertaking that appears to be starting again right now.

I have parked the Renault in a place that isn't technically a parking spot, but I don't think I will stand out from the considerable number of customers who have made the exact same decision. Still, unlike some people, I haven't parked at a diagonal or halfway up a verge of snow. The advantage of this position is that I have an unimpeded view of the back of the building. I can see the loading and transportation area, the windows of the administration wing and three different doors; I think the middle one is most likely to be the staff entrance.

Niko Kotka steps out into the bright outdoor lights; I recognise him instantly. He looks just the same as he did the last time I laid eyes on him: as though he had been cut from the pages of a men's clothing catalogue and blown into life. He walks briskly towards his white Volvo SUV, climbs in, and almost immediately the vehicle begins making a series of quick, sharp turns. My Renault and I follow Niko Kotka to the traffic lights at the end of the car park before speeding off into the flow of traffic heading towards Helsinki.

During the course of the following three days, evenings and nights, my notebook gradually fills up with annotations. I list districts, addresses, events, meetings, their time and duration, everything possible, even Niko Kotka's two-part visit to the barber – after his hair cut, the young lady working there takes him into the room at the back of the store, which he departs thirteen and a half minutes later. This event is indicative of Niko Kotka's behaviour: his manner of engaging with people is always transactional and self-serving. Most of his meetings seem to end with him smiling contentedly, strutting with the swagger of a model, leaving other people either staring into the distance or dejectedly lowering their eyes to the floor, the walls, the ground beneath their feet.

On two occasions, I have the opportunity to use the listening device that Esa has lent me. I don't know why he thought I might need something like this, but he delivered the device to my desk without asking.

The first conversation I listen in on – in hissing snippets and crackly fragments – takes place as dusk falls, by the scaffolding on a listed building under renovation. Judging by what I hear, Niko Kotka is unhappy about virtually everything, but particularly because the cost of the renovation in question has risen. The other party in the conversation (an older man, by the sounds of it) defends the rising costs, claiming this is because of the quality of the materials. First, Niko Kotka gives the man some very questionable business advice, then tells him to shove his quality materials somewhere that wouldn't have much benefit to the overall renovation. Eventually he orders the man to carry on with the work, disregarding everything they have spoken about before. However, this is not the main thrust of the conversation, at least not for me. The crux is what Niko Kotka keeps stressing, first in answer to the man's questions, then freely. He says he is the boss now; Häyrinen is gone and isn't coming back. Though the device in my hand and the headphones over my ears create a lot of background noise, the cadence of Kotka's voice is clear. He is in charge, a situation with which he is more than content. He sounds like a man who knew what he wanted, and now he's got it.

Every bit as important is my second observation, this one to do with karate.

It turns out that Niko Kotka is a karateka. He has a black belt. And though the audio I pick up from a sports centre in northern Helsinki mostly consists of moaning, groaning, panting, puffing, bellowing and isolated, unintelligible words that might be in a foreign language, this knowledge is still important in many ways and, I believe, perhaps even decisive.

It's surprising how much my espionage work has in common with my work as an actuary. I'm gathering raw data, filtering it, trying to find the best ways of processing it, boiling it down to its essence. Eventually, I gather everything together and look at the results – which, at this point, look all but incontrovertible. I am still working with probabilities, but I can't help but feel satisfied at how clear-cut things are beginning to look.

Theory and practice come together almost seamlessly in Niko Kotka, each observation and calculation supporting the next.

He is thin and of slender build. And, as I have been able to deduce from following his karate session, he has the balance and razor-sharp reaction skills of a ballet dancer. He could fit into the Beaver's tail, he has the ability to use a narrow tunnel, he has strength and punching power in abundance, both when it comes to the fatal blow itself and the emergency exit route, and all the quick moves and lifts that using such an escape route would entail.

He is in his element as the new leader of the group, and his operation is seamless. He looks so well prepared for his new role that it's hard to imagine it took him by surprise. In all respects, he looks like someone for whom assuming control of the company was a smaller step than crossing the road.

This conclusion starts to look clearer the greater the amount of snow-covered road that disappears beneath my wheels. I am approaching the Herttoniemi intersection when I finally say it out loud to myself.

'Niko Kotka meets all the criteria. Niko Kotka is the killer.'

I leave the car by the side of the road and lock it. I walk up the hill by the light of the streetlamps, my breath making me look like a steam ship, and I glance up. The windows in our apartment are dark, as I was expecting. It is two-thirty in the morning, and Laura isn't in the habit of staying up late. Soon I will be out for the count too, I think, and right now I can't think of a better moment or feeling than lying down next to Laura and falling asleep in her warm glow. I can feel the exhaustion in every part of my body. I've spent several evenings and nights with Niko Kotka – in a purely unilateral sense – but it was worth it. This thought carries something with it – a sense of victory – which in turn makes my fatigue feel an almost satisfactory state of affairs. I don't know whether being released from the suspicion of murder can be compared to winning a marathon, but right now I find it quite possible that the two have many factors in common.

Outside the front door, I knock the snow from my shoes and step inside. The night-time corridor is a quiet world all of its own, like a tunnel in outer space. A moment later I am back home, standing in the hallway, and pull the door shut behind me. I take off my outdoor clothes and shoes, switch off the hallway light, take a few steps further into the apartment and head towards the bedroom. On my way I glance into the living room. The windows give out onto a panorama of the winter's night, bisected by the lights along the shoreline across the bay. It is impossible to say which is darker, the darkness above the strip of lights or the part below it. I am already turning my attention back to the bedroom door, which stands ajar, when I notice that in among the contours of the living room, its darker shadows, there is something that I can't immediately identify as a form or shape that ought to be there right now. Then I realise what I'm looking at. There in the middle of the dark living room, someone is sitting on the sofa. And though she is sitting sideways, I instantly recognise the profile. Laura Helanto does not turn her head.

'What time is it?' she asks quietly.

I tell her it is twenty-six minutes to three in the morning and remain standing on the spot as though my feet have become stuck to the dark-brown laminate floor.

'Where have you been,' she asks, 'until this hour?'

Her bipartite question is wholly justified and understandable. I don't want to lie to Laura, but neither do I want to give her a blow-by-blow account of my current situation. Just then, I am reminded of a conversation that took place at my previous job, and though at the time I didn't agree with the conclusions drawn in that conversation, I think I might have found something useful.

'Park business,' I say. 'I suppose I still haven't learnt how to delegate properly. It looks like I'm still trying to do everything myself.'

In the strictest sense, this is true. Laura says nothing. She still hasn't turned to look at me. I manage to force myself into motion, take a few quiet steps into the living room and cautiously sit down next to her on the sofa. I don't know whether I should speak or remain silent. I don't know how common this sort of situation is in relationships – sitting in the dark in the middle of the night and neglecting to mention that you are in fact a suspect in murder investigation – and I don't know whether there are any hard-and-fast ways of approaching the matter.

'It would have been nice if you'd been at home this evening,' she says. 'There was something I wanted to tell you. It was important, and I didn't want to tell you over the phone. I really hoped you'd be at home today ... But you've been away quite a lot of evenings.'

'Three, to be exact.'

'Exact?'

'Yes,' I say. 'If we count the—'

Laura turns her head slightly, and in the stillness of the night, the movement has the power of a tsunami.

'I got the job,' she says.

For the most part, her face is hidden in shadow, but I can still make out the moistness in her eyes and see that she is both smiling and crying. I realise now probably isn't the best time to suggest counting the nights I've been away or anything else for that matter.

'Congratulations,' I say. 'That's—'

I don't have time to finish my sentence before Laura attacks me. Or, as I come to realise a fraction of a second later, this isn't really an attack in the strictest sense; it is just as quick, just as fervent, but in all respects this has a distinctly more positive disposition. She squeezes me, talking all the while.

'They called me today,' she says, 'because they knew they didn't need any more time to think about it. The budget is almost what I originally proposed; I'll still have to think where I can save a little. But that's not a problem. They want it. My works. On display. My. Works.'

I realise that rarely have I ever felt this happy. And the times when I have felt this happy have all involved Laura Helanto. It's as though I am happier about her successes than I am about my own, and I know it's something greater than just a feeling. This is far more important. I know it.

'In drawing up a budget—' I begin as Laura lets go of me and starts speaking again.

'But they've got a few requirements when it comes to the timetable', she says, and I can hear how these words have been waiting inside her all evening and she can't hold them in any longer. 'They want everything ready a month earlier than they said in the original call. Which means I'm going to have to do more work in a shorter timeframe, which means I'm going to be away from home a lot more. And that means...'

Laura stops for breath. Her inhalation is brisk and determined.

'It means that someone will have to be at home. It isn't a long time, you know that. And when you think about it, this is actually a better solution all round. The work will be ready earlier. It's a win-win.'

Laura looks at me, her eyes still glistening. I decide not to say that, in my experience, when a situation is described as a win-win, it generally means somebody else lost a long time ago. But I understand what she is suggesting: that I should be the one to stay at home. In fact, I don't have anything against this – particularly not tonight. On the contrary. Besides tying up a few loose ends, my murder investigation is essentially complete. And this in turn means I can get a better grip on the park's situation, as the conclusion of my murder investigation will have significant repercussions both for Somersault City and YouMeFun, to the distinct benefit of the latter. Laura grips my hand, and I respond.

'Things at work will quieten down very soon,' I say, honestly. 'I'll be only too glad to stay at home.'

Laura says nothing. Suddenly the darkness and the silence feel softer. We don't remain still for long. The sofa is like a great, balmy sea beneath us.

6

The atmosphere in the Curly Cake Café is tense and agitated. I arrived at the café three minutes ago, and in the course of those three minutes I have three times had to calm my employees, who have gathered around one of the tables. Everyone is there. The beams of wintry sun pour directly into the otherwise deserted space, almost with the power of an X-ray. Esa has just finished presenting his findings to me, as I was the last to arrive. The final internal glimmer of hope, the special glow I carried with me from that nocturnal moment on the sofa as I walked through the snowy morning all the way to the door of the park, is gone. The cold, incontrovertible evidence of that lies on the table.

'There's normal bolts, carriage bolts, dome nuts and wing screws,' says Esa. 'All of them taken from our equipment. I can't remember ever seeing such widespread sabotage in the adventure-park industry before. One of the slides on the Big Dipper now drops the kids to the concrete floor from two metres in the air. One of the walls in the Strawberry Maze could topple over at any moment. If we had any customers, the situation could be life-threatening.'

I reiterate that, as soon as this meeting is over, we will check every apparatus, right down to the last screw and wing nut. I am about to continue with my original point, but Johanna manages to get in first.

'I've almost had enough,' she says. 'And it isn't just about nuts and bolts. Or sausages. I can't accept this. And I won't. At all. Enough's enough.'

By her own standards, Johanna's interjection is uncharacteristically long and exceptionally emotional. She is visibly agitated, and there is a look of fresh determination on her steely, Iron Man face.

'I don't understand—' Kristian begins, but Minttu K, who appears to be smoking two cigarettes at once – one smouldering between the fingers of her left hand and the other hanging from the right-hand corner of her mouth – and whose dark-hued bottle is giving off a whiff of petroleum, interrupts him.

'Honey,' she says, addressing me. 'You know I normally keep things strictly business, nothing personal, but right now—'

'A controlled eruption,' says Samppa. 'A bilateral intervention, an encounter. Air, that's what we all need. Air. We all need to be able to draw the contours of our own—'

'Esa,' I say, though I know I'm interrupting Samppa. There is no other alternative. If I want to make my voice heard, I'll have to interrupt someone. 'Shall we watch your video one more time?'

Esa turns his iPad on the table. The screensaver claims that the device is property of the US Marines. I notice how little attention I pay to this anymore.

'The intruders didn't even bother disguising themselves,' he says as once again we watch a presentation of material taken from the security cameras. 'There, next to the Doughnut ... and here they are again, approaching the Turtle Trucks, where they remove the brakes from several vehicles ... And now he's crouching down under the slide...'

Esa continues his running commentary, which in many ways feels unnecessary. We all recognise the park's equipment; we know what they did. And when the presentation again reaches the section where two men appear from behind the Moose Chute, I ask Esa to pause and zoom in on the image. The colour freeze-frame makes identification simple.

Olavi's face is still blue.

The other man is sporting a red cap with an exceptionally long brim, so identifying him isn't quite as easy. However, I suspect this is the first of the men I encountered at Somersault City, the one who escorted me into the conference room then seemed more interested in his phone: Joonas.

Esa continues verbalising the events on the screen, or at least he tries to. It's hard because everybody else wants to speak too, and they do speak. For a moment the café, in the morning light as bright as a dentist's chair, is filled with agitated voices. This time I don't even try to get a word in, because my thoughts are still with that image on the screen, which I continue to stare at. The image itself leaves nothing to the imagination, and this helps formulate the main question.

Why?

Why would the owners of an adventure park that has already demonstrated its market dominance do something like this? What could motivate them to attack a competitor that has already lost its clients and that is now clearly the underdog? And why now?

To my mind, the answer doesn't require any particular grounding in logical thinking or an understanding of applied mathematics. This is an escalation, an acceleration. Somersault City is in a hurry. Nothing else can explain this act, its timing or target. The question remains: *why* are they in a hurry? The pressure must be coming from within Somersault City; for one reason or another they need to bring this matter to a quick resolution – that is, to get YouMeFun off the map, and the quicker the better. For an answer, I don't have to look any further than Somersault City itself, and amid all the terrible news, this might even be considered good news.

The rush, the need to get rid of YouMeFun, reveals two things I'd doubted in the past:

1) Somersault City has a strong desire to show that it is fully in charge of the adventure-park sector in and around the capital city, possibly in an attempt to monopolise the sector as a whole. It doesn't need to demonstrate this to itself, at least not at the current pace. Therefore, there must be a third party; someone or something to whom Somersault City needs to come up with the goods. Quickly.

2) Following from this, we can conclude that Somersault City itself is in acute financial difficulty. This doesn't surprise me. Celebrities and flights to the moon cost money, and free entry and free goodies won't bring any money into the till.

3) If Somersault City is unable to convince this third party, the park's cash resources will dry up, the financial woes will grow until the whole park is no longer viable and Somersault City will quite simply...

Crash.

I raise my eyes from the freeze-frame. The conversation is still raging, fervent and passionate.

'Of course I'm not suggesting a ground offensive,' says Esa. 'But—'

'I can't even get soft ice cream anymore,' says Johanna. 'And I can't and won't try explaining to our customers why we haven't got any soft ice cream. It's a red line, drawn in soft ice cream. Anybody with any experience knows that—'

'All these pent-up emotions,' says Samppa, 'are a terrible burden. Redirection. That's the key. By letting out our emotions we can—'

'All-out war,' Minttu K croaks, swishing her gasoline-filled bottle in the air. 'Sign me up—'

'We're only talking about a short time,' I say, and at that everybody falls silent. I too am taken aback at the sound of my own voice. I sound certain, as though I were making a perfectly ordinary statement. 'We're talking about days, maybe weeks. We can survive this.'

At least, so I think. My assumption is based on a very quick assessment of the situation, two simple and straightforward calculations, and a considerable number of assumptions and probabilities, but eventually we have a conclusion that sounds and feels certain. Kristian is the first to speak.

'How do you know that?'

I'm about to open my mouth, then I realise I can't tell them about my murder investigations, their progress or what the result of that investigation means for our competitors. Neither can I tell them why I think Olavi and his accomplice are largely irrelevant factors who, once it's just the two of them, won't pose much of a threat to YouMeFun. And I don't want to tell my employees about my exploits with a can of spray paint or any of my night-time activities. All the above leaves me with very little of any substance that I can actually tell them.

'We will survive,' I say.

They all look at me.

'I'm afraid I can't say any more at present,' I add. It's the truth.

Every member of staff seems to exchange glances with every other member of staff. Once this exchange of glances is over, they turn again and look at me. Reading their expressions is difficult, but I believe I know my employees quite well, and their expressions don't reveal as much trust as I might have hoped. It is quieter in the café than at any time this morning.

'Well...' Esa begins, and I can see the dissatisfaction on his face.

'Right...' says Johanna, the muscles twitching at the corners of her mouth.

'You're in charge,' says Kristian, flexing his considerable biceps and sounding as though he has to exert himself in a most peculiar way. 'You're the boss. But—'

'This requires direct action,' Minttu K completes his sentence, and draws on her cigarette so vigorously that half of it turns to ash in her fingers.

'Direct...' says Esa and nods more militarily than ever before.

'Action,' says Johanna, sounding the way she must have sounded during the darkest days of her time behind bars.

I think of my brief history as manager and owner of this adventure park. I recall the early days, when it was hard to get people sitting round this table to believe in me or the park. Then, after facing a series of challenges together, I won their trust and got them to believe that the park would eventually overcome all its difficulties, financial and otherwise. Now I'm in a situation where I have to hold them back, to stop them from taking the law into their own hands. I don't want to think where Esa's planned annexation, Johanna's cold-bloodedness, Kristian's undeniable physical prowess and Minttu K's risk-taking might take them. The result would be catastrophic – and not just from my perspective. I can hardly believe I'm about to suggest what I'm about to suggest, but I can't see any alternative.

'I'm asking for a little extra time,' I say. 'Before we look at any of your suggestions.'

Another exchange of glances.

'How much extra time?' asks Johanna, the tenor of her words implying that a wrong answer now might mean we don't have any extra time at all.

I think about this quickly and conclude two things: I cannot ask for as much time as I might need, while on the other hand, what I can ask for might not be enough. But I have to try.

'A week,' I say.

The seconds tick away. Then Johanna nods, and the others nod too.

'Three days,' they say in unison.

7

The WhatsApp messages have had the desired effect. *Le Groupe Paris* has gathered for a crisis meeting.

The open-plan kitchen-dining room in the terraced house belonging to Taneli (and the rest of his family, obviously, though they are all somewhere else) is filled with concerned fathers, mostly in checked shirts.

Taneli, whose beard in all its sizable glory has assumed a new, reddish sheen, has baked two different kinds of cinnamon buns and is now making an assortment of different coffees in a machine the size of a tractor's engine. To my ears, the fathers' orders sound rather ambitious and very complex given the home surroundings, but Taneli doesn't seem fazed in the slightest. Every now and then he wipes his hands on the front of his apron, then returns to twiddling the buttons on his barista spaceship. At least, that's what it looks like to me, or, perhaps it would be better to say, that's how it feels: while the others are all enjoying the ride on Taneli's pleasant and trustworthy mothership, I feel as though I've lost contact with it and am slowly drifting into the blackness of outer space.

Of course, I can't be certain, but it seems to me that both the frequency of the hum of speech and the overall hustle and bustle have lowered a little since I arrived. And now I am sitting on a divan section of the sofa by the window, and nobody has come to sit next to me, though there is clearly not enough seating in the room for everyone. Even Sami and Tuukka, my fellow competitors in the table-tennis tournament and my colleagues from the dads' club, are engaged in visibly fraught conversation at the other side of the space, right by the front door.

The terraced home is both very cosy and wholly impractical.

The hundred-square-metre surface area is split across three floors, meaning that, once we deduct the essential staircases from the useable floor space, we are left with an exorbitant price per square metre and an unavoidably awkward layout. Still, I find myself imagining Laura, Tuuli and myself in this cosy, den-like space, regardless of its aforementioned drawbacks. I assume this must be yet another example of the unfortunate side-effects of family life, namely its tendency to weaken one's capacity for logical thought: many of my calculations now seem to end with both positive and negative outputs.

The last cup of coffee is ready, and Taneli takes off his apron. He does this with a sense of ease, the loop flies over his head, his right hand snatches the apron from the air, and he half throws it, half hangs it on a hook on the wall. He appears to be in his element, and he shows no signs of slowing down as he begins to speak.

'Hey guys, thanks for getting together at such short notice. I think we might have a minor crisis on our hands, as it turns out we might still be a bit behind with the budgeting. At the end of the day, this is about our kids, right? We really need to come up with a budget plan to help us reach our goal – and get us to gay Paris.'

The dads all nod.

'I reckon by the end of this evening, we'll have it all sorted out,' he continues. 'There's no such thing as a silly suggestion. We're all equals here, and all ideas are valid.'

The dads nod again.

'And, we've got our new budget manager: Henri.'

This time, the dads don't nod.

'At this point in proceedings, I suggest we give Henri the floor. Henri, if you could give us a broad summary of where we are, then we can put up our hands and speak if we have any thoughts on the matter. Over to you.'

I quickly glance around the room. Naturally, I don't know whether any of the other dads are suspected of murder at a local adventure park or whether they have similar problems with a variety of police officers or threats of losing their businesses, but I think it highly unlikely. Right now, *Le Groupe Paris* is quieter than it has been for a long time. Nobody is speaking, and there are no messages pinging on our phones with every passing second.

I begin. I explain that the situation hasn't changed one iota. I remind them of the substantial and very real discrepancy between the current situation and the desired outcome and, once again, I present a rough estimate of the project's total costs and explain how many jumble sales we will have to organise if this is our only way of raising funds. Then I explore the timetable challenges involved and conclude my presentation with the express wish that our efforts remain firmly grounded in reality.

The dads look at me for a second, two seconds. Then their hands go up.

I can't see a single dad without his hand in the air.

The first hour and a half passes without a moment's respite in the deluge of questions, and ultimately I don't know or, perhaps, understand – though I am closely following the course of our conversation – how, amid all the suggestions and constant flow of ideas generating increasing amounts of excitement, the dads finally agree on the time and place of the next fête and who will bake what.

Or whisk.

Or mix.

Or squeeze.

Or gather.

Because what the group has decided, with unflagging resolve, is to expand the breadth of things on offer at the event. Cakes, of course, but also buns, organic muesli, smoothies, home-made cheese and a whole array of juices and pastries. Even honey from someone's own garden. The dads' creativity seems boundless. And this appears to be the group's response to the challenges I have outlined and my desire for realism: to expand the product range, to grow and streamline the event, and to make better use of social media. The first time there is a lull in the conversation, I raise my hand, and Taneli, who has been chairing proceedings, inviting people to speak and praising their ideas, suggests that I speak – as soon as he has finished.

'Before I give Henri the floor,' he begins, 'I just want to thank each and every one of you. I knew we'd sort this out. Thanks, guys. Right, and before we wrap this up, let's hear what Henri's got to say.'

The dads look at me, and for some reason the weight of their gaze feels particularly pressing. But I say what is on my mind: that their suggestions and decisions make no sense, none whatsoever. Nobody from outside the group attends these fêtes, and the vast majority of our clients are sitting right here in this room. And that if Hannu wants to sell Teppo some honey from his own garden, and Teppo sells Hannu some freshly squeezed blueberry juice, we won't actually make any profit. On the contrary, we will lose, both in terms of work, time and materials; and therefore the most direct and cost-effective approach would simply be to pay for the trips and meet at the airport without wasting time on any more raffles and meetings or even the WhatsApp group, which seems only to complicate and slow down literally every decision. When I finish, the dads' eyes are no longer on me. They are on Taneli, who gives a decisive nod. He almost looks in my direction, but not quite, then turns his attention to the other dads.

'Let's put it to a vote,' he says.

'Pardon?' I ask.

'Let's vote on what to do,' he says, and I'm unsure whether he has even heard my question.

'What are the options?' I ask, genuinely confused.

'Who thinks we should hold the fêtes?' asks Taneli.

The dads raise either their right or left hands. All of them, even Sami and Tuukka, who are still standing at the other side of the room. I can't put my finger on it, but there's something very ... peculiar about Tuukka's raised hand. The impression he gives is anything but community spirited, someone who enjoys baking or doing other fun things together. Though I didn't especially have him in mind when I suggested we need more concerted action, I now find myself thinking that, by all accounts, he ought to have supported my suggestion. But no. He stares at the floor in front of him and keeps his hand raised, even while most have already lowered theirs. His posture exudes what I might call a Tuukka-esque defiance, but there's something else now too, a sense of having given up, like someone shaking hands with an opponent after losing a bitterly fought game.

'Okay, that was quite a landslide,' says Taneli, sounding as though he has just seen or heard something wildly impressive. 'Right, we stick to the original decision and get things moving. And remember: all pics to the WhatsApp group, please. That'll keep us all motivated and geed up. And hey, I hope my coffee doesn't keep anyone awake all night. I grind my own coffee beans, and this blend is a bit on the strong side.'

The dads stand up, congratulate one another and Taneli for the meeting and the decisions. At first, I try looking at Taneli to catch his attention, then I wave a hand. I want to ask whether he thought the vote was missing something, perhaps knowing what other options were on the table, alternatives to the raffles and jumble sales. Taneli eventually notices me.

'Hey guys, even Henri's raised his hand!'

'I just wanted to—'

'That's the spirit,' Taneli crowed. '*On y va à Paris!*'

Outside, the temperature has dropped further. The group of fathers diminishes with each intersection, and the walk continues.

Large snowflakes are slowly falling from the sky as Tuukka and I walk side by side up to the top of Karhutie. Squirrel Park is on our left as we continue up towards the Hiihtomäentie crossing, where Tuukka will turn right and I will turn left. Our steps crunch on the fresh snow. In the silence of a winter's night in Herttoniemi, the sound is heightened, seeming to rebound from the walls of the church to our right. I glance at Tuukka. His hat is pulled down tight over his head, his expression has a now familiar sternness, his eyes stare straight ahead. He doesn't appear to be in the mood for small talk, though I'm not sure he ever is. But the matter is still puzzling me, and the crossing is fast approaching.

'May I ask you something?' I begin. 'About that vote just now?'

The snow crunches a few more times before Tuukka responds.

'That wasn't a vote,' he says. 'It was what Taneli and the others wanted all along.'

He doesn't look at me while he speaks. His black hat sparkles with fat snowflakes the size of a thumb. I admit I too think the vote had a number of shortcomings.

'It just caught my attention,' I add, 'that you too voted for the fêtes and all that baking, though...'

'Though?'

We will soon be at the crossing. Perhaps the echo of our footsteps has strengthened, the speed of our steps increased. I decide to get straight to the point.

'Yes,' I say. 'It's just, I got the impression that you too would much rather aim for decisive action and faster results. At least, that's the impression I got...'

'Sure,' says Tuukka, and by now we really are walking more briskly. 'But now we're bloody baking.'

'I might have misunderstood something,' I say, and hurry to get out the rest of the sentence. 'But it looked to me as though you weren't very enthusiastic about baking, and yet—'

'That's right, I voted for the baking and the whisking and fuck knows what else,' he says as we arrive at the crossing, and I slow my step. 'And? What's it to you?'

'It was just so ... unexpected,' I answer, honestly.

Tuukka stops, turns to me. 'Yeah, well, it was unexpected when my sales figures dried up all of a sudden,' he says as we stand at the quiet crossing facing each other, snow floating to the ground around us. 'And it was pretty unexpected that, coincidentally, my main client is about to go bust. That means I can't pay for this trip on my own, at this point in time. And that means I'm going to have to faff around with those clowns.'

Tuukka's sudden frankness takes me by surprise. It looks to me as though it takes him by surprise too. The words seem to bubble from his mouth, to spill out of him. Of course, he is still his stern self, but now there is something new to his demeanour. Almost a sense of relief.

'It—' I begin.

'And it's never going to work,' he says, now sounding more like himself again. 'It's just like you said. But now we've just got to get on with it.'

'We shouldn't—'

'Of course not,' says Tuukka. 'We shouldn't put up a fight. We should keep our mouths shut and look on from the sidelines as the whole thing goes tits up and we're left with six hundred unsold brownies.'

What Tuukka has just said isn't anywhere near what I was about to say, but something makes me wary about how to respond. Meanwhile, the snowfall has gathered pace in the last few seconds; it feels like we will soon be standing up to our knees in a snowdrift, if not inside one. Tuukka knocks excess snow from under his feet, and I take this as a sign he intends to walk off. And with that we give each other a nod, and we are about to head off in our respective directions when he slows his gait again, turns and looks me in the eye.

'Forget the whole thing, Henri,' he says. 'This is Herttoniemi. That's all.'

I shake the snow from my hat and coat before stepping into the stairwell and take the stairs up to our apartment. In the time it takes to walk up the few flights, something happens, something besides the increase in elevation from ground level and the rise in my heart rate by five or six beats per floor. The closer I get to my front door, the stronger the feeling within me.

I am living in two worlds at once.

On the one hand, there is the world into which I am ascending, both figuratively and literally – a world that is suddenly so important that the mere thought of losing it touches me so deeply that I can't identify the bone or organ where the ache is strongest. And on the other is the world where the threat to the aforementioned world grows with every step. When I finally step inside the hallway and quickly close the door behind me, I can feel all the gangsters in the world, all the police officers, the fathers desperate to get to Paris, and both adventure parks in the city hot on my heels like a many-headed monster, its sharp claws about to reach me and everything I hold dear.

Later, as we sit having supper, we go through the day's events. I have the least to share. That isn't because my day wasn't full of twists, turns and surprises. I simply can't tell anyone about them.

Then I wonder whether, in my current position and situation, there might be something good after all, however trifling.

I believe I understand the challenges of blended-family life better than ever before.

8

'I hope you're not going to have to work all night in the future,' says Laura Helanto at three minutes past eight in the morning once Tuuli has closed the door behind her and we are putting on our winter clothes in the hallway. 'I don't mean you're not *allowed* to, not as far as I'm concerned, but it just feels a bit unfair – from your perspective. Everybody working in that park is capable of keeping the place up and running, they know how to take care of it. And you work really long hours as it is.'

Laura Helanto is standing in front of the mirror getting herself ready. She tries to catch my eye in the reflection. I, on the other hand, try to avoid making eye contact, though the mirror seems to be luring me in. The attraction is raw, primitive; perhaps there is a desire to show that the mirror works, that we can establish a connection that way too. My thoughts are darting here, there and everywhere, like my mirror theory from a moment ago; these are in fact subsidiary thoughts, the point of which is to push the day's real challenges to one side, to the background, further into the future – especially the challenge that I consider the most urgent and unavoidable. And that is why it takes a moment to respond, and that is why Laura gets in first with another question.

'Or is this about the Paris trip?'

I give a literal sigh of relief. I would much rather talk about the chaos that is *Le Groupe Paris* than about the park and its affairs. Just then, Laura turns away from the mirror and looks at me.

'You're ... how should I put it? You're a little distant today.

Well, maybe I should say you seem lost in thought a little differently from usual. Or ... I don't know. Has this all been a bit much for you?'

'What?' I ask.

'The move, this ... new life?'

'This is the best thing that's ever happened to me,' I say with complete candour.

Laura looks like she is about to say something but decides against it. Instead, she kisses me on the cheek, quick but warm.

'I love your honesty, Henri. Of course, I love you anyway, but this quality has made an impression on me right from the start.'

'I don't—'

'No, you don't,' says Laura, doing up her top button. 'You don't know how to lie. That's new to me. And it's adorable.'

'About the Paris trip...'

'I knew you'd be stressing about that too,' she says. 'You're so conscientious. You need to relax a little. Go with the flow.'

'The ... *flow*?'

'Yes,' she says. 'Sometimes it's easier and nicer to trust that things will work out for the best, one way or another, and just enjoy the ride.'

We are both fully swaddled in winter clothing, standing in our small but extremely functional hallway, where, through a combination of our sensible thermal clothing and the central heating, the temperature is now approaching that of a moderate sauna. For this reason, I can't begin talking at any greater length about what I'd like to – exposure to deliberate or careless coincidence, and the risks that that entails – and I absolutely don't want to tell Laura that even to an actuarial novice her suggestion represents a combination of indifference and a reckless and potentially dangerous disregard for probabilities. Besides, Laura Helanto is often right when it comes to matters related to so-called 'real life'. Her suggestion might well fall into that category.

'I'll try,' I say, though getting the words out requires a concerted effort, 'to enjoy ... the ride.'

Laura smiles, pulls on her gloves.

'Maybe you won't even have to try all that hard,' she says. 'We're here now.'

I know that by being 'here' Laura isn't only referring to our current geographical location or to the fact that we are standing opposite each other in our two-bedroom apartment in Herttoniemi. There's something else, and it's that something else that arouses my suspicions, and Laura notices.

'I'm talking so fast,' she says. 'I don't want to put words in your mouth.'

Naturally, I can't say that in order to get 'here' once and for all, I still have to find a murderer, which in turn places demands on me, both with regard to gathering evidence and dividing my time between work and home. And given that, on top of this, I have to resolve the adventure park's other problems too, the idea of going with the flow suddenly sounds a lot like being swept away by the Seine. To crown it all, the temperature in the hallway seems to be rising by the second. I decide to tell her the truth.

'I'm already here,' I say, though I realise it sounds nonsensical. 'I'm here, wherever you are.'

Laura is silent for a moment.

'You're a poet too,' she says eventually.

I don't know quite what she means but I nod all the same, because before long I'll be in a situation where I will either have to run out into the freezing cold or start to rip off my clothes.

'I'm glad we had this little moment this morning,' she says. 'It's good that we talked about this.'

I tell her I agree and am about to turn when I hear her voice.

'Don't forget, you have to pick up Tuuli from the birthday party this evening!'

Very well, I think to myself as I drive towards Somersault City. *Go with the flow.* With the best will in the world, I can't claim this comes very naturally to me. But right now, it's starting to feel like the only way of approaching things.

Time is in short supply.

If I can't resolve this situation, in two days' time my employees will take matters into their own hands. Again, the knowledge that Esa, Kristian, Johanna, Samppa and Minttu K are prepared to get involved in an adventure-park 'war' – a word I have heard them all say at least once – makes me shiver more than the slowly brightening winter's morning around me. The temperature has dropped again since yesterday, this time by two and a half degrees. The fresh snow that fell last night has covered the brown verges along the sides of the roads and shrouded the trees once more. Throughout the thirty-seven-minute drive, the passing landscape is like one long, wintery postcard. And when I steer into the half-full car park at the spare-parts garage and Somersault City appears at the other side of the road with its enormous neon signs, I remind myself of a time restriction that is even more pressing: I have to pick up Tuuli from Itäkeskus at 19:30.

But before that...

Before that I have to work out how best to present Osmala with a watertight case against Niko Kotka. I haven't forgotten the conversation I had with Osmala. It still echoes – the words, both the spoken and the unspoken, doggedly trying to overlap with the theories and scenarios I have envisaged. In his own way,

Osmala is on my side; of this, I'm fairly certain. But even he can't work with nothing. So I need something substantial, something concrete, something that confirms my theory, either completely or well enough.

And this needs to happen soon.

Naturally, this is easier said than done. I'm not sure quite what I'm looking for; I know it's linked to Niko Kotka, but at present I can't say how.

Go with the flow.

I switch off the engine, and almost immediately I can feel the interior of the Renault cooling down. If in the past I'd ever thought about the relative wisdom of going with a theoretical flow, sitting in an increasingly chilly second-hand French car without any particular action plan doesn't exactly strengthen my belief in this philosophy. On the other hand, I've already seen the ways in which Laura Helanto has been able to achieve excellent and very concrete results by following this strategy, though it differs greatly from my own. As the temperature drops, I try to sell myself this thought, I pull on my gloves, and for a moment I find myself thinking, if only I were an actuary again, working full time in a centrally heated office block, spending my days considering the ins and outs of such commonplace subjects as how to calculate random variables or the applications of density functional theory. But this is soon over. I am a suspect in a murder investigation, I am under pressure both temporally and investigationally. My thoughts return to the car and to Niko Kotka.

Of course, I don't know anything about Kotka's schedule or movements today, but I plan to change my own *modus operandi* instead. My aim is to connive my way towards him, to get closer to him that at any point before. This comes with dangers of its own, but given the situation and the conditions, it is the most logical option: if I want either to discover something I have not hitherto found or to get my hands on something concrete, I must 1) get close to my target; and 2) do something I have not yet done.

The minutes pass. Then half an hour. An hour. And another half-hour.

Then I see Niko Kotka's SUV.

By this point, I have already warmed the car again, though doing so gives me a decidedly guilty conscience – few things feel so thoroughly confined to the past as running an engine on idle – and I am ready. I glide out of the car park and into the flow of traffic, and begin tailing him at the now familiar distance.

In recent days, I've followed Niko Kotka's SUV for hundreds of kilometres, and I quickly note that this time the choice of route and general direction are new. We are heading north-west, and keeping on his tail is difficult. This is because – in another change to the pattern – Kotka is driving considerably over the speed limit. The third new factor is that Kotka is not alone in the car. Sitting in the passenger seat is a man whom I believe I recognise, though I still haven't caught a glimpse of his blue face.

Kotka's speed picks up further once we turn off the four-lane highway and onto a smaller, winding road with only two lanes. Following him goes from difficult to nigh on impossible. And this isn't just because I don't consider speeding a particularly sensible course of action. Niko Kotka seems to be putting his foot even further down with every passing kilometre, as though his sense of hurry was increasing exponentially by the minute.

The road takes some tight bends through clusters of shadowy forest, then straightens out and brightens as we race between gleaming, snow-covered fields. The winding, the speeding up, the corners that almost see us come off the road continue for another seventeen or eighteen minutes. My estimate is imprecise because I have to keep my full attention on steering myself and the Renault along the slippery forest roads. And thankfully, I see the SUV slowing down in good time.

We reach a long, gentle turn in the road. After this there is a straight stretch of road, and around halfway along it the SUV almost stops, then turns left without indicating. I reduce my speed enough as I believe possible without arousing too much attention and give the SUV time to slip onto the dirt track. I pull out of the bend and onto the straight road and, keeping well within the speed limit, I drive past the turn-off. Further to the left, I see a two-storey building, an enclosed pen and some horses.

Niko Kotka's SUV disappears behind the building.

I arrive at the end of the straight stretch of road, and from here the road delves back in between rows of trees. Just as I slow down to turn the car, on my left I see another small, snow-ploughed road that appears to wind its way round to a livery yard. I brake, steer the car off the road and onto the smaller path. The path really does lead directly to the livery yard, and at first I can't work out why there should be two roads leading to the same place. Then I realise and manage to stop the car in time. The path doesn't lead to the livery yard but to another house, which was initially hidden behind a larger building, presumably the stables.

The house and its surroundings look quiet, and there are no cars parked outside. I switch off the engine and think for a moment. I look at the time. In my current situation, time does not at all feel like a relative concept; it is as tangible as the cooling steering wheel under my fingers. And I don't have any other realistic options.

I step out of the Renault and begin walking towards the livery yard.

Between the two main buildings is a stretch of pure, untouched snow and two rows of pine trees, presumably to cordon off the space and provide a modicum of privacy. I wade through the snow to the nearest of the trees and hear the high-pitched roar of a motor. The sound is coming from further across the fields, so I leave the first row of pines behind me and make my way across the pristine snow towards the other row.

Progress is slow and arduous, and the air is painfully cold, but luckily I have come well prepared: I have a good set of footwear and my jacket comes down to my knees. The thought of the jacket reminds me of something else too. I take the balaclava from my pocket, pull it over my head and put a normal woolly hat over that too. The jacket, bearing the logo of a dark-brown energy drink, and the black-grey, cat-faced balaclava are from the lost-and-found bin at the adventure park, and they've been there for over a year. It's unlikely anyone will be looking for them right now, and I can safely say I don't look like myself. Which, of course, is my intention.

I reach the second row of trees, stop between two pines heavy with snow, and take stock of the livery yard and the general area.

It is approximately twenty-five metres to the corner of the long, red stable building. To the door of the bright-yellow house it is around fifty metres. Niko Kotka's SUV is parked between the house and the stable. There is no movement, except for the horses. I don't have any particular timing or plan in mind, but the basic principle is clear: I need to get as close to them as possible.

I set off, and all I can hear is the revving of the motor on the other side of the farm. The sound tells me that a vehicle is moving, but not necessarily getting any closer. After taking ten steps, perhaps twelve, I realise that the din of the motor is smothering another sound. There's conversation coming from the stable. So, I turn and approach the door, which stands open a fraction.

Though I cannot see him, I recognise Niko Kotka's voice and manner of speaking.

'Elsa,' he says. 'We're so close...'

'You said that last week,' I hear a woman – presumably Elsa – saying. 'And the week before ... Money's going out, but nothing's coming back in. V-P said the same. And we've got a target to meet. Well, I should say, *I've* got a target...'

'Of course. But this is the adventure-park business. You can't turn things around overnight. And we've had to spend money on other things, those—'

'If I so much as lay my eye on them,' says Elsa, 'you know what I'll do.'

'I know,' says Niko Kotka, and I note the way he hurries to get his words out. 'But the turning point is just around the corner. That two-bit park is going to go bust any day now—'

'We need to tighten the screws,' Elsa interrupts him. 'No matter what things look like. You know what I want, but can you deliver the goods? To be perfectly frank, even V-P was starting to doubt whether you had it in you.'

'I can get you results,' said Kotka. 'You'll see. Very soon. And why are you ... still talking about V-P? He's not here anymore.'

'Does it bother you that I'm talking about him?'

'Oh, come on...'

'I'm trying to get it into your thick skull that if you think you're going to get an easy ride now that I'm running this operation by myself, you've got another thing coming. Compared to me, V-P was about as dangerous as a dead poodle. And you of all people should know, I'm not that nice.'

A brief silence.

'No, you're not,' says Kotka, and something about his tone of voice changes. 'Far from it. You know how to be quite ... mean.'

'And you love it, don't you?' says Elsa, and now there's a new tone in her voice too.

I hear footsteps, then a thud.

'Can I be your horsey again?' he asks.

As far as I can tell, this question is not only something of a non sequitur, but it has little to do with the commercial nature of the conversation thus far.

'Do I need to tame you again?'

I can't say I understand what this is all about, but I assume it is something other than Excel spreadsheets and annual reports. Just then, Niko Kotka lets out a sound that I assume must be his idea of a horse's neighing. This is immediately followed by three new sounds: the crack of a riding crop, a sharp thwack and a deep moan. Then another whinny.

'Do I need to put you in your harness again, you dirty little colt?' asks Elsa, and to my ears the tone of this question is suddenly stern and demanding. 'You want the bit too?'

A third whinny.

'What about your idiot friend, chasing around the fields in V-P's snowmobile?'

'He's not my friend...' says Kotka, now clearly panting. 'He's an idiot, you're right ... Let him chase around, he doesn't understand anything. I've been a naughty horsey ... I need a good thrashing...'

Crack, thwack, moan, whinny.

And again.

And...

I think I've heard quite enough. And I don't just mean the horseplay, but something far more significant. I back away from the door and make my way towards Niko Kotka's SUV. I don't believe I am leaping to conclusions when I assume that the V-P mentioned in their conversation must be Ville-Pekka Häyrinen, the late owner of Somersault City who had a penchant for the Wild West. Besides, he too mentioned an Elsa that he had to meet, an Elsa with demands. It's also safe to assume that Elsa and Niko Kotka have been playing with harnesses and riding crops for some time: for a variety of reasons, it's hard to imagine this is the first time they have met.

I reach Kotka's SUV and open the driver's door.

The interior of the vehicle is tidy and smells of aftershave. At first glance, I can't see anything that might help me with the task at hand. I look on the back seat, but that too is empty and clean, and looks almost untouched. I am about to pull out of the car when I glance at the pocket on the driver's side.

My heart lurches.

I take a resealable plastic bag from my pocket, open it, pull on my gloves again, and only then touch the wrapper. I try to work as quickly and effectively as possible, but still can't help myself stopping for half a second.

The protein bar is exactly the same brand and flavour, and this one has just been eaten too; the small smears of melted chocolate reveal as much. Whoever was hiding inside the Beaver ate the very same kind of protein bar. From Niko Kotka's perspective, the evidence is beginning to look indisputable.

He might be playing horsey now, but that doesn't change the facts.

Niko Kotka is a killer.

I close the car door, and despite everything – under normal circumstances I would consider spying and trespassing a direct contravention of my most basic principles – I feel a sense of satisfaction that I have achieved what I set out to. There are enough

threads tying Niko Kotka to Ville-Pekka Häyrinen's murder
that, as far as I can see, there's no way he can wriggle out of them.
Again, I head towards the stable building, and I am about to
walk right past it when I think twice, for two reasons.

The first is what I hear; the second, what I see.

I hear the motor, closer now. At the same time, I glance to the
side and catch a glimpse through the stable window. Niko Kotka
is on all fours, naked, a horse's bit in his mouth. Behind him, the
woman called Elsa is thrusting back and forth, and tied to her
waist is what at first I assume must be a lance or sword, but
which a fraction of a second later I realise is an appendage of a
rather more compromising nature. Elsa, this short, fair-haired
and, at a quick glance, stumpy woman, is also wielding a riding
crop with masterful precision. I hear Elsa shouting and Niko
Kotka neighing. Then, as though they were one and the same
being (as, at this point in time, they undoubtedly are), their
heads turn at once. They look right at me.

Just then, the sound of the motor becomes louder.

I peer over my shoulder. The sound is coming from out in the
fields. The snowmobile has changed course. Now it seems to be
heading right towards the yard – and me.

It is reasonable to say that the afternoon has very quickly
changed character and that my Renault suddenly feels a little
further away than it did a few seconds ago.

I run – and run as fast as my heavy winter boots will allow.
As I run, I conduct a few quick calculations. Naturally, I had
factored in the possibility of having to make a quick exit, but
not quite like this. And I couldn't have predicted the
snowmobile. I need a verge of snow or something – anything
that will either slow down the snowmobile or speed my own
progress back to my car. And I realise that, inside the stable, I
saw something that might be of use. I remember seeing some

kind of tool with a long handle – a rake, perhaps? Yes. If I can push, shove or throw that implement under the snowmobile's tyres or runners, the vehicle will stop in its tracks, possibly very abruptly, and this will have an impact on the driver too.

I reach the far end of the stable, turn sharply, wrench the door open, see the naked couple, who have now risen to their feet – even from behind the horse's bit, I can sense Niko Kotka's fury – I grip the handle of the rake propped in the doorway and take it with me. Only once I am outside again do I realise it's not a rake I'm running with.

I dash out across the snow with a long-handled ice scraper.

My feet are sinking into the deep snow.

Naturally, a steel ice scraper like this isn't intended as a relay baton. Running with something this heavy is hard going. But I can't think of any other way of encountering the snowmobile without coming into contact with it myself. The snowmobile is fast approaching. Its high-pitched motor screams louder and louder. The snow shines and glisters. By the time I am halfway across the yard, I can feel the lactic acid starting to gnaw away at my muscles. At that same moment, the sound of the snowmobile is like a deafening din in my ears. I turn, still holding the ice scraper.

I see the vehicle approaching along the row of pines, and at the helm is a man who for some inexplicable reason decides to take off his helmet and reveal his bright-blue face. Then I realise why Olavi wanted to relinquish his helmet: he wants to shout. But though he is brandishing his fists and shouting – very angrily – his message is drowned out. I catch my breath. My ears are ringing and throbbing with my gasping and the pounding of my heart.

Olavi bellows, the snowmobile races towards me.

With the naked eye, I measure the ice scraper and assess its qualities. In my hands I have a wooden handle almost two metres long. At the end of that handle is a steel blade almost twenty centimetres across that looks very sharp and very sturdy. It's not hard to imagine slicing your way through blocks of ice with this thing. Then I turn my attention back to the snowmobile, calculate the ratio of speed to mass, gauge my optimal timing and position. At the same time, I believe I now know why Olavi is waving his fist in the air. Wrapped around his fingers is the same knuckleduster he was wearing the last time our paths crossed. The metal glints and flashes in the sunlight.

And all of the above is hurtling towards me like a comet.

I follow my plan. I flinch to the left, as though I am about to run in that direction. The snowmobile is already almost on top of me, but Olavi takes the bait and yanks the steering wheel. The snowmobile changes course. The movement is slight, but it's just enough. Or, to be more precise: it's just enough that I don't end up getting flattened. But it doesn't help with regard to Olavi's knuckleduster. The steel makes contact with my forehead before I'm able to stick the ice scraper into the chassis of the snowmobile. The blow is hard, the pain dizzying.

I fall onto the snow on my back. Luckily, I don't lose consciousness, though my vision is blurred: the sky has lost its blueness, the snow its sheen. I try to get up right away, just manage to do so, stagger a little, and grip the ice scraper once again. Olavi steers the snowmobile around and heads towards me once more. It's clear I won't withstand another encounter with the knuckleduster, and it's even clearer what will happen to me if Olavi, Niko Kotka and Elsa get their hands on me. The idea of ending up trussed up in their stable doesn't bear thinking about; it's completely out of the question. And as for Olavi, it looks like he is after one thing and one thing only: he wants me dead. The snowmobile accelerates right towards me.

Again, I calculate the dimensions of my ice scraper in relation to my assessment of the speed of the snowmobile and try to define all the other physical factors at stake. Naturally, these assessments are estimates, but taken together they explain not only why my previous attempt failed, and was bound to failure, but also tell me how I need to proceed now.

I hear Olavi hollering above the wail of the motor. The snowmobile grows larger as it approaches me. I clench the handle of the ice scraper, my grip a suitable combination of firm and relaxed, try to call his bluff again – in the same direction as a moment ago – and trust that in his rage Olavi won't have had the chance to analyse in any great detail his previous attempt to plough into me.

My guess proves correct. The snowmobile changes direction just enough. At the same time, my hands and the ice scraper continue their upward motion. And then, once the ice scraper has reached the apex of its trajectory and the driver enters the point in time and space that I had predicted, my calculation is complete: two orbits intersect, in a very literal sense.

The ice scraper does what ice scrapers are designed to do: it separates things from one another.

Olavi's head almost seems to remain in place as the snowmobile continues on its way. But only for a brief moment, naturally. Then his severed head drops to the pure white snow, and he looks at me, his face still blue, though decidedly calmer than a second ago. I glance in the other direction as the snowmobile roars off across the open fields with a headless driver at the wheel.

I look at Olavi again, then at the snowmobile, and then I start running. Obviously, I don't know how long it takes to remove a strap-on dildo from around one's waist, a bit from one's mouth, then get dressed and enter into hot pursuit, but I doubt it can be very long. The encounter with Olavi hasn't weighed on me in a temporal sense, this was more about the density – and intensity – of events. This notwithstanding, I only have a limited number of seconds and minutes to put this bizarre and life-threatening livery yard behind me. My head is throbbing with pain, my muscles are almost completely stiff, and my lungs feel like they are on fire. When I reach the Renault I start it up, steer it towards the dirt track and press my foot to the floor. Right now, exceeding the speed limit doesn't feel like a decision at all.

I arrive at Itäkeskus at the agreed time.

9

'Pollock,' says Laura, and turns the book on the table. The book is what they call a coffee-table format and must weigh several kilos. If I've understood correctly, people only touch these kinds of picture books when they're moving house; at all other times, they lie untouched on coffee tables and bedroom floors. But Laura's copy has clearly seen some life. The spine needs some rudimentary repair, dozens of ragged Post-It notes in various colours jut out from between the pages, and the book is filled with all manner of notes and scraps of paper.

I look at the reproduction of a painting that at first glance looks like nothing but a chaotic mess, but the longer I look at it, the more I start to see order, rhythm, even beauty and harmony. Still, I'm unsure whether I can trust my own interpretation. It's very possible that the challenges I've faced through the course of the day lend my reading a healthy dose of wishful thinking, and I'm not a great admirer of that. Based on my observations and experiences, I've reached the conclusion that many of the problems we face in the course of human life stem from wishful thinking and daydreaming. Again, I realise I've become lost in thought; I take a deep breath, try to concentrate.

'One of my favourites,' says Laura.

I take my eyes from the Pollock, compare it to Laura's recent sketch, which was spread out on the dining table once I'd cleared up after supper. Assuming I'm reading her sketch correctly, Laura's new work will be an abstract explosion of colour spanning three walls, and its desired effect is one of balance. Even the sketch is magnificent. All the smaller and larger motifs repeat, forming chains, pairs, groups, swoops, and to my mind the whole work makes excellent use of the space and walls. And like Laura Helanto's earlier works, this one too seems to capture my imagination, leaves me wanting more. And all this in a way that right from the start I have found it impossible to explain, especially from a mathematical perspective.

'I find Pollock quite distinguished,' I say eventually. 'But I find your works better.'

Laura smiles, looks at me over her glasses.

'Do you remember this morning, when I said I admired your honesty?'

I tell her I do. Laura says nothing. It takes a moment before I realise what she means.

'I really do think that,' I say.

'You're such a sweetheart,' she says. 'Thank you.'

Then her expression turns serious.

'At some point, we're going to have to talk about what's going on,' she says eventually. 'I haven't said anything about the purple bruise on your forehead.'

I automatically raise a hand to my forehead, touch the bump and almost yelp, even though I've taken both paracetamol and ibuprofen this evening. When Tuuli and I arrived home, I only took my hat off once I'd reached the bathroom and before stepping into a hot shower. I didn't want to risk my forehead starting to bleed in front of Tuuli. I think it best if children's impressions of the adventure-park world remain largely positive and not bloodthirsty – or worse. After the shower, I tried to comb my hair across the bump, but quickly decided this would attract more attention than the bruise itself and, crucially, it would arouse more questions about my general mental wellbeing.

'I assume this happened at work,' she says.

'Yes,' I reply. 'I was working in the field and—'

'Doing what, precisely?'

'Precisely?'

'Yes,' says Laura, and props both elbows on the table. 'What exactly were you doing?'

Naturally, I can't tell her about my scything activities. It still shocks me, and I try hard to suppress two images: that blue face staring at me, and the snowmobile careering towards the horizon with its headless driver at the helm. My hands are still trembling, and I hold them in my lap. Despite all this, I must tell her something, preferably something that is also true.

'I'm trying to find some clarity,' I say, 'about something that's been bothering me.'

'That doesn't sound very precise,' says Laura. 'And I know you like precision.'

We look at each other, then Laura gives an audible sigh.

'Fine,' she says. 'I won't plague you anymore. I know you'll tell me if you need my help.'

That final sentence takes me by surprise. But only in this context. I know that Laura's opinion of me is largely positive, but I think she realises I'm in a tricky situation – one that might bring back memories of things she would rather forget. Be that as it may, I emphatically do not want to ask her to take any part in my murder investigation or the park's activities. Family life is about sharing everything, but to my mind certain matters are still discretionary, such as unsolved homicides and widespread threats of bankruptcy. I am about to formulate a response when Laura leans closer to me, though given the width and weight of the dining table, this is barely possible.

'There's actually one other thing I'd like to deal with,' she says, now in a lower, whispering voice, and it looks as though she glances towards Tuuli's room and the door she closed half an hour ago. 'Namely, sex.'

'I like everything,' I hear myself saying before thinking about it any further. I realise I am relieved at the change of subject, so much so that I've made a statement that isn't wholly true and that even to my own ears sounds far more open-minded than I intended.

'Well, I mean, I like it with you,' I correct myself, as my thoughts race back to what I witnessed in the stables. 'And not necessarily *everything*. What I mean is, I like very many things, but there are some things I find, how should I put this, uncomfortable. But that doesn't at all mean, in any way, that other people can't—'

'Henri,' says Laura. 'I didn't mean that. I didn't mean we should talk about it or file a report about it. I was thinking we should ... have some.'

'Now?' I ask.

'No, at Christmas.'

'It's always good to plan ahead...'

'Henri, I'm joking. Now, of course.'

I begin to understand what's happening, what must happen. And the further this conversation moves from the subject of the park, the greater my sense of relief. I even feel myself relaxing. And so, I lower my voice and almost whisper.

'I'll just brush my teeth and pick out a tie for tomorrow,' I say. 'Four and a half minutes.'

'Romantic,' Laura smiles. 'I don't know what I'll do for those four and a half minutes.'

'I find the day goes much more smoothly if you spend a little time planning it the evening before.'

'That's just what I wanted to hear right now.'

'Excellent,' I say and stand up.

I don't know why Laura Helanto shakes her head. All the same, she whispers that she loves me and says she can't wait for what's going to happen in five minutes. I correct the record, it's four and a half, and leave her at the dining table.

I brush my teeth in front of the bathroom mirror and examine the bump on my forehead. Though I've read that mortal danger and the threat of death often trigger a primitive, subconscious desire to copulate and procreate – it's hard to argue with evolution – perhaps I'm not at my most aroused, tonight of all nights. More than anything, I feel a desire to flee, to escape the events of the day, my predicament, everything in fact. And right then I realise I have read about this mode of thinking and where it can lead: addiction. People seek transitory pleasure in order to escape reality. On top of everything else, am I turning into some kind of sex addict?

10

Four and a half hours later I wake with a start, and I can safely say that I am neither a sex addict nor anything else unexpected. On the contrary. The situation is as it was before and, as such, is perfectly clear.

I climb out of bed as quietly as possible, and though it is only seventeen minutes past five, I'm already in a hurry. My breakfast is fast and simple: a glass of water and a low-fat probiotic strawberry yoghurt. This isn't a particularly nutritional repast, but it is quick and, at this point, does the job. I brush my teeth more quickly than usual, though still paying due attention to thoroughness: first the back teeth, their outer surfaces, then the inner surfaces, then the front teeth, their outer and inner surfaces, all the while making sure not to neglect the gums, running my toothbrush along the gum line, softly and in small motions, then quickly rinsing my teeth and mouth with a little water so that enough fluoride remains in my mouth to protect my teeth and gums for the next few hours until I brush them again before bed. In the hallway, I pull on my outdoor clothes, and only fourteen minutes after waking up I am already outside in minus-twenty temperatures.

I start up the Renault, though it coughs and splutters as if it doesn't like me bothering it so soon after all my recent shenanigans. I'm not concerned that someone might have seen the car yesterday. There was no direct vantage point from the stables to the neighbouring plot; the two rows of pines, the open fields and undulating, tree- and snow-covered landscape around my parking spot made sure I was able to leave under the same veil of anonymity as I had arrived. The only person who could, even theoretically, have caught a glimpse of the Renault was Olavi on his snowmobile, but without his head he doesn't pose any imminent threat. I don't say this in jest but from a purely practical standpoint. It's hard to take pleasure in what happened, even though it was a potent demonstration of what mathematics, physics and biology are capable of in such a desperate, explosive, rapidly escalating situation. But there is a certain level of satisfaction in the knowledge that all this will soon lead where it must: to Niko Kotka's arrest.

The streetlamps gleam against the road and the snow as I steer the Renault into the YouMeFun car park. It's easy to see that I am the first customer of the morning. A fresh gauze of snow, as thin as silk, covers the whole area. It speaks volumes. For a while now, there has been plenty of space at the YouMeFun car park. I drive around the building, turn into one of the staff parking spaces and switch off the engine. I open the glove compartment, take out two resealable plastic bags and place them in my coat pocket. I step out of the car, climb the steel steps up to the loading bay, open the steel rear door and step into my park.

Suddenly the dimly lit hall feels cosier than usual. I quickly realise why. As I walk, I notice that I don't need any more light than this and that I really do know every square metre of this park, every cubic metre in fact, in a very concrete, tangible fashion. At the same time, it feels as though those cubic metres are a powerful part of me too.

Whatever is meant by fate, it is surely something like this. Which, in turn, is surely that fate – which, naturally, is by its very essence an ambiguous term that is hopelessly imprecise from a mathematical standpoint – is something at once unpredictable and completely unavoidable, both quick as lightning and eternal. Nine months ago, I had no idea I would be defending an adventure park in Vantaa with my life and freedom, but now that this is undeniably my current situation, I can't imagine how things could be any different. Above all, fate also appears to be the most natural thing imaginable. I take a deep breath, draw in the scent of my adventure park.

I walk underneath the Moose Chute, turn and pass the Strawberry Maze and spin past the Doughnut on the way to my office, when I am taken aback, almost startled, at a sound I hear to the side. Knocking, banging, stamping. I am standing by the main entrance, I can see the foyer and the front doors – and two customers are standing behind the doors. Then I realise that our customers, who in recent weeks have been conspicuous by their absence, don't usually try to gain entry to the park at three minutes to six in the morning.

It turns out I am not looking at two customers but at two policemen, Salmi and Lastumäki, who do, it has to be said, dress like our customers. As I stare at them, they see me too, despite the dimness inside. I know this because they are battering on the panes of the electric sliding doors with all four knuckles. I have to accept I have no other option; I'll have to let them in. On my way to the door, I glance up at the clock in the foyer. Two minutes to six. I don't think it's very likely that the pair have come here at this time in the morning by accident. They are here because they know I am here. Which means they have either been following me or keeping an eye on the park from a nearby vantage point. Neither of these scenarios is very good news.

'I thought you were going to leave us out there in the cold,' says Lastumäki once he is standing in the foyer, but I don't think he means that for a second. He shakes his arms and shrugs his shoulders, while Salmi standing beside him knocks the snow from his white trainers. I recognise their bulbous eiderdown jackets and hoodies from before, and their loose, baggy jeans

too. If I didn't know what I was looking at, I would think the
two were getting ready to shoot a kids' music video. But the
truth is that it's six a.m., and the characters restlessly fidgeting
in my foyer are police officers, and that's never been a good sign
of anything.

'It's a good job you're here,' says Salmi. That's another lie. 'We
could have frozen.'

It's high time to put an end to this nonsense. So, at the risk of
repeating myself, I have to put the question:

'May I ask what this is all about?'

Salmi and Lastumäki look at each other, then at me.

'You may,' Lastumäki answers in faux astonishment, but his
performance isn't very convincing.

'You asked that last time,' Salmi nods. 'And everything went
just fine.'

I'm not at all sure I agree with Salmi's summation. We stand
there in silence. It isn't a pleasant silence, let alone relaxing. Very
well, I think; this is a game, and taking part in that game is not
a matter of choice.

'Is this still about Somersault City?' I ask eventually, trying
to keep my voice as neutral as possible.

Salmi looks like he's been waiting for this precise question,
and now he can get straight to the point. Rather, he doesn't look
like it, he's *pretending* to look like it.

'You're a step ahead, dude,' he says with a nod. 'Yep, that's
what it's about. We've got a few more questions to ask, now that
our investigation's coming along nicely. And we've got this
niggling feeling you haven't been telling us the whole truth.'

I say nothing.

'So,' says Lastumäki, 'I'm sure you won't mind if we ask about
your situation.'

'My situation?'

'The pressure,' says Salmi. 'The pressing pressure.'

This time Salmi isn't pretending; I can see he is genuinely chuffed at his own wit.

'Now, about this gaff of yours,' Lastumäki continues. 'The car park still looks like people aren't exactly falling over one another to get in here.'

'If you mean, are we suffering from a temporary drop in footfall, the answer is yes, we are,' I admit.

'How much?' Lastumäki asks right back.

'How much what?'

'How much are you suffering?' asks Salmi.

Trying to converse with these two vaguely reminds me of playing table tennis with the dads: the ball's bounce is quick and mercurial, and every question feels like an attempt to score an ace.

'If we look at the matter—'

Lastumäki shakes his hand and stops me in my tracks. 'What does it mean in terms of weeks,' he asks, 'or days?'

I look first at Salmi, then at Lastumäki. Something really has changed, if only imperceptibly. Salmi and Lastumäki are still trying to look as cool and indifferent as before, but there's a new element now too: there's an urgency about them, making tiny cracks in their carefully cultivated exterior. It is a deceptively small shift in tone, one deviant numeral in a large body of data. But this might be my chance, this might change the direction of the entire calculation.

'I assume you mean until our bankruptcy,' I nod. 'If we look at the takings over the last few days, admittedly the situation is challenging. But we have a buffer, we have dedicated staff, and we are still expecting a number of outstanding payments, so—'

'In concrete terms,' says Salmi, now perhaps starting to look a little frustrated, 'what does all that mean in the real world?'

It really seems I have touched a nerve, though I don't yet know which one. It is still six a.m., and the situation is far from ideal, but the very fact that these two teenage cops in front of me seem so interested in the potential collapse of my adventure park may in itself be an encouraging sign. More than anything, it reveals the new focus of their attention. And so, I decide to proceed with my boldest and most quickly concocted scenario.

'As I said,' I begin, 'we have a level of tolerance for this, perhaps much more than I previously thought. We are already planning our summer programme. We are still looking at things in the long term.'

In its own way, this is all true. In a certain light, our tolerance threshold can be assessed in terms of what I know, say, about Esa's desire and ability to defend the park, as he puts it, to the bitter end. Naturally, this doesn't even require the existence of the park itself. I can well imagine Esa continuing his ground offensive long after we've sold our final entrance ticket. And my suggestion that we're thinking about next summer isn't entirely unfounded either: Kristian and I have been talking about whether the Doughnut, which has long since reached the end of its life span, should be dismantled and given away. Kristian suggested he could dismantle it and take it away for a fixed price, which would allow him to take part in a fitness competition in Greece. In a nutshell: I have told these two the truth while tactically not specifying exactly what I mean. I realise there are entire professions that make their money via this principle, but as an actuary I believe I am trying something unusual and rather risky.

Salmi and Lastumäki glance at each other again, then both turn and look at me.

'So, to summarise,' says Lastumäki. 'Now the situation has changed completely. Now you're not in any kind of hurry, least of all when it comes to this park, and you think it's completely okay for you and your business that day after day that car park is like some kind of little ... Siberia, a snow-covered wasteland, and it doesn't affect your business at all?'

'Perhaps that's putting it rather strongly,' I say. 'But after reassessing the situation, I believe—'

'And would this *reassessment*,' Lastumäki interrupts, stressing the last word as though it felt clumsy in his mouth, like a piece of particularly chewy toffee, 'have anything to do with the fact that now another guy has gone missing from Somersault City?'

The question takes me by surprise, but I don't think it shows. Olavi's snowmobile – as unpleasant as the image is – is speeding off into the distance, but even so I find it hard to believe that it has disappeared altogether. How far can a headless man drive exactly?

'I don't know anything about any disappearances,' I reply, honestly. 'And wasn't CEO Häyrinen's death...?'

'Missing in action,' says Lastumäki, and by now he sounds a little impatient. 'Let's put it like that. Seeing as our mathematician here always wants to be as precise as possible.'

There's a hint of the frozen air from outside in Lastumäki's expression.

'Do you know a man by the name of Olavi Laaksonen?' asks Salmi.

'Do you mean...?'

'Yes,' Salmi nods decisively, and he too is starting to look like he has been waiting for something, anything, a minute or two too long. 'Olavi Laaksonen from Somersault City.'

Again, I can be perfectly candid with them.

'I've met him,' I say. 'But I don't know him. I have to say, I don't really understand what we're talking about here. Has he disappeared?'

Salmi and Lastumäki pause for a moment.

'We suspect so,' says Salmi, glancing out towards the car park. 'He hasn't been seen for a day now, and nobody's been able to contact him. His phone has been located at Somersault City.'

I realise I have been extremely lucky. On the very day that Olavi tried to run me over, he left his phone at work. Who knows, perhaps it's not completely out of the question that his snowmobile is still chuntering its way towards central Finland. It's unlikely, but how many of the things I've experienced recently ever seemed likely?

'I'm sure you'll appreciate I'm starting to see a pattern, one where you're a person of considerable interest,' says Lastumäki. 'And if you thought you could fool us by visiting Somersault City in advance, that sort of thing can only work in the short term. In future, I'd suggest a slightly different approach. Like, for example, you tell us how you killed Häyrinen, or what you know about Olavi Laaksonen's disappearance.'

There is now a new, much sterner tone in Lastumäki's voice. Still, I can't help feeling a growing sense of confusion.

'I did not kill Häyrinen,' I say. 'And I don't know what you mean by trying to fool you...'

'Let's assume we ask you to provide a DNA sample,' says Salmi, and now he doesn't sound particularly cool and relaxed either. 'You'll be fine with that, because you already visited the place, to get to know it, and you had a conversation with the owners and, in your own words, offered some financial consultancy services and what have you, and that explains why your DNA is all over the place. I bet you think you've got the perfect alibi.'

'I didn't think—'

'Exactly,' Lastumäki nods. 'That's what it's starting to look like to us too: you didn't really think this through, did you?'

I am taken aback by two things. By now, the pair are almost touching me. They have managed to get closer completely without my noticing. And now they are standing so close that I can smell their breath – chewing gum and unbrushed teeth – and I feel their presence in the same holistic way that you sometimes experience people in a lift or a crowded bus, whereby a person's corporeality suddenly becomes something you not only see but feel too. The second matter is more straightforward: the pair have now progressed to direct threats. Which only confirms everything I have already concluded about them. Paradoxically, this makes Salmi and Lastumäki even more dangerous than I previously thought – even in light of Osmala's insinuations.

'I should be getting on with my morning chores,' I say. 'Cleaning, maintenance...'

'What have you decided?' asks Lastumäki.

'About what?' I ask, genuinely at a loss.

'Confessing,' says Salmi. 'Tell us how you killed Häyrinen and where you've hidden Laaksonen.'

Despite everything, from my perspective there are a lot of good aspects to this conversation. I now know significantly more than I did before the pair's visit, and I still have some time on my hands. Both of these can be put firmly in the plus column. However, in the minus column I must put the fact that I am alone on a dark morning with two belligerent young men, and that not only are these young men police officers, they are also operating – at least in part (and, for now, to an unknown degree) – out of a motivation that does not exist within a purely legal framework. And though at present I can't say exactly what that motivation is, it is easy to calculate, and it clearly intersects with the interests of all the other protagonists in the tangled web that is the world of adventure-park intrigue. Quite how they are related, I don't know yet. But this is not my primary concern. My first task is to survive this early-morning encounter without the chewing-gum breath on my face suddenly turning into a truncheon, an arrest or something even worse. I have to calm them down.

'I often think of Leibniz,' I say. 'I've found that many of his thoughts and methods can be useful in overcoming the everyday problems we encounter, both the practical and the theoretical.'

'Does this Leipzig guy work here?' asks Salmi. 'Or in the adventure-park business?'

'Is this the bit where you confess?' asks Lastumäki.

'Leibniz,' I correct Salmi, 'is not my employee or even a colleague. If he were, it would represent quite the feat of time travel and a significant hierarchical challenge for me personally; I find it hard to imagine that the Komodo Locomotive, the Strawberry Maze or even the Moose Chute could satisfy a man of his intellectual calibre. But that's beside the point. The point is that Leibniz presented the so-called principle of sufficient reason, which I believe is a very apt way of approaching the current situation too.'

Salmi and Lastumäki are quiet. This is probably a positive development, so I continue.

'The principle of sufficient reason,' I begin, 'holds that whatever happens, happens for a reason. In other words, no state of circumstances or claim can be true unless there is sufficient reason why it cannot be otherwise. An alternative formulation might be that for every entity X, assuming that X exists, there must be a sufficient reason *why* the entity X exists.'

'Right, so X is the killer?' Lastumäki asks, so quickly that I'm certain he hasn't had time to think about Leibniz or his principles.

Salmi turns to Lastumäki.

Lastumäki swallows; his Adam's apple doesn't look like an apple at all; it is like a large, knobbly potato being turned around in a cramped space. But his moment of hesitation is only fleeting.

The youngster policemen's faces return to their default setting, now every bit as intimidating as before. That being said, my words seem to have achieved their most important objective: the pair have retreated from me, considerably. I can no longer smell their chewing gum or morning breath.

Both look at me.

'What I'm trying to do,' I begin, making sure to speak calmly and clearly, 'is to draw everyone's attention to the fundamental principles of what we're dealing with. We can look at the principle of sufficient reason such that, for every event X – and, I stress, we could use any other letter of the alphabet – assuming that X actually takes place, there must be sufficient reason why X takes place. Examining things from this angle, as Leibniz demonstrated, might help us get back to basics, to the common denominators, in other words, the things that have led us to assume—'

'Now listen, smartarse,' Salmi interrupts me, now with that familiar threatening tone again. He gives a frustrated sigh. 'We know all this. You're the man, you're a whizz with numbers, adding and subtracting and all that bollocks. Whoopy-fucking-do. But it won't get you much further.'

'This will all be over very soon,' adds Lastumäki.

'The next time we come for a visit,' Salmi continues, 'we're done with the small talk. In fact, we won't be talking at all. You'll be doing the talking when you 'fess up.'

Lastumäki visibly hesitates, then adds: 'And nobody gives a shit about X.'

The pair stand there a moment longer, then, almost in

exaggerated slow motion, they take a few steps back, keeping their eyes fixed on me as they go, before turning and walking towards the doors, their eiderdown jackets rustling in rhythm. At the still-closed sliding doors they pause and exchange slightly confused glances before I press the button on the wall, the doors slide open in front of them and glide shut behind them.

11

I have to hurry. There is little doubt about the matter now.

I walk from the foyer to my office, sit down at my desk and switch on my computer. I begin to compose a message I have been planning even before Salmi and Lastumäki's visit. But then, sixteen minutes later, I interrupt my typing, take a few steps towards the window and look outside. It isn't light yet. This is the darkest time of year, and right now it really feels like it too. The car park is empty, and the skids and swirls left in the snow by the hip-hop policemen's BMW – it seems they are incapable of leaving out the spins, even in the current circumstances – are like giant, ancient marks on the ground that future generations will interpret as best they can.

In truth, I don't know Osmala very well, we're certainly not close, but I can almost hear his voice as he approaches me through the message I am writing to him. Interesting... he would say and allow his sentence to trail off. Then his tiny patent-leather shoes would creak and squeak across the floor, and the room would be silent again, and the matter of arresting Niko Kotka would be no closer than it is right now. Because even if everything I have said is, in its own way, logical and seamless, it also relies heavily on probabilities and larger computational assumptions. This is no coincidence: one of my problems, one of many, is naturally that I can't reveal everything I know.

Yes, quite, an ice scraper, a dildo and a headless snowmobile enthusiast. Obviously, there's a perfectly sensible explanation for all this...

No.

I look at the car park a moment longer, then return my attention to my email.

I'm still trying to hone my observations, to clarify everything I can, but after seven minutes I give up. It is abundantly clear what I have to do – what I am forced to do, under considerable duress: I must take a circuitous, perhaps even serpentine route, in order finally to encircle Niko Kotka. Obviously, I will need something more targeted, more focused, something decidedly more concrete than the conclusions I have already reached. I don't take any pleasure in thinking like this: I will need to take a step or two backwards. As much as I don't like the thought, it is unavoidable, and time is running out. I have to return to Niko Kotka, and this time I'll have to get closer to him than ever before.

But – and this is something I haven't observed before – this doesn't necessarily require Niko Kotka himself.

_⋅❧_

On a cold Wednesday morning in January, the district of Vattuniemi, situated on a small peninsula on the island of Lauttasaari is quiet and suitably deserted – at least, that is, the western edge of the peninsula and the residential streets furthest to the south. I leave the car further off by the side of the road and walk the rest of the way.

The wind whips in across the sea, the bare trees and the frozen sea providing no protection from the gusts, and the chill quickly finds its way under my jacket and trouser legs. The sun has risen in the east, but it is stuck behind the clouds, like a lamp behind a badly angled lampshade; it gives a little light, but the subconscious need to adjust it is ever-present. I hear my own footsteps, somewhere in the distance is the sound of a snow plough that must have passed along here only a short while ago: it is easy to walk on the pavement, the verges along the street are lined with fresh, white embankments of snow. This stretch of the pavement will be the only unproblematic part of my morning activities.

I readjust the position of my scarf, pull my hat tighter over my head.

I don't especially like having to improvise this much. Spontaneity increases risk, and in many areas of life it multiplies risk many times over. There are good reasons why insurance companies' business practices are not reactive or whimsical. The best results come about by changing your behaviour as little as possible; if you change variables, you should only do it when the chance of success is around one hundred percent. After all, I am still an actuary – recent events notwithstanding. I like one-hundred-percent certainty, but I do not like...

I realise I am becoming agitated, and I know the reason why. The terraced house comes into view up ahead; it seems to flicker between the row of black tree trunks standing in front of it. The house itself isn't moving; I am. The terrace is the last on that stretch of the street, the house nearest the sea, and though there is a pathway running between the house and the shore, I don't expect it to be very busy on this frozen, windswept morning. I approach the house from the east, and, if necessary, I am prepared to change direction and speed. But I can't see anyone else out and about, and there isn't any movement around the house, so I cross the road, and glance up at the front of the house. Niko Kotka's SUV is parked outside; there are no other cars in sight. My quick assessment of the situation is that the other residents of Vattuniemi must have already left for work, whereas Niko Kotka has decided to have a lie-in.

This is not the optimal outcome. I continue on my way, only stopping once I have reached the protection of the terrace's gable wall. There are no windows at this end of the building, so it will be impossible to see my arrival from inside the house, even if someone happened to look out of the front windows.

It is perfectly plausible that we are standing (though, as I recall only too vividly, Niko Kotka might be doing all manner of other things) a mere fifteen metres from each other, I in the freezing cold and he in the comfort of his central heating.

My original plan was based on the assumption that Niko Kotka would already have left the house, gone off to wherever he was planning to break the law today, to indulge his predilections and above all to frustrate and complicate the lives and businesses of upstanding adventure-park entrepreneurs. I am annoyed at this turn of events and consider walking back to my car and waiting. I turn, take four or five steps, then stop.

I see Niko Kotka's SUV from a slightly different angle, and I notice an important discrepancy: a missing reflection. Either the window on the passenger's side is broken or it has been rolled down. This seems a perplexing decision. Who decides to air their car at minus twenty? Who leaves their window permanently open in January, no matter how hot and stuffy the air inside? There must be some other explanation.

I look around but still can't see anyone else. The clanking of the snow plough has faded, and now it is so far away that it will soon be completely out of earshot. Then there's nothing but the wind.

Spontaneity increases risk, yes. But I reach an almost instant decision – after reviewing the known facts, of course, and reminding myself that time is running out. I walk along the path, towards the other end of the terrace, examining Niko Kotka's house and garden as I pass. The car window has been rolled down, not broken. At least, there are no shards of glass on the snow or in the footwell. I have almost walked right past the car when I have my second spontaneous thought in a very short space of time. At this, I recall Laura Helanto's words: *go with the flow*.

I turn, take a few steps towards the car, and when I reach it, I try the door. It is unlocked. At first glance, the car looks almost empty, until I notice a brown paper bag in the footwell on the passenger's side. I crouch down and peer inside the bag: an untouched, gourmet burger meal plus a multivitamin drink. I pull out of the car, press the door shut and return to the protection of the gable wall. Something has happened, that much is easily deduced.

I'm not normally keen on using my imagination, but in this particular instance I realise I am prepared to make a number of assumptions. (The fact that I am conducting a murder investigation in a thin pair of trousers in minus twenty probably has something to do with speeding up my thoughts.)

So:

On his way back from a trip to the countryside, the hungry Niko Kotka parks his car in front of his house and winds down the passenger window. It is tempting to imagine that someone might have knocked on that window, that Kotka recognised the knocker and struck up a conversation. After this, something happened that meant that Kotka left his food in the car and exited the SUV without locking it. This last assumption is based on the evidence of an unplanned and probably swift departure from the car. Perhaps the window knocker threatened him in some way? And because Niko Kotka must have left his car, there are two possible follow-up scenarios: either the two people went into Niko Kotka's residence and are still there, or they have already left Vattuniemi. If the former scenario is true, the implication is that Niko Kotka has lost his appetite and didn't even feel it necessary to close his car window, despite the weather

– neither of which bodes well for his general wellbeing. If, however, the latter scenario is closer to the truth, this means that Niko Kotka's apartment is empty, as I'd hoped...

Which in turn...

And here we see one of the central problems of letting the imagination run riot: it is endless – constantly expanding, like the universe itself, and instead of providing answers, it keeps asking more questions, for as long as we give it the opportunity. Compared to rational thinking, it's the equivalent of racing around on a powerful motorbike without a helmet: everything will end horribly, it's just a question of when.

But the frost is beginning to bite, and so are the realities in front of me, and my imagined scenarios are starting to assume practical dimensions. Above all, this is about motivation and the nature of that motivation. The fact of the matter is that I have already taken considerable risks without making any progress with my original plan or getting any closer to achieving my goals. And ultimately, one more little risk won't meaningfully add to the overall risk.

And so, I find myself looking at the tall wooden fence at the back of the property and quickly make up my mind. I look around; there is nobody in sight. Then I begin wading through the snow. I arrive at the fence, look around once more, climb over the fence, and with that I am in Niko Kotka's back garden. I can honestly say I didn't have any of this in mind when I decided to become an actuary.

The back garden is approximately forty-five square metres in size, and it is completed fenced off. This provides me with some amount of cover as I trudge through the snow to the back door and suddenly stop.

I am not the only person who has trudged this way.

Someone has walked from the back door towards the

shoreline – not via the path I have just come from – and must have climbed over the fence to get out, because the footprints in the snow lead only in one direction. When I combine this observation with the uneaten takeaway and the unlocked car, it's becoming harder to imagine that these footprints belong to Niko Kotka. Of course, it is vaguely possible that due to the cumulative shock of the day's other events – much as I try, I cannot forget the sound of all that whinnying – Kotka lost possession of his faculties, ran famished through the house and continued out towards the shore and from there to goodness knows where. But this is an unlikely scenario.

Esa has lent me a small toolkit, which makes it easier for me to gain access to the property. But it seems there is no need for the contents of this kit. The matter is resolved much more easily: I try the handle, it turns, and I pull the door open. That's it, and straight away I am faced with another decision: should I turn around and leave or should I do my utmost to find evidence linking Niko Kotka to the murder of Ville-Pekka Häyrinen? Ultimately, the latter feels more pressing. I open the door almost fully and listen. A crow squawks by the shore, but it seems to be talking to itself, so I step inside.

The aesthetic in the downstairs room is a curious fusion of bachelor pad and a substantial income: a log burner, black leather, an enormous television, speakers, a tiger-skin rug. The most interesting feature from my perspective is a low but wide TV unit with a set of drawers. But before I can start going through the drawers or anything else in the house, I have to make sure I can do so without any surprises. And that means making sure there is nobody else in the house. I take a few steps across the room, as silently and as cautiously as I can. I arrive in the hallway, see a set of stairs leading up to the left. Once I have ascertained that everything is silent, I begin walking upstairs.

The staircase is a sturdy steel frame and doesn't make a sound. From the landing at the top of the stairs, I can see the violet-walled living room in its entirety, the majority of the two bedrooms, and half of a kitchen kitted out with black units. Everything I see represents the same aesthetic choices as downstairs. The one thing I cannot see, however, is Niko Kotka himself. I walk around the upper floor just to be certain, but now it is clear: I am alone. This means I can get to work.

I decide to start in one of the bedrooms. I am already at the bedroom door when I realise I have walked past another, closed door. I stop. My heart skips a beat. Of course, I am an amateur when it comes to this, I think to myself, but this is one of the most basic mistakes I could have made. The door must lead into a bathroom, and at first I don't know how I could have missed it. Then I understand. There are certain sounds one generally associates with bathrooms: water running in one form or another, the sound of teeth-brushing, showering, scrubbing various anatomical nooks and crannies, patting and towelling. A silent bathroom is an empty bathroom. This must have been my automatic assumption. I press my ear almost tight against the door and listen. For a long time. Nothing. My heart begins to settle again. I take a deep breath, another, and another. A false alarm, I think and take a few steps back. In future, I really must...

The door doesn't just open, it flies open – and Niko Kotka is standing right in front of me. And almost right up against me. He wraps his arms around me before I can stop him, and with that we are glued to each other, as though we are dancing a very slow song together. We are moving, but I quickly realise that Niko Kotka isn't trying to push me over or crush me; he is clinging on to me for support, and I am doing the same. By the time I am able to think straight, to process what I see, I understand why. Right in the middle of his forehead is a steel peg, protruding from his skull like a unicorn's horn. As I look at it more closely and inspect the shape and form of the peg, I assume it must have been taken from the bathroom furnishings and thrust into his forehead, rendering him essentially braindead though still – miraculously – able to function. And now, here we are, dancing together on the silent landing. Niko Kotka is leading. He tightens his grip, comes a little closer. His eyes are right in front of me; they're wide open but not looking anywhere in particular. He is breathing heavily, as though he were engaged in strenuous sports activity or simply very happy at our proximity. I try to extricate myself, but his embrace becomes all the more bearlike. Eventually, he squeezes me so strongly I can feel it in my ribs. He presses his nose tight up against me and opens his mouth wider than at any point in our dance thus far – and sighs.

It is a long sigh, and when it finally ends Niko Kotka slumps into my arms, leaving me to carry him. And just when I think this day cannot possibly contain anything more unpleasant, or more surprising, the doorbell rings.

It rings once, twice.

Then the doorbell ringer holds a finger down on the buzzer and does not release it.

I don't know what else I can possibly do but lower Niko Kotka to the floor, walk back downstairs, leave via the back garden using the same footsteps that someone left before I arrived, then climb over the fence and sprint towards the shore.

Niko Kotka has been murdered.

Niko Kotka cannot be the murderer.

12

Over the next few days, I avoid everybody and everything. This really ought to be impossible, especially in my new role within our family unit. But this is what happens, and I begin to understand what people mean when they say someone has 'mentally checked out'. I take part in our day-to-day chores, take care of the home and engage in conversations, but I find it virtually impossible to give them my full concentration, meaning that I'm never quite sure what we're talking about.

I understand only too well that this wouldn't be possible in any other situation but right here and right now. Laura is so immersed in her own project and is working such long days, getting home so late and so exhausted, that she simply doesn't have the energy to pay me any extra attention. And if we sit quietly at breakfast or supper, Tuuli always fills the silence with her own unflagging ingenuity and almost without exception shifts the conversation to something far removed from our dining table. At these times, I don't even mind that the conversation is rambling, even by conservative estimates, and that I am, again almost without exception, the listening party – and even then, only a half-hearted one.

I lie awake at night.

Or if I do sleep, I have short but all the more intense nightmares where headless men are chasing me across endless snow-covered fields, or where playboys with metal pegs stuck in their foreheads are dancing with me and won't let me go, or where I look at myself in the mirror and see that my face is bright blue. When I wake up, my heart is thumping in my chest and

I'm clenching the duvet so tightly my fingers are sore.

It's much easier to avoid people at the adventure park.

I make it clear to everybody that our timetables have changed and that due to a *force majeure* (which, for reasons of trade secrets, I cannot talk about in any greater depth) my previous promise of turning things around in three days is now impossible to pull off. I brace myself for a wave of objection – but, to my great surprise, there is none, which puzzles me for a moment, and for the most part my employees leave me in peace. Right now, that feels like the best possible solution all round. I don't know how I would answer their questions, were they about individual tasks, our acute financial predicament or, in a broader sense, our future, which still looks as bleak as everything else. Particularly because what I hear from Somersault City doesn't suggest that the departure of Niko Kotka has caused any significant problems for their activities. On the contrary: their customer numbers are growing even larger, and the park is attracting people from across the country. This is in stark contrast to YouMeFun, which can't even seem to attract customers in double figures. (It is hard to imagine a more dejected, abandoned landscape than an empty adventure park, its thirteen slides entertaining but one customer who, upon reaching the bottom, gawps around as though she's been dropped into the lifeless vacuum of outer space.) And therefore, for these very reasons, I spend a lot of time by myself without talking to anyone or anyone talking to me.

And all the while I realise that this cannot go on.

But until then...

🐾

I am sitting in my office, in the quiet hum of the north-east wing

of YouMeFun as the late afternoon darkens around me and the
whole world, when a text message from Laura Helanto wakes
me from my thoughts:

It would be great if you could pop in.
Excited to hear what you think. 😃

I stare at the message for a moment, then put my phone back
on the table without answering. Right now, even the most basic
communication feels overwhelming, let alone the idea of
formulating a remotely coherent overview of recent events and
planning my next moves. It all seems impossible, no matter how
I place the pieces of the jigsaw.

And as for my thoughts that Laura Helanto really wants to
hear?

At this moment in time, they're not even thoughts. They are
erratic, panicked calculations that always lead to the same dead
end and that right now seem as pointless as ... everything else.
My theory, which was supposed to prove my innocence and help
me save my adventure park, has proved useless. And there is no
alternative theory. Which means that my thoughts always return
to where they started and ... I find myself in the same dead end
as a moment ago.

And yet, it's easy to see what will happen next.

Salmi and Lastumäki will arrest me for murder, YouMeFun
will go bust. Johanna, Esa, Kristian, Samppa and Minttu K will
lose their jobs, Somersault City will become the one and only
adventure park in the capital, and by default the market leader.
Of course, these things might happen in a slightly different
order, but they all lead to one and the same place: the end.

And this is it.

This really is the end.

And I must take responsibility for it.

The thought doesn't offer me any relief, let alone the satisfaction of finding a solution, but, I think, at least it is logical. I sigh, pick up my phone and tell Laura I will see her in Otaniemi in half an hour. Obviously, I can't tell her that I might not get there at all, as I find myself in a situation from which not even mathematics can save me. From which mathematics was supposed to save me, but didn't. That makes me no more than a murderer and a failed entrepreneur who wheedled his way into her home.

I'm not in the best frame of mind. Having said that, I don't even know what frame of mind I ought to be in. I've never believed in what people call 'positive thinking', not even when I wasn't an adventure-park owner. Now it feels even more impossible than before. I don't believe a threat can become an opportunity just because you call it one; that can only happen if the prevailing circumstances change. Now the circumstances remain unchanged, no matter how much I whisper in a soft and suspiciously intimate voice, like my former boss Perttilä, that inside each and every one of us there is a sleeping bear, a fearless creature that will come out if only we can find it, and that this will happen if we growl and howl together. I remember how hard I found growling back then, though it was compulsory and all the other employees at the risk-management department of our insurance company spent an entire afternoon growling at one another. I didn't turn into a bear that day, and I'm not going to turn into one now either.

I am an actuary.

An actuary whose own calculations have betrayed him. And as such, an actuary who has betrayed everybody else too.

It's time they heard the truth.

I begin with my employees. I ask them to gather at the Curly Cake Café. Naturally, the café is empty. Johanna has already switched off some of the lights, though where we are sitting the lights are still on as we wait for Esa, who is uncharacteristically late. Samppa is sitting furthest from me, either flicking his long hair from side to side as if trying to find the most favourable position for it without ever finding one, or leaning forwards, a hand on his forehead, staring into the distance like a mild-mannered national poet lost in thought – until he starts fiddling with his hair again. Kristian is eating a tub of protein-rich vanilla quark, and he seems to be doing this with meticulous concentration, so much so that I wonder whether he's doing so on purpose. Minttu K is sitting nearest to me, drinking coffee laced with some kind of potent liquor – the smell is like a cross between two-day-old Nescafé and a flamethrower's torch – from a mug that must hold at least a litre, and puffing away at a filterless French cigarette in a space that is technically non-smoking. Johanna is doing nothing. Except staring at me. She has been looking at me for a long time now but still hasn't said a word. I've never been able to read her facial expressions, and I hazard that the reason for this is that she just doesn't have any.

I can neither see nor feel in the room the kind of heavy sullenness I am carrying around inside me. I realise this is because my staff don't know what I know – they don't know that I'm about to tell them I have failed and that it's all over. Instead, there is just a peculiar atmosphere – which I put down to everything we have been through together, everything we're still going through.

'Raspberry Ripper?' asks Johanna out of the blue.

'Excuse me?'

'Do you want one? There's some left.'

'No, thank you.'

'Pink Panda?'

'No, thank you.'

'Zebra Banoffee?'

'No. Thank you.'

'Hedgehog éclair?'

Just as I think we really might be about to go through a list of everything Johanna hasn't managed to sell today and all her frozen delights, Esa arrives.

'Apologies for being late, sir,' he says as he sits down sombrely at the table. 'Setting up the tripwires took longer than anticipated.'

I don't know what Esa is talking about, but right now I don't want to get into a discussion about it. I intend to get straight to the point.

'Thank you for coming here at such short notice,' I begin, and look at each of them in turn. 'And thank you for stoically carrying on with your work and maintaining our excellent standards just as before, though our situation has been rather difficult for some time now.'

Everyone is silent; nobody says anything. The only sound is Kristian scooping the quark onto his spoon, Minttu K taking another gulp of jet-fuel coffee, and an ominous, low-pitched rumble emanating from some part of Esa's tract.

'As I have explained before,' I continue, 'I was unable to find a solution within the timeframe I promised. It is now clear that finding such a solution may prove—'

Esa loudly clears his throat, but he doesn't look at me or say anything, so I continue.

'Yes, as I said, I've done my utmost, but I cannot expect your patience anymore, or anything else for that—'

Again, Esa clears his throat. He is still staring right ahead. It seems that something about the atmosphere in the café has changed. Now it feels like we're waiting for a thunderstorm. Minttu K interrupts my train of thought.

'Honey, you don't need to say anything,' she says.

'The fuse is lit,' says Esa, and now he looks at me.

'What does that mean?' I ask.

'It means we couldn't just leave you here, alone,' says Kristian.

I don't know how many thoughts are racing through my mind at once, but it's not an inconsiderable number.

'What is this about?'

My five employees are silent.

'Look, honey,' says Minttu K eventually. 'After all that palaver between you and your brother, we all signed new contracts with new T's and C's. We all wanted to wipe the slate clean, start afresh and yadda, yadda. And we did this at your suggestion. Remember?'

'I remember very well,' I admit. 'And there was a good reason why—'

'So, now we have the right,' Minttu K continues once she has sucked enough smoke into her lungs, 'if we decide to use it, that is, and all five of us agree on it,' – she points at each of them in turn with her French cigarette – 'to make decisions for the good of the park.'

'Correct,' I say, still trying to recover from the direction the conversation has suddenly taken. 'This clause was added to your contracts in case the park's leadership were to change unexpectedly, for one reason or another, and the new ownership were to prove detrimental or outright hostile to the park's interests. In such a situation you would have the right to take action to protect both the park and your jobs.'

By this, I mean the precautions and safety measures I took because of Juhani: if they wanted, my trusted employees Johanna, Esa, Samppa, Kristian and Minttu K could object to him and his profligate lifestyle or any other madcap ideas of his. But I don't see what this has to do with what I'm telling them. It must be a misunderstanding. I decide to be more direct to avoid any further digressions. I intend to say – emphatically and unequivocally – that this is the end. The real end. No remainders, no rounding up, not a single decimal point. We have reached absolute zero.

'This is my confession,' I begin. 'I have done my best—'

'We know that,' says Esa, 'and we want to do our part. We want to give more than just back-up. We're going to widen our front, undertake a number of tactical manoeuvres.'

I am genuinely, whole-heartedly perplexed. Esa's interruption has jumbled my thoughts once and for all.

'Fox Tart?' asks Johanna.

'What?' I say, again trying to pull my head back above the surface. 'No, thank you. What exactly are these tactical manoeuvres?'

'We've taken out a loan,' Esa explains. 'In our own names. For the good of the park. To strengthen the balance sheet, shore up the fortress.'

'So we can get through this,' says Johanna. 'And now we will.'

'And there's more,' says Minttu K, blowing smoke from the corner of her mouth. 'That money has already been transferred into the park's accounts; it's already being used for acquisitions. It's enough money to buy a couple of new attractions or something. We'll do some proper ad campaigns. And above all, we'll show Somersault City who's boss.'

'You have…?' I begin, and feel myself sinking beneath the surface again.

'Yes,' says Esa. 'You might say we've gone all in. It reminds me of Normandy.'

I look at them all. Only then do I realise that Samppa hasn't said anything. He seems to notice this himself too. Could he yet prove a voice of reason...?

'Problem, solution, love,' he says. 'On a meta level. Maybe a workshop where we can explore our feelings and come closer to what...'

I want to make sure I've understood correctly, so I ask: 'You mean to say you have taken out a loan ... at your own risk ... all for the good of the park?'

They all either say yes or give a decisive nod. I think of their homes, their belongings – which they are about to lose. Inevitably, inexorably.

'And you all understand that—'

'We know you'll do everything in your power,' says Johanna. 'Like you always do. There isn't the slightest doubt that we'll get through this. Together. Under your leadership.'

13

I leave the Renault parked behind the adventure park, then take first the bus to the train station, then the train to the Central Railway Station, then the escalator down into the metro and continue all the way to Otaniemi. I'm not exactly lost for thoughts on the journey.

The knowledge that my employees are counting on me, that they trust me with all their worldly assets, doesn't do much to calm my mind. On the contrary, it feels as though the combined weight of their apartments has been placed on my shoulders, as though I were both carrying it and dragging it behind me, inhabitants and all. And here I am, as darkness falls on the January chill, the man because of whom they will now lose everything. My steps feel heavier than ever before, as though the snow were crunching and crackling louder, drier, more ominously than ever.

Built only a few years ago and with glass walls, the office block is easy to find, and the same goes for the entrance. I come to a stop in front of it. I can see the foyer and Laura Helanto inside. She is working, giving it her full concentration. Just seeing her makes me feel both better and worse. Better for the simple reason that she is Laura and therefore my everything; worse because I am losing her. I'm losing many other things too, but above all I'm losing her. The feeling wells up inside me, settles somewhere deep inside my chest and radiates throughout my body, chilling me many times more than the air around me.

Laura is painting with a narrow, long-handled roller, which she is wielding almost like a paintbrush, skilfully and with the utmost determination. The result is a series of streaks in brilliant okra, and the more streaks that appear, the more they start to form regular patterns. Though everything looks improvised, as though Laura had decided to daub okra paint across the wall at random with a three-metre roller, I know this isn't the case. I've seen dozens of sketches. But the difference between the sketches and the final result is like night and day. Now everything looks a thousand times more vivid, more impressive, in all respects more alive.

The wall that she is now painting is part of a larger work that will fill the whole foyer with its joy and power. It isn't finished yet, but right away I know that I could spend hours staring at it, as I have Laura's other works. And this time I don't seem to be suffering from the need to try and explain everything or to understand why Laura's works, as it were, carry me away, why they continue to open up to me long after I've finished looking at them. Quite the contrary; I enjoy the fact that I forget about everything else. And at this point I sense, though I didn't think it possible, that I like this work even more than I liked the murals at the adventure park, which I can safely say changed my life.

For a moment, I don't even notice the biting-cold wind.

Then Laura's roller stops, she looks like she is considering something, and, as though she knows she is being watched, she turns a little, releases a hand from the long handle of the roller and gives an excited wave, inviting me inside. At that moment, I snap back to reality, to the frozen day that has lost its sheen, to today's events and, of course, to my manifold problems. I open the door and step into the foyer.

Laura Helanto smiles as I walk towards her. She is wearing a pair of dungarees and a sweatshirt, both so dappled with paint that you really have to look for their original colour. The roller handle stands next to her like a vaulter's pole, and she looks like someone who has been concentrating hard for hours, as though she too has snapped back from somewhere else.

'Great that you could come,' she says, once we have exchanged gentle kisses which, I realise today more clearly and more painfully, still don't come very naturally to me despite our continual practice. I notice that the smile quickly disappears from her face too. 'And so soon. I wanted to ... I mean, I want to hear you say it.'

This is it, I think. Word has got back to Laura, I don't know how or when, and now we are about to have a conversation that I know isn't going to end well for me. The words don't come out very easily, but I say I am ready, and Laura takes me by the hand.

'Let's walk a little, take your time, look around in peace,' she says, then lets go of my hand.

At first, I don't understand what we're doing, then I realise that this is ultimately a very simple procedure. We are to wander around the foyer and, as Laura put it, I should take my time, look around in peace. The latter might cause me some difficulties, though hopefully only internal ones.

'Do you see what I see?' she asks before we even reach the end of the first wall.

I quickly realise four things: how I enjoy looking at the work, how it seems to increase in power the longer I look at it and examine it, how inexhaustible it is, and how, to my great surprise, of the two of us Laura Helanto is the one who seems more burdened. Though I don't think it likely that she's been dancing with the living dead like me, wading through snowdrifts to escape murderers, felt her theories come crashing down and become responsible for five people's futures, she is still the one of us whose worries look greater. And as a result of this, in the literal blink of an eye, my own worries seem smaller after all, somehow less significant. We avoid a group of young IT consultants darting through the foyer, and I wait until they have all got into the lift. And with that, I make one final observation, one that now feels the most important of all.

'I think you have excelled yourself,' I say. Honestly. 'Everything I see here is, frankly, extraordinary.'

This is true. And I tell her that what I see and what I expect to see later, once the work is complete, will surpass even the murals at the adventure park.

'Maybe wait until you've seen the finished piece?' she suggests, as if she hasn't properly heard what I said. 'Once it's ready?'

Laura Helanto sounds more uncertain of herself than I've ever heard her. It takes me a little by surprise, but I say nothing. We walk all the way around the space, and gradually I find it easier to forget everything and concentrate on what I see. I let the work carry me away; the shapes, the surprises, the colours. The boundless ingenuity.

We are back where we started, but I could easily walk the whole route again. I say this and tell her the work has exceeded all my expectations. Laura Helanto looks at me, then glances around.

'But don't you get the feeling this is … somehow … bad?'

I look at her, and I see that she is actually quite tired; in fact, she's utterly exhausted. She avoids eye contact. And she could not be more wrong.

'This is magnificent,' I say. 'It is breath-taking. Fascinating and endlessly interesting.'

For a moment, she remains silent.

'Really?'

'Really.'

'Then why do I have the feeling this is going to turn out to be rubbish, a complete failure?' she asks quietly, as I look around.

The patterns take shape, repeat, split apart, then they are reborn, constantly forming new connections. Laura's work is alive. I don't understand how she can even contemplate the possibility that it won't be a success.

Then – while still allowing the work to impact me on its own terms, not mine – something happens. It flows straight out of the work and into me, and vice versa. As a feeling, it's something between a river and an electrical current; it's certainly immaterial, but it exists all the same, this ... invisible exchange. And with this, all of a sudden, I understand her troubles. And not only hers.

I understand my own too.

At the same time, I realise this has happened to me once before, and that too was caused by...

Laura's work.

The shift in my thought process feels almost physical, like a large object turning and finally slotting into place, as though the dark side of a pyramid is finally brought into the light. The change is everything a change can be: gradual, incremental, then final and earth-shattering.

The patterns are perfect; they perfect one another.

The colours glow; the entire foyer glows.

'The fact of the matter is...' I begin, trying to find the most suitable words, the most precise expression of my thoughts, which are now soaring at the speed of light. And while I am confused at my previous blindness, I understand that this must be closely related to what Laura Helanto is currently experiencing. Once again art – and, again, it is Laura's art – has opened my eyes. And I understand what has gone wrong – for both of us.

'Linear regression,' I say, and continue examining the work.

'What?' she asks.

'No vector is entirely straight,' I begin. 'It might look straight, even when we examine it closely, but its straightness is only ever approximate. But that's a side issue. Most important is our tendency to adapt linear regression to almost everything, and sometimes, as I believe is happening to both of us right now, we apply it to things to which it cannot be applied.'

'Really?'

'Oh yes,' I reply quickly. 'Linear regression is a very useful way of perceiving things when we have to combine different data sets and understand which variables affect what and in what ways. And this is precisely the approach we should take to assess the correlation between the use of yellow paint and the resulting remuneration.'

Laura says nothing. I take this as a good sign: she may very well see the matter the same way I do.

'But what if the phenomenon being modelled isn't linear?' I continue. 'Then we might end up assuming, for instance, that a rocket will continuously rise along a given trajectory. After all, we've already carefully calculated this with regard to the combined factors of speed, time and perspective. But a rocket or, more specifically, the rocket's trajectory is a phenomenon that doesn't fit this type of assessment. As we know, sooner or later, the rocket will fall to the ground.'

'I'm not sure I...' Laura Helanto begins.

I nod.

'Exactly,' I say. 'Few things have the propensity to lead us so astray as linear extrapolation.'

We stand next to each other in silence. I realise I've been speaking rather passionately. Yet, I must continue a little more.

'I assume your eyes have fixated on the spots you're not happy with,' I say, 'and you've combined them in a way that is quite logical, perhaps even compared them to your sketches and other works that have inspired you. You might even have placed this entity in the context of other similar entities and tried to position it among them. But though the parameters of this examination are essentially correct, the result – or, in this case, the positioning – is flawed, as the phenomenon behind the parameters doesn't abide by the principle of linearity.'

I pause briefly, then try to make sure there is sufficient weight behind my words:

'Furthermore, this isn't a case of omitted-variable bias, I'm quite sure of it.'

I look Laura in the eyes.

'The fact is, this is going to be far from rubbish. This is going to be your best work so far. Right now, the only thing that matters is that you keep working and get this finished. It's going to be your masterpiece.'

The IT youngsters now hurrying past us are different from the previous group, though they look almost identical.

'So, what you're saying is, it won't be rubbish,' says Laura once we are alone in the foyer again. 'It's going to be a full-blown catastrophe, right?'

'As I've said,' I reply with a shake of the head, 'the correlation is completely different, and once we dismiss any random variables, we—'

'Henri,' she interrupts me. She also smiles for the first time since my arrival. 'That was supposed to lighten the mood. Thank you for your kind words.'

Laura steps closer to me, presses her body against me.

'I love your stories,' she says.

I am about to say what I've said isn't a story in the strictest sense, but my thoughts on mathematical principles that help us make sense of life and our actions. They are the foundation upon which all sensible and successful ventures are predicated and have been since time immemorial. And that though I doubted this for a moment, that doesn't change the facts. Mathematics has always saved me, and it will save me in the future too. This is both a matter of faith and knowledge. But there is no time or opportunity to voice these thoughts right now. Laura kisses me gently on the lips.

'I don't know,' she says eventually. 'I had a sneaking suspicion you would sort this out for me.'

This is a flattering claim, of course, but it is wrong all the same. I tell her this.

'No, your work did it,' I tell her, honestly. 'It has that kind of effect.'

Laura smiles. There is something a little moist in her eyes, something that highlights their grey-green, making them gleam like jewels.

'Nobody has ever talked to me the way you do,' she says.

'Maybe that's because I'm your first actuary.'

Laura smiles, shakes her head.

'No,' she says. 'I can assure you, it's not because of that.'

I don't fully understand what she means with these words, this tone of voice, but right now that's largely irrelevant. Her lips approach my own. Something happens, something in me too.

'I think,' she begins, 'we're a pretty good couple.'

'I think so too,' I say, and the following words I mean more emphatically than I've ever meant anything: 'Both quantitively and qualitatively.'

That night, after we have completed each other the way adults can do, I sleep like a log.

My dreams are logical and sensible.

I am an actuary once again.

14

Very well, I think, at seven-thirty the following morning as I make Tuuli her breakfast: my problems might be larger than before and their solutions might require more resources, but at least I can start solving these problems with, as they say, a clear slate, free of my previous theories.

As I hand Tuuli the milk so that she can pour it onto her cereal and thus regulate the amount of milk by herself – the border between an acceptable and an unacceptable amount of milk is very precise; even a line drawn in water leaves a bigger margin for error – I consider once again that this realisation might never have come about in different circumstances.

Laura's work has consumed me, wiped away my deep-seated ideas. And not just my theories, but the calculations that sustained them, calculations that for some reason I had been clinging on to, searching for the root cause of my failures there among the details and decimals. Perhaps most decisive was letting go of the final elements of an unworkable theory.

I finish making my own cheese-and-tomato sandwich, take my steaming mug of tea from the kitchen counter and sit down opposite Tuuli at the table.

At this point, I think I can conclude that though I don't necessarily understand art, it seems to understand me. It gave me a moment's respite, a moment somewhere else, in order that I might understand something important, something I can use to carry on. And though saving a desperate actuary-cum-adventure-park-owner from his own theories isn't quite the point of art, it seems to help, at least.

It would be an exaggeration to say I already have new theories or plans – or even in the singular: a new theory or plan. I do not. But the greatest difference to the recent past is that I believe I now have something much better, something at which – and understanding this last night was perhaps the most important thing of all – I didn't particularly excel. Now it feels almost like a superpower, a secret weapon.

I have the capacity to change my mind.

The morning is cold and dark as Tuuli and I set off. I've promised to walk her to school. This isn't because the journey is at all dangerous or because she doesn't know the way, but because of her skis and poles, which I'm carrying. The PE teacher plans to take the children skiing in the nearby woods, and Tuuli is visibly excited.

On the walk, we go through the fundamentals of skiing and talk about how to grease one's skis properly, the principles of speed distribution, we even mention a few notable Olympians. Tuuli seems to know a great deal more about all things skiing-related than I do. Again, I am struck by her ability to shift seamlessly from one topic to the next: a few sentences can touch on two or three different subjects, complete with associated questions, only to give way to new ones a moment later. The overall effect is similar to my encounters with art: it feels as though my brain is constantly in danger of being sprained by unexpected changes of track, which can even occur while going around a metaphorical corner. Still, this is not an unpleasant feeling. In this respect too, family life is very different to how I had imagined it.

In the frozen air, we cover the journey at a brisk pace, and we arrive at school ten minutes before the morning bell. Tuuli takes her skis and poles from my hands and thanks me for my help. I am about to say the pleasure was all mine and that our conversation about skiing was especially fascinating, but she is already on her way. I can't help thinking that her disappearing like a flash might be an inherited trait. I set off towards the Siilitie metro station.

I've been walking for a few minutes when I hear someone call my name. I turn and look behind me, but I can't see anyone. I look to the side and the pavement opposite. Behind the pine trees, their branches weighed down with snow, I catch a glimpse of an egg-yolk-yellow eiderdown jacket whose bearer is walking towards the end of the road and is soon on the same pavement as me. Sami quickly catches up with me.

'Haven't seen you around,' he says. 'All good?'

I look at Sami, his large head and enormous red cheeks, which have now broadened into a smile gently steaming in the cold.

'Everything is fine,' I say.

'Brilliant,' Sami nods. 'And you've replied to Taneli?'

I know what he is referring to. Alongside all my other attempts to avoid people, I have been deliberately avoiding, indeed, taking great pains to avoid *Le Groupe Paris*. And I have taken particular care to stay out of any discussion of the one factor causing the liveliest conversation and, judging by the tenor of that conversation, the greatest enthusiasm: the fast-approaching fête. Everything has happened very quickly: renting the space, dividing responsibilities, advertising on social media. I still don't believe we will sell our wares to anyone but the other mums and dads. But the truth is, this is one more issue I cannot avoid forever.

'I'll reply as soon as—'

'Brilliant,' he says once again, and I realise that the reason for this is not that he thinks my answers exceptionally well formed or that they have made a great impression on him, but that this is merely an expression he uses both as neutral confirmation, as a conjunction and as punctuation. 'Speaking of which, we're all meeting at Tuukka's place for a baking session. As well as making our individual stuff, obviously. The idea is to have a nice evening baking together and see what we can come up with. I'll send you the time, the exact address and the door code.'

'That's—'

'Brilliant, but I've really got to be going,' says Sami, as though I were the one holding him back. 'I've got an exam coming up. Cultural anthropology. I guess it's not as straightforward as your insurance maths. You've always got to wing it a bit.'

Sitting on public transport first to Itäkeskus and from there to YouMeFun, I try to follow Sami's example and ... wing it. I decide not to pay any attention to how little he understands about actuarial mathematics, not to mention the array of situations to which I apply these principles every day, but try instead to emulate his cultural-anthropological approach. Thus, I take care not to resort to solving matters using the methods I have been relying on thus far and instead try to look for new factors, new perspectives. And eventually, as the large, colourful *YOUMEFUN* letters appear along the horizon, I believe I have come up with something. I take my phone from inside my winter jacket, send a message, return my phone to the warm confines of my jacket, head towards my office and wait.

Forty-one minutes later, I have company.

Detective Inspector Pentti Osmala of the Joint Division of the Helsinki Organised-Crime and Fraud Units is dressed in the now familiar attire that he seems to wear all year round: an asphalt-grey blazer, a light-blue shirt, trousers with the trademark baggy knees and a pair of too-small, laced leather brogues. He has the same angular and serious expression as always, the same guarded look in his light-blue eyes. Osmala folds himself into a chair and takes stock of me for a few seconds before speaking.

'I understand the artist's work is coming along nicely,' he says after a pause, seemingly referring to Laura Helanto. 'And that we are in for something quite fascinating.'

'Correct,' I say, and decide not to think about where Osmala has heard this.

He looks at me, I respond in kind. Neither of us appears to be particularly fond of small talk, so without further ado I get straight to the point.

'Last time we met, we spoke about Salmi and Lastumäki,' I begin, 'and you suggested we engage in an informal exchange of information, assuming I've understood correctly.'

'That rather depends on the nature and quality of the information,' says Osmala. 'And whether there is any information in the first place. But in general, I can confirm that your assumption is on the right track.'

Not quite the enthusiasm I was expecting. Not that I was expecting Osmala to leap out of his chair with glee. But still.

'They were here,' I say.

'Under the circumstances, I think that's understandable,' Osmala says with another nod.

'Their business was twofold,' I tell him. 'First, they wanted me to confess to the murder of Ville-Pekka Häyrinen, former CEO of Somersault City.'

'Very well.'

Again, not quite the answer I was expecting.

'Obviously, I did not confess,' I add.

'Of course, you didn't,' he says, 'because you didn't do it.'

We sit in silence for a moment.

'They were pressed for time,' I say eventually. 'They were talking about days.'

Now Osmala looks as though something has lit up inside him. It isn't a big change, only manifesting itself in the way he places his elbows on the arms of the chair, as if to assume a better listening position.

'Did they say anything more specific? Any particular timeframe, perhaps even a deadline of some sort?'

'No, nothing like that. But they must have a timetable in mind – why else would they talk about days?'

For a moment, Osmala is silent.

'They're in a hurry to get a confession out of you,' he says. 'In a hurry to bring the investigation to a close, to shift attention elsewhere...'

'That's what I've been trying to say,' I nod, unable to hide my frustration. 'I was thinking that, at this point, the reciprocity you mentioned might—'

'Horses,' says Osmala.

It takes a few seconds to convince myself I have heard him right. But it doesn't change what he actually said. My first thought is that perhaps Osmala isn't the wise, senior detective I've taken him for all this time, and that until now he's been able to hide this unbalanced side of himself very well indeed. At the same time, I hope that my surprise – shock, even – isn't obvious. It is one thing to share information within a carefully confined conversation; quite another to be identified holding a particular ice scraper at a particular livery yard where a particular headless man is still hurtling towards the horizon on his snowmobile.

'Horses?' I ask in as neutral a tone as I can muster.

'Horses,' Osmala nods. 'I can't go into the details, by that's where we might find a connection. And perhaps all these shenanigans have their roots somewhere in the same soil, as it were.'

Again, I repeat Osmala's words in my mind and conclude that his answers are actually questions and that he doesn't formulate things like this by accident.

'When you say "connection" and "shenanigans", you mean…?'

'I mean, for instance, that you didn't kill Niko Kotka either.'

Osmala's eyes have remained fixed on me throughout our conversation.

'No, I did not,' I say, though this is probably unnecessary in light of what Osmala has just stated. I remember his lukewarm enthusiasm at the beginning of our exchange. 'But you wanted to make sure. That's why—'

'I wanted to make sure,' he says. 'Yes.'

We sit in silence for a moment. It is a brief moment, but it reminds me of the similar silence I experienced during our very first conversation. It seems we are still on the same side.

'About the horses—' I begin tentatively, but Osmala interrupts me right away.

'I don't need to know any more than is necessary,' he says. 'And the same goes for everything else I've mentioned. My primary focus remains unchanged.'

I know what – or whom – Osmala is referring to. An icy chill ripples through me. Of course I know Osmala is most interested in Salmi and Lastumäki. However, the role that he has reserved for me is not only chilling, it also begs a number of questions.

And I think it gives me permission to ask the following question:

'What stops you taking direct action against Salmi and Lastumäki?' I ask. 'Wouldn't it be easier to—'

Osmala nods, interrupts me.

'Again,' he says, 'I can't go into the details, but as a general observation one could perhaps say, even of life itself, that sometimes you have more room for manoeuvre, sometimes considerably less.'

He looks at me. I can see he has told me everything that he is going to on the subject. But I'm not out of questions yet.

'Aren't you interested in who killed Häyrinen, who—'

'Of course,' he says, so calmly that one might think he and I have been talking about the weather or a football match in the lower divisions. 'But in my experience, criminal rackets like this typically start to unravel once – how should I put it? – once the tightest knot has been undone. And here we are, undoing it, you and me, together.'

I'm aware that I invited Osmala here myself, to my office, my adventure park, and that I myself suggested this kind of collaboration and exchange of information. More to the point, I've already got what I wanted: new information. And Osmala doesn't even suspect me of murder.

'Exactly,' I say. 'Thank you for that.'

Osmala seems to be considering something.

'If I might ask,' he begins. 'There is one thing I've been thinking about quite a lot.'

I swallow. Have I calculated everything wrong after all? What have I overlooked?

'By all means,' I say, trying to sound as calm as possible. 'I'll answer as best I can.'

'I don't doubt it,' he says then pauses. It isn't a short pause; at least, it doesn't feel short. 'Does Ms Helanto's new work make direct reference to other artists, other works? In her murals, I particularly liked how she—'

'Pollocks,' I say. I doubt anyone has ever spoken the name of an artist with such profound relief.

'Jackson Pollock,' says Osmala, sounding as though someone has just given him a bunch of roses. 'This is the best news I've heard all day.'

He gets up from his chair. He's not looking at me anymore but gazing around the room. 'Jackson Pollock,' he says another three or four times, presumably to himself, before he reaches the door.

Just in front of the doorway, he stops repeating the name of the American modernist and, without turning to face me, says: 'Salmi and Lastumäki. There's more than a little of the Wild West about those two, don't you think?'

A second later, his Italian shoes squeak and clack along the corridor. Then, silence.

15

The Renault is cooling down, the streetlamps flickering into life. The long, straight road ahead doesn't provide any cover, but I believe I've found a suitable parking spot, at the end of the road where the asphalt ends and the outer edge of the cul-de-sac almost falls away across a pathway and out towards thick woodland.

The house is situated almost exactly halfway down the street. I can see lights in the windows.

I have to pay attention to two things. The first one – keeping out of sight – is already taken care of, largely because light is fading from the sky: the woodland will soon be indistinguishable from the surrounding darkness, they will be one and the same thing, and the only way to tell the woods from the dark, the dark from the woods, will be by touching them. Which I don't think anyone will be doing any time soon. In fact, I think it is almost certain that, taken together, the -22°C temperature, the knee-high snow and the encroaching darkness will keep anyone's desire to go fumbling about in the woods in check for a good while. With that in mind, I continue sitting in the car and turn my attention to what's most important: making sure that the small white BMW parked up ahead isn't out of my sight for a second.

I am watching the two policemen who want to arrest me for murder.

It's not an ideal scenario.

I've already spent a few hours tailing Salmi and Lastumäki. All our previous stops were new to me too, as is this house in darkest Espoo. Only one place we stopped at was even vaguely familiar to me: Somersault City. But our pit stop there was nothing more than that: the pair got out of the car, walked inside, and only a moment later walked out again; as though they had been expecting some result inside, been disappointed, and marched out again. Or perhaps heard that what they were looking for wasn't inside after all. Of course, this is purely conjecture on my part, but to construct a new theory, you have to start somewhere.

It is hard to imagine the sheer volume of problems that would arise if my cover were blown. On the other hand, it is hard to imagine the sheer volume of problems that will arise if I don't start to see some results. Though my staff's dedication and desire to take risks has rescued the park for now, this is merely an exercise in life support. Without a greater shift in circumstances, the doors will close sooner rather than later, with predictable results. At the same time, I am paradoxically relieved that I no longer have any other options; the phenomenon is familiar from mathematics, and perhaps this is why I find it so compelling. Sometimes, when looking for answers, it is easier to start by ruling out certain outcomes than by trying to go straight for the solution. The arc of probability leads in only one direction, a direction indicated by my recent conclusions and Osmala's words.

Salmi and Lastumäki.

Another half-hour sitting in the car tells me three things:

The temperature is dropping, Salmi and Lastumäki are still enjoying the central heating, and alongside all the joy and fulfilment it brings, family life involves many things that produce a sense of badly defined guilt.

This guilt has nothing to do with the fact that there are parties who would like nothing more than to frame me for murder or that I have resorted to some not strictly mathematical methods in defending my park and myself. It is something completely different: a feeling not unlike the chill slowly but surely settling inside the car. Its roots seem to lie in the fact that I am not where my family is. I notice that when my geographical location is different to theirs, the feeling becomes all the stronger. It's hard to find a rational explanation for this, because Laura Helanto thinks of my travails at the adventure park with the utmost understanding – and my current situation is certainly one such travail – and she hasn't been making demands one way or the other. Besides, we have agreed on the day's schedules, and Tuuli is safe and has been properly fed. Everything ought to be in order.

And still I feel I've neglected to do something or that there should be more of something and, above all, that what I'm doing right now affects them too. (Of course, it *will* affect them if I end up with a lengthy prison sentence, but right now I'm not doing anything except sitting in my Renault nineteen kilometres away from them.)

The fact is, I haven't taken any of this into account.

When I made my decision to move in with Laura and Tuuli, and form a family unit together, all I could see were the positives. On the whole, I felt as though I'd been saved – from what, exactly, I don't know – but as though I had jumped from something at the last possible moment, just managed to reach safety, and that this jump had changed the direction of my whole life. What I didn't know, however, was that along with this would come a constant nagging feeling that, having saved myself, I had let them down, and that looking for a rational explanation for this feeling – or even for what was happening in reality – was ultimately futile.

I sigh; it's so cold that my breath steams inside the car. I return my thoughts to the here and now, and not a moment too soon.

There is movement outside the house. I am certain I can make out both Salmi and Lastumäki's puffy eiderdown jackets in the lamplight outside the front door. The jackets then disappear into the white car, the car backs out of the driveway and into the road, the reverse lights switch off, I hear the sound of the engine, the BMW performs a few handbrake turns before finally straightening up and continuing along the street. I wait for the car to glide out of sight, start up the Renault and speed to the house that the pair have just left. I look at the name on the letterbox, then add it to the list I've been making all day. After this, I speed away again and catch up with Salmi and Lastumäki at the next junction, where they are waiting for the traffic lights to change just like the six cars in between us.

The evening draws on. Salmi and Lastumäki order a couple of kebabs and spend time in a large sportswear shop. As it approaches nine o'clock, they leave the shop – visibly in a hurry. Their urgency is clear for all to see: for the most part, their deliberate attempts to look relaxed only make them appear more ungainly, and it is easy to spot an ungainly person in a hurry – their speed picks up, their step becomes increasingly uncertain, unnatural, their posture oddly ineffectual. Nonetheless, they reach their car and set off. Of note is the fact that they do this without a single skid.

Salmi and Lastumäki maintain a speed slightly over the limit for the seventeen minutes we spend on the city's ring road. We then take the exit to Pukinmäki, drive underneath the train tracks, and then, slowing down surprisingly and suddenly and dramatically, the BMW turns into the car park outside a block of flats. I avoid making rash decisions, I neither slow nor slam on the brakes, which is more likely to attract their attention, but continue along the main road at exactly the speed limit. Once I am far enough away and have made sure my car is out of sight, I perform a U-turn and drive back the other way, this time slightly under the speed limit. And I see Salmi and Lastumäki.

The pair are standing under a streetlamp next to their car. And now there is a third man with them.

At the next junction, I turn right and see an empty parking space outside the supermarket. I steer the Renault into the space, switch off the engine, and think for minute. I calculate the relationship between the risks and the potential profit, make my decision, get out of the car and start walking. I have no reason to think that the duo – now a trio – is expecting anyone else to join them. Not that I was planning to join in their conversation. I need to find out the identity of the third man. If what I saw in passing is confirmed, I might be making some progress.

I walk along the pavement, which offers me no protection whatsoever. To my left is the wall of the building, to my right the highway. There are people walking towards me, but they are not police, or anybody else I know. When I finally reach the gable of the house and peer around the corner and into the car park, I recognise all three men standing in the pool of light.

Salmi, Lastumäki – and Joonas.

Whom, I now realise, they had not located at Somersault City.

16

When Tuuli asks me a question later in the evening, I'm taken aback. The reason for this is twofold. I am sitting at a dining table in Herttoniemi, but my thoughts are still in the car and I'm trying to put the elements of the equation together in an order that produces the most probable outcome. Additionally – and, right now, most acutely – I have been of the firm belief that she is quite capable of reading by herself. However, it turns out that her question is more to do with the final minutes before going to sleep (Tuuli, that is) and of how that time might be usefully spent together. Laura and Tuuli glance at each other while Laura explains the nature of the question. The matter becomes clear to me, the tone of their glance not so much. In any case, they smile, and when Tuuli asks again, I tell her that I'm only too happy to read to her.

Of course I am.

I arrived home an hour and thirteen minutes ago and took a long, hot shower, which I normally consider inefficient, particularly with regard to energy use, though I think being chilled to the bone in the course of a murder investigation can rightly be considered a *force majeure*. I have warmed up and eaten a portion of delicious soya and funnel chanterelle lasagne and drunk my evening tea, so the timing is optimal all round. When I ask Tuuli whether she would like to hear my recommendations from the bookshelf, she tells me she has already selected a book and that we are going to read a story from that.

She lies in her bed, I sit on a stool I've taken from the hallway. (I don't dare use the chair in front of her desk, as its proportions and visible structural flaws tell me that my sitting on it would result only in significant back pain and a pile of scrap aluminium.)

I open up the book *Accidental Andy (and Other Super-Useful and Mega-Exciting Stories)* at the place Tuuli shows me, and I begin.

Accidental Andy and the Break-Time Lesson

'Whoops,' said Andy when the coat stand in Nan's hallway toppled over, and the hats and coats and gloves and scarves scattered all over the floor. 'It was an accident.'

'Oh, Andy,' said Nan. 'You only arrived ten seconds ago, and that's already your second accident! But it's alright. It's nice to see you again.'

Nan never got angry. Almost everyone else got angry, though Andy never toppled anything over, never ever shoved, knocked, poked, crashed, crushed or broke anything on purpose. Nan was always happy when Andy visited her whenever he had a late start at school.

This term, that was on Wednesdays.

And now it was Wednesday morning, and here he was, in Nan's sunny living room that smelt of wood.

'Nan?' asked Andy once again. 'I can help too.'

'No, Andy,' Nan replied. 'You sit there on the sofa – and do not move an inch. I'll bring you a plate of biscuits in a minute. On second thoughts, I'll bring you some sponge cake wrapped in kitchen roll instead.'

That was another nice thing about Nan. She always gave Andy cake, even when he had accidents. Mum often sighed and said in a tired voice something like, there goes your dessert, when Andy dropped a bag of blueberries from the balcony when he was supposed to take them out of the fridge and bring them to Mum. But even when the bag of blueberries went flying over the railings, this was an accident too: Andy had just picked up the bag when a big bird flew past, and Andy thought he recognised it as a white-tailed eagle, so he quickly pointed his finger at it, and a few seconds later Tarmo Ilmarinen's cycling helmet got a new splash of colour.

Nan was still trying to catch her breath when she handed Andy the sponge cake wrapped in kitchen roll and sat down in her armchair.

'How is your new detective agency coming along?' she asked. Nan was the only person Andy had told about it.

'I'm still waiting for my first case,' he said excitedly. 'But nobody has gone missing yet, and nobody has lost anything either.'

'Now that you have your own detective agency,' said Nan, 'it will only be a matter of time before something happens.'

'That's right,' Andy nodded as he threw a piece of cake into his mouth. At least, he meant to throw a piece of cake into his mouth, but he missed, it flew behind him, and then came a crash, and when Andy looked over his shoulder, half of the cake was lying on the bookshelf on top of Grandad's photograph, which had been knocked over too. Grandad was dead, so he probably didn't mind, but Andy felt bad for Nan. 'Whoops, it was an accident, I'll clear—'

'I think it's time for school,' said Nan. Andy looked at the time and knew he would have to run.

Andy made it to school in the nick of time, and Janne told him that Neuvonen the janitor wasn't in his hut that morning, so *they wouldn't be allowed to borrow the American football at break time. Andy was so annoyed at this that he didn't listen to anything throughout the whole lesson – which was doubly annoying because he liked biology, mostly because Mum was always calling him a biological miracle.*

When the bell rang, Andy headed to the janitor's hut and noticed straight away that the door had been left ajar. Andy remembered that Neuvonen the janitor always locked the hut door after him, no exceptions. There must have been at least a hundred keys jingling and jangling on Neuvonen's belt, and he used these to open all the doors in the school and carefully lock them behind him. Andy crept into the hut.

A brightly coloured magazine lay open on the table, beside it a coffee cup, and beside that ... the janitor's set of keys! Andy knew that Neuvonen the janitor never went anywhere without his keys. On top of this, there was a strong smell in the hut, or a scent, as grown-ups called it, something that Andy had sometimes caught on Mum's breath in the mornings after she had been to the theatre with her friends. Now Neuvonen smelt of the theatre too. Andy touched the coffee cup, the way he had seen the police do in detective shows on TV. The cup was cold. There could only be one explanation: Neuvonen the janitor had disappeared!

Andy backed out of the hut. At least, that was his intention. But he had forgotten that his fingers were still gripping the coffee cup, and when he tried to return it to the table, it fell and the coffee spilled everywhere, and when Andy tried to rescue the janitor's magazine by quickly tugging it out of the way so it wouldn't get wet, it tore and ripped and fell into the puddle of coffee on the table. The table looked like it had been hit by a brown tornado.

'Whoops,' said Andy – to himself, of course, as he was all alone. 'It was an accident.'

Now he was in a hurry! The detective agency had its very first case, and he only had the thirteen minutes of break time to get to the bottom of it.

Andy knew that, when looking for missing persons, the first thing you had to do was look for any traces they had left. But there were no traces of the janitor's sandals or any of his other belongings either, neither his worn-out old leather satchel nor the grey cap that he wore all year round. Andy kept his eyes on the floor because he was sure that Neuvonen the janitor must have walked across the floor and hadn't turned into a vampire bat.

Andy was close to the steps when he noticed something on the floor. The blotch was small, maybe only the size of a small coin. To the right of it was another blotch. Soon, Andy was underneath the steps, where there were more and more blotches, almost as if it had been raining. Andy got down on all fours, the way he had seen detectives do on TV, inhaled deeply through his nose and smelt ... the theatre.

Neuvonen must have been here!

And there were blotches on the other side of the steps too!

Andy looked at his watch. Only eight minutes left! He followed the blotches and hurried after them all the way to the second floor, where everything was quiet.

Andy walked along the deserted corridor. The blotches were getting smaller, then they stopped altogether.

Andy stood in front of the small library. Just then, he heard a sound coming from the back of the room. It sounded like a low growl, an angry snarl, a deep sigh, then a yawn to round it off. Until all the sounds started from the beginning again. Then, from the back of the room came a bright clink, a bottle rolled to the floor, and Andy knew this wasn't a wild animal that had got lost in the school.

Andy carefully approached the sleeping janitor.

'Break time will be over in four minutes,' he said, but Neuvonen did not move. 'And you shouldn't be asleep at school.'

The snoring stopped.

'They turned down my poems,' Neuvonen blubbered from under the bookshelf. 'They don't understand beauty, these publishers.'

Neuvonen sounded very unhappy indeed. Luckily, Andy had some good news.

'The detective agency has found you,' said Andy. 'You were missing, but we've discovered you now.'

For a while, everything under the bookshelf was quiet.

'Discovered me?' asked Neuvonen after a moment. 'Have they really discovered me? And my poetry too?'

Andy thought about this for a moment. If Neuvonen had been discovered, didn't that mean the whole janitor had been discovered too?

'That's right,' Andy told him.

Neuvonen rolled out from under the bookshelf and staggered to his feet.

'I knew it,' he panted. 'Words will always win.'

Neuvonen looked like a newly born foal trying to stand on its own legs for the first time, the kind Andy had seen in nature documentaries. At first, he looked as though he was thrilled at being discovered, then a shadow fell over his expression.

'Why, it's you, Andy,' he said. 'Don't come any closer...'

'I only started the investigation thirteen minutes ago, and I've already...' Andy began as he gripped the upright bar of the bookcase to support himself while helping to steady Neuvonen the janitor. But the tall bookcase was wobbly, and only then did Andy remember that the library was due to be renovated because some of its fixtures were old and unpredictable. And all

of a sudden, the bookcase started to topple over. Andy stepped back, and with some quick thinking he managed to save Neuvonen too. Andy grabbed the old school pointer and used it to push Neuvonen to safety on the other side of the bookcase. But the pointer fell from Andy's hand, it went past Neuvonen and hit the plaster bust of the school's founder, Elviira Kolehmainen, which came off its plinth and wobbled off the top of the chest of drawers and fell on the music teacher's kantele *zither. Books and bookshelves rained down on the janitor while heads rolled and the* kantele *rang out.*

'Whoops,' said Andy, once it was quiet in the library again. 'It was an accident.'

'And it all turned out for the best,' Andy said the following week when he was sitting on Nan's sofa again, his mouth stuffed full of sponge cake. 'The detective agency solved its very first case, and I got to my history class on time.'

Nan nodded. 'I think you've learnt a very important lesson. Looking and finding really are different things. Sometimes I don't even know which is supposed to happen first. In fact, sometimes it's only by finding something that you realise what you should have been looking for all along.'

Andy threw a piece of cake into his mouth. Or rather…

Tuuli has fallen asleep. I close the book and quietly place it on her desk. Then I switch off her reading lamp and leave the room. Standing in the kitchen drinking some water – my mouth feels dry but my mind is alert – I believe I truly have read something both mega-exciting and super-useful.

17

There are people in the park; we have customers. The hall is once again filled with shouts and squeals, the rides are clanking and clattering. From early morning the Curly Cake Café has been giving off the delicious aromas of everything from Red Nose Buns to Dragon's Delight, and the spirits of each and every employee can reasonably be said to be very high indeed.

However, this isn't quite as good news as one might think.

By late afternoon I have done several tours of the hall, I have talked to each of my employees and established what is really going on at the park.

My staff paid for a radio advertising campaign out of their own pockets. Kristian wrote the advert, Esa was the sound engineer, and Minttu K booked the slots – and in return we had a total of eighteen children and ten adults at the park.

In a single day.

Of course, eighteen children can make a lot of noise, and ten adults will buy around ten cups of coffee and a certain (though still very limited) amount of savoury snacks and pastries from Johanna's already vastly overstocked café, but the day's total takings reveal the cold truth about the correlation between investment and profit. This investment is neither profitable nor sensible, neither in the short term nor the long term, and the solution is far from sustainable.

However, perhaps most illustrative of the current situation is the fact that I do not share my thoughts on the matter with the staff: I do not say out loud what a simple calculation would have told them straight away or what the earliest and most basic accounting practices in human history would have shown them. That they are possibly walking towards destruction on two fronts: the loss of their job and the collapse of their own finances, and their future.

To put it mildly, the atmosphere throughout the day is conflicted.

On the one hand, I feel a growing sense of terror and pressure when I see how overjoyed my staff are at the customers and witness their newfound enthusiasm all across the hall. Johanna is cooking, baking and frying. Kristian is moving between the different rides like a panther that has learnt how to use power tools, hunting down the smallest flaws, screws, bolts and nuts loosened a thousandth of a millimetre. Esa is scouting around, carrying out precision security reconnaissance and, if I have understood correctly, has also started counter-intelligence operations. Samppa is offering talking therapy both to our customers and their mothers and fathers, and at times he is so engrossed in the topics of discussion, he doesn't notice that his audience has already walked away. And Minttu K has informed me that radio by itself isn't enough anymore, we'll have to move to television 'and beyond', as she puts it. On the other hand, I can honestly admit that I have never experienced such a deep sense of attachment to my staff or been as proud of them as I am right now.

Therefore, I constantly feel as though I'm not moving quickly enough, though I'm doing everything I can think of to come up with a solution and to understand the twists and turns of recent events. Drawing up a new theory is always slow and laborious, and the constantly growing pressure doesn't make it any easier.

I'm sitting in my office. The park closed its doors almost two hours ago. Once again, I am trying to compare the information I have gathered thus far to what has already happened and what

I know in general, based on these two data sets and various probability ratios, when Esa knocks on the door and strides in without waiting for me to invite him.

'They're trying to come under cover of darkness,' he says. 'I knew it. Hence the tripwires.'

I try my best to understand Esa – in theory. He is speaking proper Finnish, and I remember him mentioning these tripwires. But, once again, I must confess I'm not entirely sure what we're supposed to be talking about, and I don't know what he's doing in the park at this hour.

'What exactly is this all about?' I ask him.

'The alarm came from the northeast,' Esa nods; he clearly hasn't heard my question. Then he continues: 'But not to worry, I've made sure the drone is in the air, and we've got a thermal camera following him too.'

I'm not sure whether what Esa has just told me is strictly legal, but the situation is gradually becoming clearer.

'Someone is approaching the park?' I ask him. 'Someone suspicious?'

'More than suspicious,' he says. 'And he's carrying something with him.'

I lower my eyes to the table, look at my calculations, my timeline, my formula. I have a thought.

'We have cameras outside the park too, yes?' I ask.

'I've just fixed the—'

'So, very soon, we will be able to see exactly who is approaching?'

Esa looks at me, perhaps even with a ripple of excitement. 'Are you expecting someone?'

'I think it's possible,' I begin, then hesitate. 'No,' I add almost immediately. 'One could even say it's probable.'

Two and a half minutes later, we are in Esa's control room.

I had no idea that Esa's at times over-the-top approach to park security would give me a tactical advantage like this, but that is exactly what has happened. At first, the dark figure is unrecognisable, but soon – as the colour image comes into focus and the figure appears on three different screens at once – I see that my calculations were right. I watch Joonas; he is pulling something behind him, something that looks like a sled, only larger and more angular.

Esa's expression tightens; he is about to bound out of his chair. I place a hand on his shoulder.

'We should activate our defence protocol without delay,' he says and is still about to get up; I can feel his muscles tense beneath my palm. 'And we should prepare a counter-offensive too.'

I stare at the image of Joonas, who looks as though he doesn't really want to be where he is right now, doing what he's doing right now. This is obvious in all respects: his expression, his posture, the way he is dragging the box behind him.

'We're not going to activate anything,' I say. 'On the contrary. We're going to help him inside.'

A few seconds pass, during which Esa gives up his attempt to get to his feet and eventually relaxes. Then he spins around in his chair and looks at me.

'Patton,' he nods, looking me fixedly in the eyes. 'A classic sideways manoeuvre. And an excellent deployment of it, if I may say so.'

Esa spins back and turns his attention to his monitors once again. I have no idea what this brief exchange meant, but the main thing is that Esa stays in his chair a moment longer, helping to carry out my plan. He remotely unlocks the back entrance, switches off the lights both in the corridor leading from the entrance and in the hall itself and makes sure that there's only one possible route Joonas can take. I've drawn up this plan in a hurry, on the hoof, as they say. Nonetheless, this is far from improvised. I have taken into account all the calculations I conducted today and all the observations I made before.

Joonas arrives at the back door, pulls something out of his backpack: a crowbar. He has already lifted it and is about to wedge it between the lock and the doorframe when he stops in his tracks. He lowers the crowbar and tries the handle. Naturally, the handle turns and the door opens. Just as it should do. Joonas looks around, returns the crowbar to his backpack, hauls his angular sled up to the door, crouches down, lifts the sled, props it on his chest, and steps inside.

We watch Joonas as, with some difficulty, he makes his way deeper into the park. He has switched on a torch, but pointing this at the route in front of him is all but impossible while carrying his heavy box. He doesn't look like a man who has planned this operation himself, let alone one who believes in the plan. Esa appears to have reached the same conclusion; he shakes his head but says nothing.

Joonas reaches the main hall, but because his use of the torch is a little approximate, he can only walk where there is already some faint lighting. That is to say, he can only walk where I have decided he will walk. And once Joonas is exactly where I want him, I give Esa the signal. He presses three buttons at once, and the entire hall suddenly seems to explode with light. Even seen through the monitors, the brightness is dazzling and revelatory. The sudden illumination seems to affect Joonas even more powerfully, and he does exactly what I was expecting him to do: he looks for cover as close as possible. And because he cannot leave behind his box, he must choose a hiding place with enough room for a man and his belongings.

Once Joonas and his box are inside the Banana, I ask Esa to

lock it remotely. I'm almost certain I can hear the lock clicking
shut all the way up in the control room.

The Banana is not one of the park's current array of activities,
but it has nonetheless proven its worth, both with regards to
capacity and location. And due to its bright-yellow hard plastic
casing and amusing curvature it is an important part of the park's
interior design. In practice, this provides temporary storage
space for all kinds of things needed either in the immediate
vicinity of the Banana or that we need to access quickly. And if
in the past I have wondered and asked Esa quite why we need a
remote locking system in the Banana, now I will never wonder
or ask such a thing again.

We cautiously approach the Banana. I don't know whether
there is any need for such caution. Even if Joonas's box is in fact
a bomb, I can't imagine him using his explosives to blow up the
bare interior of a seven-metre-long plastic fruit and, thereby,
himself too. Of course, anything is possible, but having met
Joonas before and having watched his reluctance a moment ago,
I don't think a strike of this nature is especially probable. We
arrive at the Banana and listen for a moment. The hall is quiet,
and so is the Banana. I knock on its wall.

'Joonas,' I call out. 'What's that you've got with you?'

Silence. I knock again and ask again.

'Who's there?' I hear from within the Banana.

I tell him who I am and explain that he and I have met before.
I inform him that I am here with the park's head of security, who
received training in how to detain trespassers from the Israeli
secret services. As we were walking towards the Banana, Esa
insisted that I add this piece of information, and I had neither

the time nor inclination to begin assessing the probability or veracity of the claim.

'Ants,' comes Joonas's voice. 'An anthill. I've got a million ants with me in here. If you don't open the door, I'll let them loose.'

This is certainly not the answer I was expecting, but in its own way it is perfectly logical. This is a classic attempt at sabotage, and one that we have only just succeeded in scuppering.

'If you let a million ants loose,' I begin, 'then it'll be you and the ants inside the Banana.'

'We can secure the Banana,' Esa says to me. 'Seal it off completely. In the storeroom, I've still got a few camouflaged tarpaulins used for siege situations that I got from the Romanian special forces. I guarantee not even a fart would get through that material.'

I look at Esa: either he is one of the best-equipped people in the world, come rain or shine, or it's something else altogether. I return my attention to the Banana, recall the calculations I made earlier that day and the information I have already gathered, in part by following the underage detectives. I realise I am about to take a huge risk, but as I see it, the risk is carefully controlled and based on a very limited number of highly probable outcomes.

'Joonas,' I say. 'I know who sent you.'

Silence. I am about to ask my next question when Esa raises his voice.

'We can open the box of ants from out here, you know,' he shouts. 'We use a heating system developed by NASA that can take that box apart at the seams. So you can look forward to a night in the sauna with ten million ants.'

'Thank you, Esa,' I say, keeping my voice calm because I can feel him getting agitated. 'Until we've exhausted all diplomatic means, I suggest we—'

'Is that true?' I hear from inside the Banana.

I glance at Esa. The answer seems obvious.

'At this point in time, I think it's highly likely,' I admit, keen to return to my original topic. Just then, I make a decision and take the risk factor up a notch. 'I know Salmi and Lastumäki sent you, but I want to know why, and why now?'

Silence. There comes a thud from inside the Banana.

'If I tell you,' shouts Joonas, and now I can hear the panic in his voice, 'how can I be sure you'll let me out of here without opening the box?'

I don't imagine Joonas is well acquainted with game theory, at least not very deeply, but even a cursory understanding of the basics might help him see that, to use a gambling analogy, he doesn't have many aces up his sleeves.

'What are your other options?' I ask.

The Banana is silent. For a long while.

'I don't want any of this,' he says eventually. 'I hate adventure parks. All adventure parks. They piss me off. And now I'm stuck inside a fucking banana. What do you want to know?'

Naturally, I'm no expert when it comes to interrogations and associated techniques, but I have a strong suspicion that Joonas has broken comparatively easily and, at the very least, quicker than most. I ask the same questions again.

'They're in a hurry, Salmi and Lastumäki,' he says. 'They said they're in a hurry. They got hold of this box and forced me to bring it down here, tonight. Or try to. Meaning there would be a major incident at your park, everyone would be terrified, then nobody would ever come here again because, like, the ants would eat their kids or something.'

Joonas's outburst is short and frantic and contains an amount of hyperbole (it is hard to imagine ants either partially or wholly gobbling up our customers in the Strawberry Maze – or anywhere else, for that matter), but it allows me to take another approach.

'Did they tell you why?' I ask. 'Why you have to do it tonight?'

Another silence.

'How the fuck should I know?' Joonas almost shouts. 'This whole business is like a loony bin. Häyrinen gets it in the neck from a giant ice-cream cone, Niko takes a peg in the forehead, the kid cops are extorting money left right and centre, and now you're threatening to melt me in a banana. You can stick your fucking park—'

'Alright,' I interrupt him. 'Let's take a few steps back. When Salmi and Lastumäki appeared at Somersault City after Häyrinen's death and—'

'After...?'

'Yes, after Häyrinen's murder...'

'What do you mean, *after*,' says Joonas. 'They were there long before it happened.'

'Before the murder?' I ask, as I feel a shiver run down my spine, so literally, in fact, that I have to glance quickly to the side and check that Esa hasn't touched me with some kind of ice-cold metallic object.

'Yes!' Joonas shouts. 'Before, for God's sake. They've been hanging around there since the beginning.'

I try to organise all these people, their connections, the events and the weighting and probabilities I have calculated between them, and place them on my timeline, but realise just as quickly that almost all the parts of the puzzle are in motion, all searching for a new constellation. At the same time, I recall my conversation with Osmala.

'Is that good enough for you?' I hear from the Banana. 'Now let me the fuck out of here.'

I understand Joonas. He is here against his will, in a variety of respects, and he has agreed to cooperate with us. Esa and I will have to release him soon.

'One more thing,' I say. 'Do you know how Häyrinen and the police – that is Salmi and Lastumäki – knew one another? What was their connection?'

'If I know, will I get out?' asks Joonas. 'Because I happen to know, but if that door doesn't open…'

I give Esa a nod, he presses the remote control in his hand, and there is a click from the side of the Banana. Joonas cautiously pushes the door open, peers out, then locates me and Esa. In a way, he resembles a fledgling hatching from an egg, albeit an enormous one.

'It's something to do with horses,' he says. 'Now, can I get the hell out of here? You can keep the ants – and your park. I'm done with this shit.'

18

The following morning, I receive a WhatsApp message that complicates the situation even further, though in all respects this shouldn't be possible.

I'm drinking my morning tea, and trying to take part in the simultaneous conversations going on around me, at least some of which appear to involve me in some way or another. Right now, as it is approaching eight o'clock, and while reading the message on my phone, it looks and sounds as though Laura is having one conversation with Tuuli, another with me, I'm having a third conversation with Tuuli and a fourth involving both of them. I realise this is what people call family life, but when I compare this to what my mornings in Kannelmäki were like when it was just me and Schopenhauer, the difference is considerable. Whereas before I would have prepared for the day ahead by reading the day's papers while enjoying my bread and tea and sour yoghurt in peace and quiet, now it feels as though I'm trying to gather my thoughts at a crowded, half-feral market place. For this reason, I can't keep up with some of the conversations, let alone understand them, though I have quickly picked up another survival skill for family life: there is no point trying to catch a metro for which you're already late, because the next train is already pulling into the station. Based on my short but all the more intense experience, in family life there is no shortage of things that have to be agreed upon together.

The WhatsApp message is from Sami, and it is alarming to say the least. Time and matter seem to be shrinking around me, in opposition to what usually happens in an ever-expanding universe. Sami and the other dads have moved things forwards in an unexpected way. The fête is now in two days' time. The dads have been talking about a pop-up fair, which might explain the greatly expedited timetable. They have rented a space at an old shopping mall for the day, and in their own words, social media is already awash with posts, likes and comments about the upcoming event. And another matter further curtailing my timeframe is to do with what is happening later tonight, this very night: we are meeting for a group bake-off where we will plan and confirm the eventual budget for the fête. My presence is now doubly important: I have been appointed to both the redcurrant jelly and budgetary teams.

'So, that suits you too, right?' asks Laura.

In all likelihood, she asked this question a moment earlier and I only register it now. First, I peer out into the dusky winter's morning beyond the windows, then I turn my head towards Laura. I haven't the faintest idea what we've been talking about. Then suddenly, I'm certain I do know. This can only be about one thing, the same subject we were talking about a moment earlier: a simple trip to the supermarket. As I now realise, the matter has advanced without my noticing.

'I'll take care of it,' I say. 'Gladly.'

Laura kisses me lightly on the temple, then disappears into the bathroom. Tuuli smiles, she looks as though she is suddenly curious about me, then gets up from the table without saying a word. I load the dishwasher. After this, the three of us head off to take care of the day's chores.

As dawn gently breaks and the morning traffic flows smoothly, the drive to the adventure park gives me the opportunity to examine my theories one at a time, theories that I have been mulling over through the night as I lay awake. In this respect, Joonas was a treasure trove of information. Thanks to him, the number of unknown factors in the equation is now drastically reduced, though there are still plenty of variables left.

The fact that Salmi and Lastumäki have one way or another been involved with Somersault City since its very inception explains a lot and makes it easier to see the bigger picture. My primary assumption is now that Salmi and Lastumäki have murdered both Häyrinen and Niko Kotka. My secondary theory features a homicide too, but this time only one: Niko Kotka. This theory assumes that Niko Kotka is the one who murdered Häyrinen, only then to be murdered himself. But, right now, the question of whether Salmi and Lastumäki have one or two victims to their names is largely irrelevant. What's relevant is that both trains of thought lead to the same conclusion: Salmi and Lastumäki need a scapegoat. And that would appear to be me.

All of the above is both logical and apparent.

But how can I best present these ideas to Osmala so that it will lead to the outcome I want – fast? At present, this seems like an insurmountable task. In his own words, Osmala has very limited room for manoeuvre when it comes to Salmi and Lastumäki. And to the extent that I can say I know Osmala, I assume this is a euphemistic way of saying that there isn't really any room for manoeuvre at all. Thus, if I tell him about my suspicions right away, he might simply say that my information is 'undeniably interesting' and that he will promise to 'look into it' (words I can already hear him saying), while in fact we are both still at square one, or at most only a step away from it.

Meanwhile, Salmi and Lastumäki could continue hounding me. If they were prepared to go as far as they did with Niko

Kotka and possibly Häyrinen too, what or who will stop them treating me the same way? The answer is, manifestly, nothing and nobody. I'll have to come up with a better solution – very quickly. And by better, I mean a solution that doesn't end up with me in prison or conducting one final, brief calculation.

Naturally, not all the information that Joonas provided is equally fruitful with regard to these considerations. I don't think the horse connection is especially important. To my mind, it is immaterial where Salmi and Lastumäki originally met Häyrinen or what the horses have to do with their interpersonal relationships. This is irrelevant for me and with regard to later events. Besides, I've been conducting investigations of my own (and a highly unpleasant self-defence operation that still leaves me with flashbacks second only to the Book of Revelations) into a livery yard that may or may not have anything to do with the case, but even still I don't know whether this will have any bearing on achieving my most important aim: finding incontrovertible, watertight evidence to prove Salmi and Lastumäki's guilt.

At the junction, I turn and head into the now familiar emptiness of the YouMeFun car park. The radio advertisement campaign has had only a minimal and temporary effect. I steer the car round to the back of the adventure park and leave it in my own parking space.

It isn't a busy day – in any respect. The park is quiet, my office is quiet and, worst still, quietest of all is the sector of my brain usually dedicated to problem-solving. This isn't because I haven't come up with enough theories, performed enough calculations or tried to think through all the various potential scenarios. It is because those theories, calculations and potential scenarios can't yet find one another. The truth is I'm missing something that will tie all these details together, and I don't even know how or where the missing link might be found.

I don't imagine I will find the answer at the Curly Cake Café, but this is where I head.

I walk through the silent hall, and I can't help feeling a certain melancholy as I listen to the echo of my own steps. Things shouldn't be like this, I think. Normally I wouldn't even hear my own thoughts, let alone the gentle slap of the rubber soles of my shoes against the concrete floor. My throat feels dry and constricted. This forces me to swallow, though the very act of swallowing feels suddenly difficult, and there seems to be less air around me, though the oxygen levels in the hall are probably higher than in months. I walk into the café and see all my employees gathered there.

I notice right away how their expressions shift, even their seating positions, when they see me. As I approach the table, they all smile, sit up with their backs straight, and I can see they're not really smiling and they're not actually remotely energetic or receiving customers with their usual bubbling enthusiasm. I also notice that my throat and chest now feel tighter than a moment ago, when I was walking past the Doughnut, the Komodo Locomotive and all our other empty activities. I don't have to ask what is on their minds; I know only too well.

When we greet one another, I can see they are still trying to be upbeat, but then, once I've sat down, their forced smiles start to become visibly hard to maintain, and their shoulders begin to sag, as though pressed down by a great, invisible power. Just then, for the first time that day, I realise something. Right away, I know why I see everything so clearly, why seeing it feels so different now from how it would have felt in the past.

Family.

I don't have only one family. Nowadays, I have two.

That's not to say I am one of those men who have two families that know nothing about each other, one in Helsinki and one in Hämeenlinna, and who never feels it necessary to tell anyone, or that Esa was a child I was caring for, Johanna my sister who has just got out of prison and Minttu K my eccentric aunt – though naturally such a dynamic can be perceived in our relationships. I mean everything we are when we are together, what we have survived together, achieved together, and the bonds that those achievements have caused to grow between us. Thus, I feel the need to bring good news, to give them hope, though in all honesty I don't where I'm going to find either.

'We will get through this,' is all I can come up with. 'Better days lie ahead, sooner or later. Right now, things might feel difficult, but this is only temporary. Everything will work out for the best. Spring will come, the sun will rise, the park will flourish. We will get through this. And we'll get through it together.'

At first, I'm not sure where these words are coming from – or why they're coming right now. I know that in the past I would have thought words like this flat and banal, even corny; in fact, given what we already know, they would not withstand the least scrutiny. Then I realise it's my thoughts on the notion of family that are making me speak like this. Of course, I don't think being a member of a family carries the duty to share untruths or unconfirmed predictions, as I have just done; it is merely the simple truth about where I position myself and what I will dedicate myself to, totally. We really will stand or fall together. And that's the only thing that matters.

'In the entire adventure-park business, there is nobody better equipped or with a better knowledge of park security and defence systems than Esa,' I continue. 'And nobody runs a marketing strategy as fearlessly and open-mindedly as Minttu K, nobody can beat Kristian in tirelessly developing new business ideas, nobody can touch Johanna when it comes to menu innovations at adventure-park cafés, and nobody has developed such a vast array of play-therapy techniques for adult and child alike as Samppa. Each one of you is unique, and as such you are all vital to YouMeFun. And together, you are indomitable – you *are* YouMeFun. Nobody can beat you.'

There is silence in the café. If I were to say my employees look confused, that would be misleading. Admittedly, there is an element of confusion in the air, but this is something else. Kristian wipes the corner of his eye.

'Nobody's ever said anything...' he begins.

'...so damn beautiful...' Minttu K continues and downs what's left in her mug.

'Or valued us,' says Esa, his voice hoarse, and is only just able to finish his sentence, 'or understood the challenges of my role in that way.'

'Agreed,' says Johanna with a curious nod of the head. She might even be a bit moved.

'In an adventure park, we encounter one another person to person, spirit to spirit, our caring dynamic is fused with the power of the awakening mind, and everything opens up...' Samppa begins, but by this point everyone else has already stood up from their chairs.

They walk towards me. Instinctively, I too stand up. I don't know what to expect, I don't know what they are doing. And I don't have time to think about it any further. They are around me, then I am standing between them. Crushed, yes, but very gently. I understand what I am experiencing is known as a group hug. I also understand this is something embarrassing, something

to be avoided, and I've never before been in danger of being
involved in one or becoming the object of one, but I must admit
that the procedure itself doesn't feel entirely unpleasant. In fact...

Quite the opposite.

'This is so super fabulous,' says Samppa, his voice heavy with
emotion, from somewhere near the centre of the maul. 'A
spontaneous love cluster, all this energy-transferal, the empathy,
the emotional current. I surrender!'

This time, nobody even interrupts him.

19

Team Redcurrant Jelly, to which I have been assigned, is working at the windowless side of the small dining area in Tuukka's apartment. The other end of the dining table, facing the window, has been reserved for the Jammy Dodgers, as they call themselves. Their official name is Team Strawberry Jam, but for some reason the nickname they came up with almost immediately is more to their liking and seems to amuse them more and more as we try to prepare our products – in virtually impossible circumstances.

It's not only the size of this operation that is causing problems – a total of six teams working in an apartment with three rooms and one kitchen – but also the fact that, with the exception of Team Knit-One-Purl-One, everybody constantly needs the kitchen. Thus, there is always a queue for the kitchen and at times the atmosphere is a little tense as the dads jostle for access to the taps, the oven and the cooker. But despite the frenzied atmosphere, the dozens of smells, some pleasant, some less so, the decidedly elevated temperature and occasional cross words between the dads, the project is making progress.

I consider this not only surprising but also quite encouraging.

As buns and cakes rise in the oven and mushroom sauce bubbles on the stove, the rows of jam and jelly jars on the table grows and decorative woollen socks and colourful mittens start to appear from nowhere, I find myself thinking that perhaps there is a slim possibility we might meet our targets and arrange our trip to Paris after all.

It has already been several hours since the group hug at the adventure park, but something of that moment is still with me. And though I appreciate that part of the warm atmosphere was due to my own words, improvised on the spot (though I meant every word), something about that shared moment is still smouldering. Being a member of a family and taking care of that family seems to be in large part about creating hope, building something abstract. Families need bread and warmth, but they also need a vision, something they can believe in together. I've never been a fan of such thinking, and I don't mean that family life should be founded on the least rational thought possible or on a wholesale rejection of logic, but now I understand something that I didn't understand earlier. Becoming a member of a family and operating within that family is above all a leap of faith: in moving away from the safety of pure reason, you get warmth in return. And if I can create hope and vision, it seems I will get them in return too.

This sort of leap gives me food for thought with regard to my investigation too. I am almost certain that there is only one missing factor that, when found, will explain how all the pieces of the puzzle fit together. All I have to do is let go of my most recent calculations, even those I carried out immediately after our group hug, invigorated and looking at things with fresh eyes, but without reaching any new conclusions.

I have to find a new approach – and family membership doesn't actually feel like such a bad option. We need trust and warmth and benevolent, patient progress from one situation to the next – and eventually, when the time comes, the right kind of action. Of this, I have recent experience. Whether I'm thinking about Laura or Tuuli, or my employees at the adventure park, the truth is that I've always got my best results by taking a leap, by jumping ... on board. And perhaps, if I behave in the world as I do in my family (or families plural, minus the whole

Helsinki–Hämeenlinna dynamic), the world will respond just as my families have responded, and I will finally know exactly what I should be looking for.

I focus my attention on the various stages of jelly production. I'm not familiar with this process and follow the instructions I've been given. It doesn't feel especially difficult. The only significant challenge seems to be in my neck and shoulders, which are beginning to feel sore after being hunched over the pots and jars and the viscous redcurrants for such a long time. Therefore, after around two hours of work, I straighten my back and tell the dad standing next to me cleaning jars that I have to stretch a little. At first he recommends a complicated yoga position, but eventually lets me go my own way. Which in this case means the balcony at the end of the long living room.

The living room is divided between Team Knit-One-Purl-One and Team Honeycomb. The latter is working on top of a tarpaulin, which is understandable. It is hard to imagine anything stickier and messier than Team Honeycomb's operations.

I am stretching my neck when I suddenly notice someone beside me. I explain to Tuukka that my neck is stiff from all those hours on the redcurrant-jelly production line, and now I have to try and revive it.

'I noticed,' he says. 'But you're stretching all wrong.'

'Wrong?'

'Right,' he nods. 'The tension isn't just in your neck. Start here.'

Tuukka points at his feet. And right away he raises one of his feet from the floor, and catches his ankle from behind, stretching the front of his thigh. The entire movement lasts only a second. He then repeats the movement with his other leg. I recall his background in sport.

'I don't know...'

'And then,' he says, as he lets go of his ankle and drops down into a crouched ski jumper position. 'Then you expand the movement.'

At first he retains his ski jumper's descent position, then starts moving his feet across the floor, and before I've even straightened my head from the first stretch, he has done the splits.

'Stretch the whole body, from the bottom up,' he says, then starts getting up as though pulled by an invisible lift until, somehow, he is standing in front of me again. He raises his arms, stretches them upwards, then starts moving them like a windmill. His arms swish past, his shoulders are loose and strong. I note how flexible and tensed he is at the same time: while his limbs are supple and flexible, his face is as taut and harsh as before. He lowers his arms, shakes his hands and feet and, it seems, his entire body too, then looks at me for a moment.

'Do that,' he says, and I can't tell whether this is an order or a recommendation. And with that, he walks away.

It takes a moment before I realise what I've just seen. I think about it but push the thought away. It's impossible, I think, and there's nothing to warrant drawing such a conclusion. It's just a coincidence. I try to stretch my neck once more – I won't even attempt to replicate the contortions I've just witnessed; they are far too daring after over twenty years of desk work – but I cannot. All of a sudden, I am considerably tenser than I was a moment ago, huddled over the jam. I see the winter outside, the streetlamps, the illuminated windows across the street, identical to the one I'm standing next to. The window reflects things too: I can see myself, people making honeycomb, people knitting and crocheting. I see Tuukka. Then someone calls his name, says they need a set of pliers. Tuukka says he will have to fetch them from the garage. His tone of voice suggests he isn't exactly thrilled about this. The calculations I conducted earlier today now start to rearrange themselves; theories are discounted as new ones arise. The tracksuit top disappears from view, and a moment later I hear the front door opening and closing.

Go with the flow.

This is at the heart of my revelation. And it would never have come about without recent events, recent emotions, what I might genuinely call learning new things. Becoming a member of a family, admitting that mere knowledge doesn't always tell me which direction to take or where to aim. And finally, Laura Helanto's art and everything it has taught me. This is about learning to look and, thereby, to see new things. And if I will only let it, the picture will start to come into focus by itself, facts and meanings flow, constantly joining in different configurations, again and again, at times differing wildly from previous assumptions, at others almost exactly the same. But always revealing something new, time and time again.

Go with the flow.

In part, this refers to motion, also the physical kind.

The living room is filled with sound and action. But there are immobile elements too, the kind that one could easily overlook because of the movement going on in the foreground. I too have overlooked them. Not entirely, of course; I've seen them, but I haven't incorporated them into the larger picture – my calculations. I haven't looked at them carefully. I look now.

Behind a glass door on the bookshelf there is a collection of trophies with photographs behind and between them. First prize in show jumping, immortalised jumps in which it looks as though man and horse are frozen in the air. Prize winners on the podium. For a long while I look at a picture in which the rider is holding the reins in his left hand, while his right is placed on the neck of a majestic, dark-brown steed. What particularly catches my attention in this image is that the man is smiling. I've never seen him do anything like this in the past. He looks happy and content, and it's easy to imagine this isn't just because he won a race.

Tuukka is in his element; he is doing what he loves.

At the same time, my mind is flooded with words and images. Tuukka at the parents' evening, where I met him for the first time. Tuukka's temperament, his rashness, his short temper, his competitive instinct. The sportiness I have seen for myself, his explosive power, the suppleness I witnessed a moment ago. Tuukka trying to get himself out of financial difficulty in a way that confused him too, telling me that his biggest client was about to stop putting in orders.

And eventually ... of course.

I move as quickly as I can without attracting attention. I pass the dining area, tell one of the dads that I'll be back to the jam in a moment. He doesn't look very happy, but I'm relieved that he doesn't want to discuss the matter any further and turns his attention back to spooning jam into small jars.

The hallway is narrow and claustrophobic, and next to the front door is another door leading into one of the smaller bedrooms. I don't walk that far but stop by the tall coat stand in the hallway where I took off my shoes when I first came inside. Back then, I paid some attention to the items in the tall, slender display cabinet, various pieces of sporting equipment and drinking bottles, but I didn't look behind them. I look now. I am familiar with these protein bars – or their wrappers, that is. I return my eyes to the coat stand.

The lanyard is hanging on one of the prongs. It has Tuukka's photograph and, more importantly, the name of his company:

Sure Build Ltd. The name is neutral; it tells us something but leaves a lot of room for interpretation. The name could cover such a broad spectrum of work that anyone who didn't know would find it hard to work out what the company actually did. Unless, that is, you happen to know a thing or two about adventure parks, the details of the construction and maintenance of their rides and, specifically, if you have recently learnt new things from Esa. (I think of the benefits of family life as having an accumulative effect.) We too use all manner of professionals to inspect and calibrate the attractions in the park, for instance when we need to test the optimal friction levels for a type of flooring: the floor mustn't be too slippery but it mustn't unnecessarily slow down our customers as they rush from one activity to the next. It should be a quick surface, but above all it should be…

Sure.

The person inspecting the structures of our attractions and assessing their safety must know those structures in advance. He must know not only the structures but the equipment too, both inside and out.

He knows Somersault City, and he knows the Beaver.

I stand in the hallway conducting dozens of calculations. This isn't difficult any longer. Now I have all the variables in the equation, I have gathered plenty of data, and I have experience. The only problem now is how to…

The door opens. I manage to turn just in time so that it looks like I'm on my way to the door. Once again Tuukka looks as though he is about to lose his temper.

'The toilet's the other way,' he says and looks me right in the eyes. 'By the kitchen.'

'Right,' I say. 'Thank you.'

Three and a half hours later, there are only two people left in the apartment: me and Tuukka.

I could never have envisaged myself packing jars of redcurrant jelly with such care and attention. Naturally, I would never have conducted the packing sloppily, let alone thrown or tossed the glass jars around, but now my sense of care is heightened, and I am taking my time. Very deliberately.

Tuukka is busy in the living room. He is very upset at the quality of Team Honeycomb's clean-up operation and has made this abundantly clear to me. One other thing is clear too: Tuukka's wife and daughter are not coming home for the night. The lack of women's clothing in the apartment speaks to this fact. On the coat stand in the hallway there isn't a single coat or other item that, given its size and style, one might conclude belonged to a woman. And the smaller bedroom with its loft bed is suspiciously tidy for a child's room; it looks more like a museum than a space belonging to one of the adventure park's typical customers. It is easy to conclude that Tuukka lives in his three-room-and-kitchen apartment – if not wholly then at least primarily – alone. I can't help thinking that there is something very fresh about the situation, something recent.

Tuukka walks into the dining area just as I am slotting the last jam jar into the cardboard box. I fold the four corners of the lid in on one another. The jars are ready for transportation. This I say aloud.

'Okay,' Tuukka replies. 'Put the box out in the hall with the others.'

'Won't it be in the way if—'

'It won't,' he interrupts, 'be in the way.'

Tuukka has been standing between two light sources. It looks as though neither the light from the dome lampshade in the dining room nor the spotlights along the ceiling in the hallway can properly reach him.

'If someone—'

'They've gone,' he says.

Of course, I could ask a few follow-up questions such as *who?* or *do you mean your family?* or even *gone where?*, but the matter is clear enough.

'I'm sorry,' I say. 'I didn't know. You're still involved with the...'

'With all this ... I promised Noora. Though none of it makes any sense. You said as much yourself.'

I decide not to tell him that these days I think it all makes a great deal of sense. Perhaps not from a business perspective, but in other ways.

'Well,' I say and nod towards the bookcase in the living room. 'I see equestrian sports are something of a hobby for you.'

Tuukka shakes his head. In his expression I detect the same tension, the same harshness I've seen whenever he is challenged, in competition or otherwise.

'It's not a hobby,' he says. 'I ride horses. Well, I used to.'

I say nothing. Tuukka looks into the living room, presumably at the riding photographs on the bookshelf.

'They took away my horse,' he says after a pause.

I know I have reached a crossroads. I know I'm not very good at reading people, something I have realised quite recently in my short experience of family life. On the other hand, I know my own strengths: when it comes to calculating probability ratios, I am all but unbeatable. And, as curious as it might sound, I feel that I understand Tuukka. He is in trouble; I am in trouble. He is a murderer; I am suspected of the murders he has committed. But what brings us together also keeps us apart, and this is what I need to prove. And I can't do that just by saying so – *believe me, he did it, I did not*. I'm going to have to spur Tuukka into action.

'Wouldn't another horse be—'

'Another horse?' he asks, his voice as icy as the evening outside. 'Another horse is not an option. I want to win. That's only possible with one horse.'

Once again, it seems Tuukka has said more than he was planning to, just as happened the night when we walked home together in the snow. And again he looks as though he has taken himself by surprise. Perhaps this is what prompts him to continue.

'Keeping a horse costs money,' he says. 'Training, stable fees – it all costs money. I lost my largest client. Then I tried to combine work and riding to sort things out like that, but it only made things even messier, so I had to look for a livery yard I could afford. By the end, I couldn't even afford that, so they took my horse. I think that was their plan all along. And they won't give it back. I've tried. Everything.'

Now I am more convinced than ever that Tuukka simply had to let all this out. It's easy to believe everything he says and form the beginnings of a theory about what happened. Horses might be what initially brought Tuukka into contact with Häyrinen and Elsa. Having run into financial difficulties, he asked them for help and perhaps even offered his professional expertise in return for a place at the livery yard. This is how the horse ended up at Häyrinen's yard and how Tuukka ended up working at Somersault City. One thing led to another, and eventually Häyrinen took ownership of the horse. Knowing Tuukka, he probably flew off the handle and tried to dissolve their agreement. And when that didn't work out, for good or ill, he finally lost his temper and reached for the steel ice-cream cone. Of course, I don't know if this is precisely what happened or whether it was in this particular order, but I don't think I'm far from the truth. Probabilities aren't probabilities by accident.

'Do you happen to know,' I ask, 'where the horse is now?'

20

How do you get a murderer to murder? And, more specifically: how do you motivate him to do so?

This question and various other possible solutions are in my mind again as I head to the fête with Laura, Tuuli and a consignment of marmalade. The morning is like something straight out of an old postcard: the cloudless sky is dazzling, deep and blue, the sun is glistening on a fresh layer of snow, and the whole world looks pure, gleaming, still. At least, superficially, I add to myself. So far this morning I have already received one text message from Esa, who tells me that Salmi and Lastumäki are looking for me again and have even visited the park. I know it is only a matter of time before their investigations lead them to Herttoniemi. In all respects, time is of the essence. The fête, or Paris Pop-Up, as it is now officially known, is set to begin in half an hour's time.

I have spent the morning driving between Tuukka's apartment and the shopping mall, loading and unloading the car, and now I have stopped in at my own house for my last delivery. At least, I hope it will be my last, as that will mean we have managed to sell the majority of our products and nobody will have to go home with two hundred jars of apple compote.

Tuuli and Laura are in high spirits; this is clear from their light, rapid-fire chit-chat, their high-pitched voices and volleys of laughter. Naturally, this has an impact on me too, to some degree. But although I voluntarily agreed to take care of transporting the goods to the venue, this doesn't mean my mood is as bubbly as that of my fellow travellers or that I am in any way over-excited at the prospect of the long-awaited fête. I have other reasons: it gives me a chance to get closer to Tuukka.

Thus far, I have been largely unsuccessful.

Besides, Tuukka no longer seems as open to conversation as he did before his outburst late the previous evening, surrounded by boxes of redcurrant jelly in the dining area of his three-room-and-kitchen apartment. The moment was quick and short, as was the answer to my question. Tuukka knows where the horse is. We haven't spoken about the matter since.

Again, my thoughts wind their way back to the original question as I slow the car to a crawl. I don't want the speed bump to spell the end for the boxes of marmalade. And, naturally, I don't really want Tuukka to repeat his actions, to murder anyone *literally*. I want him to *try* to murder someone. (Though, obviously, I confess that even expressing such a wish, even if only in one's own thoughts, brings with it a certain amount of mixed emotions.) The fact is that I cannot see, let alone construct, a picture that would lead to a successful outcome from my perspective. And regardless of how I might possibly encourage or otherwise motivate Tuukka to act, in all imaginable scenarios I will be forced to improvise more than ever before.

Which brings both me and my thoughts back to the car, as we leave the speed bump behind us. As I listen to Laura and Tuuli – for a fleeting moment, I get the gist of the conversation: the sights in Paris and the history of the city – I realise why I am no longer as averse to improvising as I was in the past. Because that's what being in a family is all about: continuously acting in the moment, reacting, adapting, learning, constantly reassessing things. But it goes without saying that this isn't the only thing I trust in. After all, I am still an actuary. If not by profession or in my familial relations, then at least in my heart, just as all real actuaries always have been. As such, I've never left everything to mere improvisation. I have plans, different ways of moving forwards which, just as they always have been, are strongly grounded in probabilities, which I have used a great deal of my expertise to calculate.

I park the car, and Laura and Tuuli help me carry the boxes of preserves into the venue.

As I set up our table, I try to locate Tuukka. I sigh with relief when I finally spot him next to Team Honeycomb's table. It seems he hasn't run off to kill anybody – yet. From my perspective, this is essential.

I can't hear the conversation between Tuukka and Team Honeycomb, but I can clearly see that Team Honeycomb's view on the subject differs from Tuukka's. With some degree of probability, I assume the conversation must be about the quality of their cleaning skills. I believe I know Tuukka well enough to be able to say that letting things go, accepting things and letting bygones be bygones is hard for him, if not impossible. In fact, I'm counting on it. And what I see now confirms my theory. Tuukka is like an indefatigable bulldog, only slimmer. He always has to have the last word, always has to win. My hope is that that instinct will soon kick in again, and not just in a honey-laden showdown with the other parents.

Finally, he turns and starts walking towards my table. There is so much noise and movement in the space that I give him a wave just in case; I specifically want him to come to my redcurrant jelly/apple compote stand. The beanie that Tuukka wears even indoors looks very tight indeed, somehow encapsulating his mood. He doesn't look any happier than before.

'Not the sharpest tools in the box,' he says, 'the honey gang.'

I wait a little. Whatever he and the honey dads were arguing about is, as far as I'm concerned, of secondary importance.

'I was thinking,' I begin once I'm sure the rest of Team Redcurrant Jelly is out of earshot, 'about our conversation the other night. Especially ... the horse.'

'What about it?' he asks and looks at me fixedly. I've learnt that this is his way; he looks at *everybody* fixedly.

'I am an actuary,' I say.

'What's that got to do with it?'

I remind myself that I'm talking to a murderer, and it is crucially important that he gets angry and channels his anger in the right direction, at the right people, instead of focusing it on me. Therefore, whereas at a juncture like this I might illuminate my ideas with reference to the great mathematicians and their solutions to classic problems, perhaps even going through the basics of the history of mathematics along the way, I decide to take a shortcut, though this approach has its risks too.

I tell him I have been calculating probability for years, decades in fact, so I speak with a certain expertise, and that what I am about to say is based on a series of meticulous calculations. I can see that even this briefest of introductions is causing him some discomfort, so I get to the point even more directly.

'It is *your* horse.'

Tuukka looks at me.

'I know,' he says. 'I've tried to—'

'What's the probability that anyone else could ride that horse better than you?'

He doesn't think about this for long. 'Zero.'

'What's the probability that you are and will continue to be happy that somebody else now owns your horse?'

This time he doesn't even need a fraction of a second to answer. 'Zero.'

'What's the probability that the person, who currently has your horse, will ever give it back to you?'

'Zero.'

I pause briefly. I need Tuukka to count. I can see in his eyes that he is with me. I'm certain of it. And so, I ask him:

'And what is the probability that there's any other way than the one you're thinking of right now that will guarantee you get your horse back?'

Tuukka doesn't answer. Instead, he glances in both directions, leans forwards a little so that our faces are approximately forty centimetres away from each other. I look the murderer deep in the eyes. I don't recall ever having to carry out calculations under such pressure in my previous job at the insurance company, though admittedly back then I hadn't been trained and hardened by the twists and turns that life can throw one's way. And I didn't have the steely, durable warmth that the adventure park and family life have given me.

'Who are you?' Tuukka asks, and I can see that his face muscles are working hard.

'I've already told you', I say. 'I am an actuary. I know everything there is to know about probability. What's the probability that this situation will get any better by waiting?'

The fête is a roaring success. This is obvious as soon as the doors open. There is a crush of customers at all the stands; some even have a long queue. It looks as though there is a certain allure to the dads' pastries, preserves and delicacies, one that I hadn't personally predicted.

While selling my wares, I keep an eager eye on Tuukka.

He is clearly not enjoying himself, stuck behind a table selling loaves of sourdough bread; he looks as though he is desperate to get out of here, as though he is in a hurry to be somewhere else. As, indeed, he is. Horses don't come galloping back to their owners through wishful thinking alone nor even by exacting revenge, and I am certain that, today at the latest, Tuukka has come to realise this. Life looks rather different once the weight of probability truly dawns on us.

Selling and packaging preserves and marmalade, I feel happy for our shared success. Taneli walks past every now and then, and each time we slap the palms of our hands together. The first time this happened I didn't quite get my hand out in time, but I soon learn the technique, and when Sami appears at my stand to fill up his own basket of goods – he has set up a roaming one-man kiosk to increase sales – I even take the hand-slap initiative myself. He is clearly a little taken aback, and eventually we end up shaking hands, rather warmly. Our travel budget is growing by the minute. Particularly pleasing is the fact that people have come to our fête from across the city. This is all thanks to Sami's social-media team: in a flash, they spread the word far and wide.

I am about to give a customer a marginal discount for a bulk purchase when I notice Tuukka leaving his stand and heading for the door. I act quickly. I take my phone out of my pocket, switch it on and click up the two text messages in my draft folder. I check to make sure they are up to date, press Send for both of them, and with that the messages disappear on their way. Having done this, I tell the dad standing next to me organising jars of preserves that I have to take care of a few work matters. In a way, this is true. Ultimately, everything always comes back to my adventure park. I don't have time to think about it any more deeply, but even a quick consideration shows that most things in my life these days are intrinsically, viscerally linked to the adventure park, and that perhaps all roads lead to YouMeFun. The dad says he will survive just fine for the rest of the fête. We slap our palms together, I pull on my coat, and leave the stand behind.

I've already reached the front door when I hear my name. Laura Helanto is standing barely two metres away, in a spot where she was not standing only a moment ago. Somehow, she has simply appeared there and takes a few steps towards me. She reaches me, and we stand close to each other. So close that I can smell her, my favourite smell in the whole world. I can sense her next to me.

'You'll be careful,' she says more than asks.

I look her in the eyes. It's as though perhaps suddenly I can't read her expressions as well as I'd thought.

'I will...' I begin.

'I know,' she says. 'I know you're going. I just want you to be careful. I want things to work out soon. And...'

Only now do I notice her slight hesitation, one that disappears again almost immediately.

'If you need any help,' she continues, 'you only have to ask.'

'I didn't—'

'Know,' she nods, raises her hand, touches me. 'You didn't know you could do that. But that was then. I think nowadays you do. I know you, Henri Koskinen. I can tell when your mind is elsewhere and you're worried about something. And it doesn't take much to guess what that something might be. I don't know what's going on, but I really hope this is the last time.'

There is only one possible answer to this. I don't even need to think about it.

'It is,' I say, and at the same time I know it is the truth. 'This is the last time.'

I kiss her, she kisses me. She gently caresses my face; I touch her wild, bushy hair. Then I set off, and after rounding the corner, run to my car.

I start up the Renault, perform a U-turn, and drive in the most probable direction.

21

I catch up with Tuukka and his white Toyota Corolla outside his house. I'd expected him to stop at his house before heading off to carry out his plan, which, of course, isn't a plan in the strictest, optimal sense of the word. What Tuukka is doing is rooted in his quick temper; it undoubtedly has a direction, a focus, only without any precision or accuracy. Right now, this kind of plan suits my own plans perfectly.

We are heading in the direction I hoped. The further we drive, the greater I allow the distance between us to grow. Every kilometre we travel confirms my theory, and I don't need to keep an eye on his every brake and acceleration. Our destination really does appear to be the one I'd assumed. At times, I glance at my phone to make sure it still has service. It's important that I'm able to send one last text message, and even more important that I am able to receive replies to the two I've already sent.

The winding dual carriageway is familiar now. The afternoon begins to darken, the woodlands start to thicken, before closing completely, like curtains on either side of the road. Our progress is so calm and steady that I can concentrate on thinking and, moreover, completing and confirming new, final calculations.

Proving that Tuukka is the killer has turned out to be the key to understanding Somersault City. Right from the start, this was all about horses. Of course, at first the intention was to destroy my park and to capture the market as quickly as possible, but the reason for this wasn't a passion for the adventure-park business or a burning desire to offer our young customers unique experiences – especially not in the long term – but simply the desire to eliminate the competition, monopolise the field and start making money.

Money that would ultimately be funnelled into the horse business.

But in entering the adventure-park business, Häyrinen, Elsa, Niko Kotka, and all the others involved in Somersault City or who sought to profit from it either financially or otherwise (I now include Salmi and Lastumäki in this group), made their first miscalculation. They didn't know anything about the business and its commercial opportunities or methods, and they knew their competitors only superficially, if that. Thus, they could not know that I, my park and my employees would never give up. Another fateful error on their part, and one that was especially serendipitous from my perspective, was the forced expropriation of Tuukka's horse. I don't believe any of them imagined what Tuukka would be capable of once he lost his horse. I doubt even Tuukka himself could have seen it coming.

Naturally, this doesn't mean that I am in any way happy about the murders he has committed (or manslaughters – I will gladly leave making that distinction to others) or that I can somehow bypass them in my mind. I know I will have nightmares about my tango with Niko Kotka for a long time to come. And I haven't forgotten about Häyrinen, his mouth splayed open for all eternity; or the headless snowmobile driver, whose journey is presumably still continuing across far-off snowy plains. So far, I have heard nothing to the contrary.

I am no expert when it comes to economics, I only have a grasp of the basics (though naturally I understand the mathematics that underpins it), but one of my favourite quotations is attributed to John Maynard Keynes, who is said to have responded to his critics when they accused him of being a turncoat, saying: "When the facts change, I change my mind.

What do you do, sir?" Keynes was right here too: in modern parlance, you simply have to go with the flow.

Tuukka, the horses, the dance with death; Elsa, the dildo and the economically unsustainable marketing gimmicks at Somersault City; Salmi, Lastumäki and their two-man blackmail enterprise. All part of the same web that only now I can see clearly. And that still threatens both me and my park.

Unless my own plan today is a success.

Until now, everything has gone just as I had hoped. Throughout the journey, Tuukka has been driving slightly over the speed limit, but now he slows a little, bringing him just back within it. This doesn't surprise me; I had accounted for this too. I slow down accordingly and allow the distance between us to grow even further. Then I brake a little more, steer the car towards a bus stop and eventually come to standstill. I wait for two minutes, check my phone – still none of the replies I was expecting, though there are victorious messages from the members of the *Le Groupe Paris* – and set off again.

Before reaching the livery yard, I see a clearing in the trees on my left-hand side. A narrow path leads somewhere deep into the darkest recesses of the woods. I don't know where the path leads, but right now that is irrelevant. What is relevant, however, are the tyre tracks. They are fresh. Tuukka has turned onto this path, and his car has disappeared from view. I continue onwards.

Once again, I drive past the end of the road leading to the livery yard, just as I did the first time I visited the place. I see horses in the darkening evening light and the long, red wall of the stables. I drive a little further and then, when I see the familiar private road, I turn and drive noticeably more slowly.

The road hasn't been ploughed for a few days. As almost always and in almost every respect, this too has both positives and negatives. The positive is that nobody has driven up to the house next to the stable, so I can park my car without anybody noticing it. The negative is to do with my Renault, which wasn't designed for such terrain or conditions. I drive cautiously, with the lights off. I don't even want to imagine what would happen if I got stuck in the snow. I don't have an alternative exit strategy. And I'm not prepared to hop on horseback either.

I leave the car slightly further away from the house than before and take some more appropriate clothing from the back seat to keep warm. The park's lost-and-found department has saved me once again. I get dressed quickly, and I realise I look a little out of place here (or anywhere else), but right now I can't be overly concerned about my attire. I'm not going to a fashion show, I tell myself as I step out of the car and into the frozen dusk.

I am hopefully on my way to a crime scene.

The yard is familiar. The fresh covering of snow has softened my tracks, but if I look a little more closely and recall my last visit to the property, I can see the indentations I left as I fled along the swerves left by the snowmobile. I can't hear anything that catches my attention. The late afternoon is still, there is virtually no wind at all; somewhere a crow gives a squawk, feebly, almost out of a sense of duty. Then my jacket vibrates, I take off my mitten and pull my phone out of the inside pocket of my thick borrowed jacket.

Esa's message reveals yet again just how often I underestimate his abilities. He doesn't just tell me that all the people I want are already en route to the livery yard, he even tells me their estimated time of arrival given their current speed. This, he explains, he knows because he is following them in real time. I

don't fully understand how this is possible, but I can already hear
Esa explaining that it all has something to do with the time he
spent at a training facility run by the South Korean secret
service. I drop the phone back into my pocket and approach the
thick stand of spruces, behind which the stables await.

The spruces scratch me; clumps of snow fall from their branches
and drop inside my collar. The thinner the row of trees, the more
cautiously I walk forwards. The thinning of the branches means
that I have reached the edge of the woodland, but it also means
I can be seen either from the stables or the house before I realise
I have been seen – assuming someone were to look out at the
dusky, wintry forest at that precise moment. I don't think this is
particularly likely, and my aural observations don't suggest that
the area is buzzing with people. I stop again and wait a moment
before pulling back the final edge of the curtain of spruce.

Just as I had expected, there is one car in the yard. It belongs
to Elsa. I recognise it from my last visit.

I don't know how experienced Tuukka is at trudging through
snow, but in practical terms I believe with almost one-hundred-
percent certainty that he is not in the slowest percentile. He is a
man in excellent shape, sporty (he probably practises dozens of
sports) and planning an imminent horse heist. It is reasonable
to assume that he has both the skill and the passion to carry out
such a task. The woodland path, along which he drove his car,
runs slightly further away from the livery yard than the road I
took, but taking our relative physical capabilities into account,
it's highly probable that he has already arrived.

My next task is to locate him.

Every minute is darker than the previous one. This, after all, is what sunset feels like: as though the dusk were somehow in a hurry and speeding up. Eventually, a light switches on along the side of the stable. And once the artificial light finally subsumes what is left of the natural light, I see movement on the other side of the yard. The distance between us is perhaps one hundred and thirty metres, but I have no trouble identifying the new arrival. I know Tuukka's figure, know his way of holding himself. He stops several times, presumably to listen and to look around him, and even before he reaches the forecourt, I can see he is wearing a balaclava.

Under cover of the spruces, I do the same: I pull on my own balaclava and a woolly hat bearing the logo of a popular chocolate bar that I took from the lost-and-found box. I realise this makes me look like a chocolate-obsessed bandit, but that's my intention. I don't want to look like myself. Again, I take my phone from my pocket and look at the latest information Esa has sent me.

I will be the first to admit that my plan is far from perfect; it comes with more temporal challenges than I care to think about. Which is precisely why my own part, and the perfect timing thereof, is so important. I assume I will both have to draw events out and speed them up a little. With regard to the overall timing, Esa's messages give me reason to feel moderately positive. It is only a matter of minutes.

Tuukka arrives at the edge of the yard. I'm unfamiliar with the mechanics of stealing a horse, but I imagine it must be a significant procedure involving various logistical challenges, and for that reason I remain in my position. I think I still have time.

And when I see where Tuukka is heading, this only confirms my suspicions. He is nearing the stable; he appears at the corner of the building, creeps along the side wall until he arrives at the main door. He stops, looks over his shoulder and towards the house, then opens the door and slips inside. The door closes behind him, and with that, Tuukka is reunited with his horse. Or so I assume.

I check my phone once more – only a minute longer, two at most – and begin making my way towards the house. I reach the cover of the pines standing outside and try to make a snowball out of the frozen snow. It's impossible. I back away from the pines, find a branch that has fallen to the ground, break it in half to give myself a short stick. Then I wait.

I wait until I hear the sound of a car approaching from the main road. The sound of the motor tells me it is moving at quite a pace, and I believe I recognise it: I've had the opportunity to witness its quick accelerations, sudden brakes, slides, skids and spins so many times that I would recognise the sound anywhere. I follow my plan to the letter: I throw the stick at the house's window. The thump is louder than I had expected. The entire building seems to shudder. The sound must surely wake up anyone still lingering in the dim of the house. At least, so I assume.

I keep my eyes fixed on the window; that seems most logical. I imagine that anyone would appear at the window where the thump came from. This too is part of my plan, as it gives me enough time to carry out the next stage. But nobody appears at the window. At the same time, the sound of the car first dips, then revs again, then approaches with ferocious speed. I quickly try to work out where my calculation has gone wrong. To my mind, the fact that Elsa's car is parked outside suggests that she is at home. And – I ask myself, somewhat puzzled – if Elsa is at home, why hasn't she come to the window...?

Just then, a white BMW swerves into the yard, and its driver immediately kills the engine. Salmi and Lastumäki leap out of the car, pull their weapons from within the folds of their eiderdown jackets, and begin sprinting towards the stable where, to my surprise, the inside lights suddenly come on.

A moment later, I realise why Elsa hasn't come to the window.

The front door bursts open, and Elsa is standing at the top of the steps. She too has something in her hand, something I can only assume is a shotgun.

I turn and run.

A lot can happen in a few fractions of a second. I have time to consider that my calculations have been reset and that it is now clear I will have to improvise many times more than per my earlier assessment. At the same time, much to my annoyance, I have to abandon my original plan to use any conversation between Salmi, Lastumäki and Elsa to prove their connection to the crimes and to one another; such a conversation would probably have ensued once the trio had found a suitable scapegoat for their criminal enterprise: Tuukka, the horse thief and murderer.

But this doesn't happen.

Now something else is happening.

Salmi and Lastumäki have already reached the stable door. They wrench at it, but it appears to be locked. It *is* locked. There is no other explanation: Tuukka must have bolted it from the inside. I realise what Elsa sees – the stable she thought would be dark is now bathed in light; the loathed detectives, the black-mailers, weapons in hand, are rattling the door and trying to gain access to her stable, her sanctuary – and this she puts into words.

'Horse thieves,' she shouts louder and more enraged than I have heard anyone ever shout anything. 'Nobody lays a fucking finger on my horses.'

The shotgun goes off.

Salmi and Lastumäki's BMW seems to explode. The windows shatter. Salmi and Lastumäki hit the ground and almost immediately begin returning fire towards the house. Elsa fires again, shouts; Salmi and Lastumäki fire again, and shout.

Everybody is firing and shouting.

Everybody except me, that is. I'm running faster than I've ever run in my life, snow or no snow.

I have to take a slight detour; I have to run away from the line of fire and take cover by the house. Behind the house, the yard slopes towards the verge, gently leading downhill and back to the stand of spruce trees where I came from, but I am a hundred metres from where I want to be. I hide in among the spruces again.

From what I hear, I conclude that Elsa is used to handling a shotgun. It takes her no time at all to reload and fire another round. She doesn't stop shouting for a second. Salmi and Lastumäki's pistols sound almost shrill compared to Elsa's cannon fire.

The stable lights are burning bright. I can't understand why. I catch glimpses of the stable from between the branches, then I put my head down and charge forwards. I no longer have a clearly defined plan; that was smashed to smithereens like the teenage cops' sports car: I hear the shotgun hitting it again and again, and from this I assume that Salmi and Lastumäki must still be lying in the snow somewhere nearby.

Then, once I am finally where I want to be and again peer between the branches, I observe three things at once. I hear the sound of an approaching car and see blue lights licking the surrounding landscape, then, much closer to me, I see an open door at the far end of the stable.

'Police,' I hear a familiar voice through the megaphone. 'Everybody drop your weapons.'

The pistols obey almost immediately; they stop cracking and, judging by what I can see, drop to the snow.

But Elsa and her shotgun do not stop.

Elsa carries on shooting and shouting.

Osmala repeats his command about the weapons and asks Elsa to stop shouting too. She replies by shouting something, and the shotgun booms again.

'Now, now, take it easy,' says Osmala. 'Let's see what this is all about.'

Even through the megaphone, his voice exudes a stoic calm; as always, he's playing the long game. And perhaps this has the desired effect on Elsa. Perhaps her decision to stop firing has something to do with the exponential increase in blue lights flickering across the landscape, and with the fact that the sound of cars seems to multiply and that everybody and everything now seems to be approaching the complex.

The sound world of a rural livery yard changes dramatically when you subtract the shotguns, the handguns and the mindless yelling.

I mentally thank Osmala once again. He has acted exactly as I hoped and predicted, precisely and one hundred percent. But at the same time, I sense that he is perhaps the only one who has done so.

I hear more cars approaching, their motors quietening, the sound of car doors opening and slamming shut. I hear men's and women's sharp voices: commands, questions, instructions. And though I can't see it, it is clear that on the other side of the large yard officers are arresting suspects, securing the area, checking the surroundings and checking them again. Before long, that checking will reach the place where I am standing right now.

But despite that, there's still one thing I have to make sure of.

Very cautiously, I approach the stable door and peer inside. I cannot see anybody or any motion. I step inside. There is a pungent odour of animals, hay and manure; the combined smell is distinctly earthy and, somehow, almost cosy.

There are horses in the stalls, equipment hanging on the walls.

The door to one of the stalls is wide open.
The horse has gone, and so has the rider.
I do the same.
I disappear.

TWO MONTHS AND EIGHTEEN DAYS LATER

The spring sunshine warms my back, and the friendly taps on my shoulders provide even more warmth.

I am standing in Taneli's kitchen, in front of the window, one bright and sunny Saturday, and have just concluded my budgetary statement.

To put it mildly, the atmosphere in *Le Groupe Paris* is optimistic – one could even say, ebullient. The dads are chuckling, shouting out coffee orders and various French words and phrases (at least, they sound like French to me) and slapping not only my shoulders but one another's palms too. Part of the reason for this exuberance is my statement: the second fête was an even bigger success than the first.

I wonder that, if all this around me, all these people and everything we have achieved together, is – as Taneli mentioned at our first meeting – special, and perhaps even a little odd, then a tight-knit, open-minded group of dads who don't think only about themselves but who work together for the common good is … fine by me. I am only too happy to be a part of it. And if this is the third family I have had the privilege of joining over the last winter and spring – and these days I call it a *privilege* to join these families, not an obligation or something I've been forced to do – I consider this a badge of honour and admit that I was wrong. In this regard too.

Which doesn't mean that I'm no longer an actuary. That hasn't changed; I will be an actuary for the rest of my days.

Which reminds me of my meeting.

I tell the dads I have to go and barely escape ending up at the centre of another group hug, akin to the one I had in my adventure park, where such a thing now occurs on an almost weekly basis. I exchange a few words with Taneli, and while he presses, rattles, programmes and fiddles with the buttons on his space-station coffee machine, making it churn out coffees, each more complex than the last, we agree on the timing of our next planning meeting. And as I am leaving, I tell Sami I would very much like to join the dads' urban orienteering group, which sounds suitably challenging, and something I believe I can give a lot to when we compete as a team. I don't tell him that I have experience running under pressure or that I am adept at finding the kind of routes that others might not notice at first glance. Sami is visibly thrilled at this news and adds me to another WhatsApp group there and then. Whereas in the past my phone used to sit quietly on my desk or by my bed for days at a time, nowadays it is filled with messages that increasingly I find myself only too happy to receive.

The sun almost blinds me as I step outside. The air is cool, but it carries the hint of spring, the promise of something better.

This is a good sign, as I'm not at all sure what lies ahead. Except, that is, for Osmala and his small electric car. Detective Inspector Pentti Osmala of the Joint Division of the Helsinki Organised-Crime and Fraud Units is dressed the way he always dresses, heedless of the weather or season. His familiar statuesque, Easter-Island appearance doesn't reveal any more than usual; his large, expressionless face gives no clue as to his current mood. Of course, I have my suspicions, though we haven't seen each other since January.

'Shall we go for a drive,' he asks when I reach his car, 'to toast the spring?'

As ever, Osmala seems to communicate in riddles. I don't consider it very likely that he is genuinely enquiring as to my willingness to take a drive with him, or that we are doing anything simply because it's a nice day and the sun is warming us after the long winter. And so, I say as neutrally as possible that his suggestion suits me very well, then I walk round to the passenger's side of the car and we both get in.

'I'll be honest,' he says as soon as we have set off. 'I've been busy. And I've been trying to put this meeting off.'

As I said, I am still an actuary. I calculate things. And though Osmala's tone of voice reveals precisely nothing, I believe I have made the right decision by agreeing to meet him away from Laura and Tuuli, and away from the park. I want to protect both of them.

Osmala has a startlingly gentle touch when it comes to his car; there is something about the way he grips the steering wheel that reminds me of his balletic footwear. Our progress is smooth and soft, but clearly deliberate. This isn't a drive; this is driving. And perhaps it is this subtle revelation that makes me look around with such a sense of melancholy. All of a sudden, it feels as though I am watching the sights of Herttoniemi passing and falling behind us for the very last time.

We arrive at the Herttoniemi roundabout, take the first exit, and head towards the city.

'You see, I've had quite a few loose ends to tie up, as they say,' Osmala continues. 'Though personally I don't like making loose-end comparisons like this. They sound a bit old-school detective; amateurish, even. And you and I, we're not amateurs; we're professionals. Me in my police work and you ... as an actuary and owner of an adventure park.'

'That,' I admit, 'is correct.'

After this, neither of us speaks for a long while. Osmala switches lanes, checks his phone while we are waiting at the traffic lights, reads something on his phone that leads him to comment, 'good, good,' almost with an element of satisfaction, then we continue on our way with the same smoothness and nimbleness as before.

It is only once we are almost there that I hazard a guess as to our final destination. Of course, I don't speculate out loud. I considered this option so unlikely, so practically impossible, that I only draw my final conclusion once we arrive in the car park. My assumption is confirmed as Osmala drives across the almost deserted car park, pulls up right in front of the main door and switches off the engine. The car stops humming, and we remain sitting there, both, I believe, gazing in the same direction.

'The guard will come and open the door,' he says. 'He confirmed by text message as we were driving here. I must admit, now I'm nervous.'

I don't tell him the feeling is mutual, though that may well be the case. I note that if Osmala ever gets nervous, it certainly doesn't show; he sounds virtually the same whether he is talking about the weather or trying to calm someone brandishing a shotgun. We see the guard in the foyer and begin getting out of the car.

'I have a distinct feeling,' Osmala begins as we step outside, then making us pause for two seconds, 'that this is going to be the cherry on the proverbial cake.'

Osmala tells the security guard that we'll find our way from here, thanks, and, his keys rattling and jangling, the guard disappears through a dark-green steel door at the far end of the building. It is a Saturday: the office building is quiet, nobody is dashing through the foyer and the lifts aren't constantly pinging to inform us of their presence.

Which, naturally, has a positive impact on what one might call the ambience.

Laura Helanto's work is able to shine in all its glory; we can look at it, take it in and examine it without gaps or interruptions, without any distraction whatsoever. We can let it carry us away; we can surrender to it in peace. Above all, we can allow it to affect us. At least, that is how I interpret what's happening. Osmala's sighs, his turn of the head, shifts of posture, his pensive steps, gestures and nods, all of which last a total of fifteen minutes, strongly suggest as much. I don't have anything against silence *per se*, especially when I am able to behold and admire the fruits of Laura Helanto's labour. But right now, everything feels a little uncertain.

'Yes,' Osmala says eventually, then turns on his Italian heels. 'Great things come to those who wait.'

We look each other in the eyes; we are standing about as close to the mathematical and geometrical centre of the room as is possible without undertaking more detailed measurements.

'In so many ways,' he continues. 'I even postponed my retirement, you know.'

I shan't pretend to be surprised at this, to tell Osmala that it's hard to believe he is about to retire, he seems so young. This wouldn't be honest in the least. In a way, he looks as old as those statues that he resembles so strikingly.

'But there were people in the force who, to put it bluntly, smoked me out,' he says. 'Salmi and Lastumäki foremost among them. And now we know why. For a long time, they have been involved in precisely the kind of activities I suspected them of – and more. But when it came to them, I just didn't have any room for manoeuvre. Until I did. And Elsa Häyrinen has been only too happy to talk. She seems to have well and truly lost her rag at them. Which is hardly surprising. I feel the same. I feel myself getting agitated just speaking about them.'

Osmala holds a brief pause. He looks about as agitated as a rockface or an old country road.

'In any case, I should thank you,' he says eventually. 'I won't ask how you got everyone to do exactly what they did and when, but I have my suspicions.'

A quick, cold shiver courses through me.

'I suspect it all comes back to mathematics,' says Osmala.

I open my mouth to speak, but he gets there first.

'I thought as much,' he nods. 'And that's why all this is confidential. You could say, you and I have a core skill set, the kind that we don't need to explain to people who won't understand it. There's no point explaining a complicated formula to someone who would have difficulty with two plus two, right?'

Again, I am about to say something, but again he speaks first.

'And so that this isn't just words,' he continues, 'I can guarantee that my successor will not be interested in your involvement in the disappearance of that horse...'

'I did not—'

'Or its rider,' says Osmala, as though he hasn't heard my attempts at protestation. 'Perhaps I should formulate this differently: we know who we're looking for and why, and before long we'll find both of them: horse and jockey. That is, my successor will. Without your help, mathematical or otherwise. Ever again. I'm sure you understand what I mean.'

I believe I do understand. I say this, and after a moment's thought Osmala looks satisfied with my answer. So satisfied, in fact, that he allows his attention to return to the walls of the foyer, where it remains for the next thirty-one minutes.

The drive back to Herttoniemi isn't unpleasant. Osmala tells me about his plans. On Monday – his first official day of retirement – he and his wife are heading to Italy to take in the art galleries: 'I can't seem to get enough of the Uffizi.' But before that he has to make a few final notes in his final case report. As we cross the Kulosaari bridge in the slightly surreal light of an early-spring evening, he asks me whether there is anything I'd like to tell him that might be of interest, one way or another, but I can hear from his voice – and judging by the stage in our little excursion at which he asks this – that he isn't really looking for new information.

Osmala pulls the car up in front of my new house, though I've never officially told him my address. He stops the car, and we look at each other.

'We'll meet again,' he says, then yet again continues before I can answer. 'As breath-taking as her work is, I can tell that Ms Helanto is only just getting started. I shall be keeping a keen eye on her.' After a brief silence, he adds: 'As an art lover, that is.'

Osmala doesn't smile, but I think there's something approaching warmth on his stern face.

'I suggest you take the same approach,' he says. 'When you're on to something good, keep hold of it.'

I tell him that nothing is more important to me. Then I thank him for the ride and step out of the car.

As I open the front door, I glance over my shoulder one last time.

It looks as though the small electric car is chronically sloping to one side, due to its heavy but all the more dignified cargo. I would never say this out loud, especially not to Osmala, but, as topsy-turvy as it might sound at first thought, he too has become something of a family member. In my mind I wish him a pleasant retirement and exhilarating experiences in all branches of the arts, and with that I start walking up the stairs.

On the way up, my mind is awash with images.

I see and hear the lawyer handing me a bunch of papers, breaking the news of my brother's death and informing me that I have inherited an adventure park. I see the entire dramatic arc – the story of how the adventure park's initially reluctant employees became my trusted musketeers, my friends, and ultimately – my family. And how yet again, after the challenges it has faced, YouMeFun is flourishing and competing with Somersault City, which recently filed for bankruptcy and which now, under new ownership, has instigated a policy of sensible pricing. And how together these two parks are helping to grow the dignity and value of the entire sector. I see bodies too – buried in the freezer under mounds of chicken wings; deep inside a green plastic crocodile; sunk in a dark pond in the freezing rain; soaring through the sky on a snowmobile – but in these situations I simply don't know how I could have counted or calculated any better or more accurately. And besides...

I know very well why I did what I did.

I have reached the final step. I can only conclude that the journey that led me to the other side of this door was longer than the geographical journey from northern Helsinki to eastern Helsinki, from cost-effective Kannelmäki to functional Herttoniemi. It is a journey that has lasted the entirety of my life thus far. And now I understand better than ever before that it was only possible when two factors that I had always considered mutually exclusive finally came together. In fact, it isn't too great a stretch to suggest that this journey is the key to the world and to life, to all the wonders hidden inside them.

Happiness resides where love and mathematics combine.

I open the door and step inside.

After taking off my shoes and coat, I walk straight into the kitchen, which is bathed in spring light and where the aroma of garlic potatoes hot from the oven is almost intoxicating. I am certain I can feel the warmth of the oven dish metres away. But this is nothing compared to what I feel next. I give Laura a kiss, then another, and hug her as tightly as I dare. I hold her for a long time. Eventually, I let her go and look into her blue-green eyes.

'Everything okay?' she asks, though she looks as though she already knows the answer. This I conclude from her smile and the familiar wisdom in her eyes.

'Everything's okay,' I confirm.

I don't even ask whether she knows I've just met Osmala. Instead, I tell her what Osmala thinks about her work and career. I tell her I think the same and add that though I feel the most extraordinary relief that so many things have now reached their conclusion, nothing, absolutely nothing can conceal the joy I feel in the knowledge that our adventure is only just beginning.

Our shared adventure.

An adventure where none of us will ever walk alone again.

ACKNOWLEDGEMENTS

As always, I would like to thank a few people who made this possible – *this* being the process that turned the Finnish words on my computer into the readable or audible English version you have just finished (and enjoyed, I modestly hope).

I am very much indebted to my agent, Federico Ambrosini from Salomonsson Agency, whose support and wisdom have both saved me and helped me over the years. What a privilege it is to be working with you, Federico.

I don't know how David Hackston does it, but he performs miracles in turning Finnish into English in such a fantastic way. David, thank you again for another brilliant job.

West Camel has expertly, precisely and steadfastly edited this book. Thank you so much, West.

And words are not enough: Karen Sullivan is the hardest-working publisher in the world, and then some. Karen, thank you for your continuous work, support and kindness over the many years we've worked together.

Finally, we come to the most important part. Anu, there wouldn't be any books without you. I love you.

—Antti Tuomainen, Helsinki, August 2023